*Wood, Talc and Mr. J*

## Foreword

They say each of us has at least one novel to write – while only a few of us are prepared to sit down and do the deed. Reason being, at some point in our lives, we will all experience feelings covered by a novelist: love and happiness, hate and sadness; jealousy, anger; sexual thrill, excitement, frustration; there'll be gain, there'll be loss, and on, and on…

Themes eternal, in other words. Life.

We never write anything new, theme-wise, perhaps only of newly-encountered happenings always subordinate to the real themes; we write of old themes in a new way.

And one such way *I* have chosen to play with themes eternal, in *Wood, Talc and Mr. J,* is to have my favourite writers from previous centuries – Blake, Dickens, Delancey, Milton, Stevenson, Shakespeare, Shelly, Wilde, along with the odd 'anon' and piece of ancient Chinese wisdom – comment on the book by way of chapter-headings, chapters set in northern England during the late 1970s.

When poetry works for me, it tends to imprint itself on the wall of my photographic mind – something I came to realise over the years. For this book, then, during the writing of these chapters, each chapter-heading quotation came to *me* rather than me having to look for *it,* from books I have loved and will love again.

What my experience taught me, or confirmed, was that the above authors were wasted on me during my school years. We need to stand up and live before sitting down to write, as someone once said.

I hope you'll find as much life in reading my book as I did reliving similar experiences.

Chris Rose, May 2014

*'... It touches secret reservoirs in your heart... It presses buttons inside your head – which you can respond to. You may not be able to put it into words... Umm... But you feel it, it communicates in an invisible way. And it doesn't just communicate through the head, it communicates through the gut as well...'*

Dave Godin

For Nathalie and Phillip

1

# 1

'... stop,' echoed the honeyed tone. 'It's your stop.' For another evening it belonged to the rare attraction one seat on, in the coat – real mink from where I was sitting. Pushing thirty-five and still as sexy as Venus. As long as she parked herself upfront, so would I.

I sprang to jump the stairs before my 49 pulled away, when my rare attraction's hand seized my hood's furry bit, restraining me between top and bottom. She leant over the banister and thrust her glass-blue eyes into my own.

'I smoked your cigarette,' she said. ''Thought it'd be a waste hangin' in your mouth. And one o' these days, you must to take me to that place you dream about. Màlaga, is it?'

Màlaga? Now who was dreaming? But a "place" I frequented too often.

'And who's Jess?' she wanted to know.

'You... mean Jed?' Though there was something else: 'I... didn't swear, did I?' You never swore in public back then.

'No,' she said, releasing my furry bit with a smile I couldn't quite read.

My dirty double-decker stammered away analysis-free for a more urgent concern: a stagger from bus stop to house via a near third of the estate, nights drawing in. It wasn't Hell but a close ally. I was acquainted with Hell, I'd just spent the day there.

As one house resembled the next, I tugged at the old swathe for warmth, when from a side-street emerged an intense beam. My routine attempt at self-preservation was to prod my fingers into my ears and produce the loudest Johnny Weissmuller yodel possible – something I'd learned watching Saturday morning *Tarzan* films. For if ever I'd need reminding where I was and at

1

what time of year, I could rely on one of these here indifferent machines blocking my path. Most people referred to them as ice cream vans.

Hearing its route wouldn't be my own, I might have made a dash for it. But not on a Wednesday. The world still had it in for me on a Wednesday.

The candidate for Britain's worst TV theme tune emanated from a house in whose privet I was now enmeshed. The digits were re-prodded.

'I say,' nudged some woolly-coated lady, out of the dark, 'you're setting my dog off. He thinks you're crying.'

The more-wiry-than-woolly animal was hurling a distressed glare, and so I told her I'd got a bit of *Curly Wurly* in my pocket if she was interested, disentangling myself from the bush's clutches and patting the dog's head. The trouble, she said, was that the toffee tended to get stuck in his teeth, which made him panic.

I then stumbled on the notion this episode had happened to me yesterday, while I was sure they'd never air *Magpie* on consecutive evenings...? I hoped the answer lay with the lads leaning against a lamppost, looking every bit an ad for *The Fenn Street Gang*. I knew the brother of one; the other was a stranger. I approached with a nod.

The former nodded back and produced a packet of *10 Park Drive* from a *Birmingham Bag* knee-side pocket faster than *Kid Curry* drew a gun, assuming I was about to request one of his short white sticks and space against their grimy-green prop. The stare was perplexed, on my enquiring which days *Magpie* came on. 'Tuesdays and Fridays,' he said.

'I thought you said he was cool,' spat El Gringo, as I lurched away with an unwanted truth.

However long it took from here, intuition dictating, I'd raise my head and sight her. Silhouetted by our more neighbourly streetlight, she neared the house's side-garden gate. That figure. That indefatigable soul. A generator of the spirit vital to all working-class households – in November, November was the worst.

That's what she was for me then: a midweek beacon in the dark.

She called round after work Mondays, Wednesdays and Fridays. Her fiercest comment, scurrying through the kitchen, would be 'By heck, it's a cold un!' Her prey would suffer a frozen-handed slap on the back of the neck, usually mine. 'Sod off' or 'Git' would be my typical, light-hearted response to her fun-loving, laddy antics. I kept my more honest sentiment for the place called Under My Breath. How else to react before the lady's glee? She was my grandma after all.

It was a stop-off between work, bingo and home. Why then would she miss 'nippin' by on the way'? Even if her nippin' bys lasted two hours and, as a rule, ended with 'Christ, I'll miss my tombola at this rate!' Tuesdays and Thursdays were reserved for her other maternal duties: calling on her younger son's family. I was thankful my dad didn't have more siblings.

We not only met in front of the house, but, along with that younger son, worked in the same mill. The authentic satanic type. The only thing lacking was cholera, which I'd have accepted to keep me away. My grandma, or 'grom', never saw it like that. She was of an old breed: 'What do you want, *The Ritz*? 'Should be grateful you've got a job...'

She'd been a truck driver in World War Two, as a transporter of steel for arms. She'd also lost my granddad to seventy-a-day forty years previous but had naturally remained faithful to his name. They said work kept her going. I'd not turned eighteen and it was killing me off.

The reason we worked in the same place but met in front of the house was down to an impasse on my part, even if she finished an hour earlier than me. There were two bus routes home: the longer, ugly one; and the shorter, uglier one. I took the former, she the latter, the one that penetrated Hell's bowels like a lion into the night, while mine ducked and dived, helped on by a handful of trees.

I'd only once committed the gaffe of asking her to wait for me at her stop, to accompany her *chez nous,* since every evening she'd indulge in a little tripe-hunt first, hence the lost hour. I didn't so much learn anything that day as have my worst fears confirmed.

\* \* \* \* \*

3

Instead of waiting at the bus stop, she'd suggested for all ears that I meet her in the market, to treat me to 'a bit o' grub' before home. She loved that indoor market, it was 'buzzin' with life', whereas I'd have bought a plane ticket to avoid it – she'd taken me for such treats when I was a wee boy, when I had a better view than the grownups. Half of the "life" was on at least four legs.

'Enjoy your treat,' snorted my old boss through clouds of tin-solder smoke, as I rinsed off the Sworfega, which should have left me feeling fresh and clean...

My riposte would be eaten by the crash of the weighty door, or shared between that and the resonance of the machinery.

Clocking-out card clinked, I'd made it to the gate before the first of this evening's assaults: a cry from across the yard, penetrating my abdomen like a sword through butter and pinning me to the wall. Its source was an ex-steel-grinding, now silver-plate-buffing workmate of my grom's, another who'd never see sixty-five again. Bertha. 'See you in the mornin', duck.'

It was like they couldn't wait.

She wouldn't hear my colourful rejoinder either; the buffers were all 'machine deaf'. Hood up, head down, I feigned the same ailment.

At the indoor market, I soon rooted out the old soul: the lady with the audience. She was caressing a hot tea's pre-war mug the way I would a pint of *John Smith's*.

''Want one, Phillip?'

I nodded like I meant it.

Parking my legs on my reserved plastic seat, opposite hers, I began to soak up the scenery. We were in the days when tattoos were not so fashionable, more skull and crossbones than Celtic love sign, and if I succeeded in deciphering the odd denizen's neck-scrawl, it turned out to be the kind I would have preferred to be too far away to read: 'Made in England', 'Kill a Greaser' and 'Screw me'. Scary women...

But it wasn't like I was being rude, because my grom seldom looked into her interlocutor's eyes, when she talked or listened – not that I'd let that fool me, she was more astute than most. She had a way of absorbing her surroundings. Or she'd appear to take

4

a trip, as if to report back to the man she'd planned to spend her life with. And then she'd spring one on me, with a Joe Frazier-in-his-prime left-hand 'decker', as I thought of them.

'That's Bert,' she said, and called over my shoulder: ''Want a tea, Bert?' At least the name sounded like it belonged to an old man, which he turned out to be. He was in a bit of a hurry, too, was Bert, and wondered if he might take up her offer the following evening. What she forgot to tell him was, 'By the way, Bert, *This Is Your Life*. But don't you worry yourself, Bert, because I'm going to recount it all to my grandson.' She also enlightened me on two thirds of the market: names, jobs and lack of, who'd 'gone down' for what, number of kids. It all had me thinking everyone was related.

'You could write a bleedin' book about it,' I said, in my best *Harold Steptoe* imitation. She loved those.

'Heyup, Edith,' rang the welcome from every corner.

And if ever she got the impression I felt left out, she introduced me as her 'Soul dancin' grandson'. She knew how to fly my kite: ''Stays up all night. Wigan Pier...'

'I bet he does, the dirty sod,' shot one of the younger sorts, like the bullet was a bit too fat for the barrel. She stubbed out what remained of her cigarette tip into the bottom of her mug: ''No wonder he looks half-dead...'

My short-lived majesty deposed itself, slid under the table and scurried off to play with the four-or-more-legged creatures.

If I was amused by my grom's fame, I was disturbed by the idea most of these people perhaps spent half their lives here. My grom was lonely enough, despite our love, but...

My mind had no sooner chugged away on another answers-to-life reconnaissance trip when it was propelled back. 'Let's have that treat,' she said, wiping away tears of mirth. As much as I loved to see her laugh, even at my expense, I'd forgotten about ''that treat''. Arm in mine, her other fluttered to wholehearted cries of 'See you tomorrow, Edith', and had me feeling like the Queen Mum's bodyguard.

Treat Land was known as The Fish Market, just over, this evening via the thumping bass-line of The Jam's *Down In The Tube Station At Midnight* reverberating from a second-hand record booth. Rumours the place attracted a Neanderthal-type clientele were confirmed, although it wouldn't have surprised me to learn she was acquainted with them as well. As the fishy hum grew stronger, I realised I would rather have been down in some tube station, at midnight.

She now proffered the pin-pulled grenade: ''Had a win this week.'

She not only spent the rest of her leisure time in the bingo halls, but had a permanent winning streak, which, in most circumstances, leaned in my favour. This wasn't one of those circumstances. I'd be obliged to yield to her force-feeding.

Years later I'd be forced to view Sly Stallone's *First Blood,* by a brother-in-law of the very Yorkshire persuasion – who'd leave my upper-arms in bruises with his How's-it-goin'-lad greeting and my achy face feeling like the false smile had set in for good. *Johnny Rambo*'s ex-Vietnam guru – *Colonel Sam Trautman* – would describe our young muscles in a bandana as having been *'trained to eat what would make a billy goat puke.'* In doing so, he'd half-define my doting grandmother, who'd trained herself to eat what would make *Rambo* puke.

'What would you like?' she asked me, hovering over a stall.

I faked interest in the emporium of delights, to my dad's voice grating round my head like a steel wire against a windowpane: *'Don't ever let her buy you owt from that hole, there's nowt in there ever seen the sea.'*

She was served her usual before we reached the counter. She then granted me a moment's breathing space by sprinting off to another stall, where she was again catered for without reaching for her purse, as if she had some sort of season ticket. So much for the bingo win.

I requested a tray of what, for me, were still a tad too pink and measly-looking – I didn't say as much. I also went with a rushed expression, to be served before she got back, though not too many, patting a 'full' belly, naughty but nice.

But my efforts proved pointless when, making to place that second crustacean between my lips, I was made to jump out of my own skin.

'Kevin, get 'ere!'

I did, I jumped, prawns to the floor, vinegar down my trousers.

Without batting an eyelid, the man behind the counter refilled my tray with a greater quantity, while Kevin, the five or six-year-old waif, gaped up like *Oliver Twist*, wiping his nose on a tattered sleeve. And so I offered Kevin a prawn, two, three, more – he was doing me a favour – until Dr Marten-booted mum wrenched him to a corner among other young wretches and another post-apocalyptic-like elder of indeterminate sex.

'This place gets worse,' sputtered my grom, between chunks of raw sausage, like some... like an insatiate cormorant. And it was all *Candid Camera* rescue-free.

As she wiped herself off with a tissue no less ancient, by the looks, I compared her to the unfortunate friend I'd recently made and lost. She'd been a waif her whole life in a sense. She'd battled through two World Wars, the second one alone. For Kevin, I couldn't fathom it, not in 1978. If there was mass unemployment, there was always social security.

'What have I done with the thing?' She rummaged through her shabby, taupe bag, that once endless supplier of goodies those three evenings a week, with or without a bingo win. Into its magical depths her leathery hand would slide, and out would materialize a comic. *Dr Who and his war against the Daleks...*

The second *Doctor* was my second hero when I was a lad, second to my dad. Who could forget the day Mr. Hartnell plummeted to the *Tardis'* console room floor and transformed into Mr. Troughton? I was at the impressionable age of five and, like all, had never before witnessed the act of *Regeneration*. In later years I'd prefer to trust the programme's opening sequence of psychedelic imagery and spaced-out music had been my main attraction, had made me hip in spite of my tender age. But it was more down to scenes as when, around Christmastime, the *Cybermen* were popping out of grates in central-London and one of the slinky, silvery fellows hounded my favourite *Doctor* down a side-street. That shot up the bum left him hopping, skipping and jumping off to the *Brigadier* like a secular turkey, and my sister and me rolling around the floor for the next two years.

My grom wasn't teasing now, shattering my daydream with 'I am a bloody fool!' She'd since recovered the flimsy sachet housing her main dish, which had split and allowed the juice to seep havoc. She was more concerned the raw tripe would be all

7

the tougher without its vinegar base. 'Stand here, darlin',' she said, tugging at my sleeve, that I shield her from other eyes. 'It's already a sod for gettin' stuck in your teeth.'

I didn't concern myself with her next move for a looming crisis of my own. My dad's words had turned out to be wise words.

Except my grom would jerk me back like only she could.

With thumb and middle finger, she thrust aside her cheeks, yanked out the choppers, which she slid into the sodden sack, replaced them with the offal-load, and commenced mastication, otherwise defying description. Maybe she resembled some, as yet undiscovered, deep-sea species. Or something from another solar system.

I opted for the space theme with 'Beam me up, Scotty.'

'I know I shouldn't when I eat out,' she began to explain, spitting on my coat again, 'but my gums are harder than my teeth.'

She'd one day end up sprawled across one of these slabs, I warned, with a hook in *her* mouth. All it then took was my resigned *'Bon appétit'*, to catapult us to Planet Hysteria, tears driven by the day's smoky intake, by the vinegar's sting, by her riotous self. And maybe by a thought spared for needy little Kevin, too...

I was grateful to snatch whatever fresh air I could in the city's centre during the rush hour, though couldn't help noticing we had a lot of space to ourselves, in the queue and on the bus. Things became clearer when people sitting downstairs developed sudden urges to go upstairs, as if remembering they were smokers, surrendering their seats to anyone.

''Lights are nice,' said my grom. ''Best in England, Sheffield's lights. They come from Blackpool to see these.'

'It's September.'

'It's October turned.'

Which changed everything and implied I was being my usual humbug. I didn't dislike Christmas just the four-month build-up, even at my green age. The faintest jingle of Wizard's *I Wish It Could Be... Everyday* played like a repellent. I'd reach the shop doorway and spin on a heel, denying myself the window display shirt I'd studied for the last two months.

8

Famous lights behind us, our once white bus entered the once famous industrial estate on the east side, its heart not so much pumping as ticking over. The glory days were gone for our erstwhile empire-building men of steel, and while a few were throwing admirable rearguard punches, an iron lady was glaring on from the ringside. And she'd neglect the Queensbury rules…

… or so they'd say. I came to life on Fridays. And all but died on Mondays, when resumed the narcolepsy, the falling asleep standing, the reverie, the pining for Friday to work its too drawn out route round again. I suffered from an incurable disease: a fear of factories. It was hereditary. During many of his The-Fifties-were-better-than-today tirades, my dad would brag of having had sixty different jobs in a week, that you could do that then, just nip from one place to the next. He never clarified why he'd had sixty jobs. I knew why.

Our conductor proposed an assortment of coloured square tickets from his tinny machine, colours depending on the price of the journey. I paid ten pence and got a red one, which might have taken me as far as Barnsley without my grom's guidance. She waved a free-travel pass, indicating she was retired. ''Somebody died on here?' he said, handing me my ticket, other hand clasping his nostrils.

'Nay, it's a fact,' added a flat-capped chap opposite. ''Awful, that is.'

I was less prepared for what was to come.

'Too fuckin' right!' a more raucous voice resounded, belonging to someone hankering after camaraderie-type approval.

She was sitting at the back like some contender for Big Daddy this coming Saturday. A mirage: fireworks; Roman Candles ejaculating their multicoloured balls, our perennial host, Dickey Davis, sporting the blinding edge of silver-tinted tuff. That whatever-could-*Grandstand*-offer-you-more way of his…

No doubt aggrieved at having been forced to occupy three seats of our lower deck, the wrestler chewed on an un-tipped, un-lit cigarette.

But she'd backed a loser this time.

Vulgarity before women was unacceptable – and from women? Even the market lot only did it in print. It was the case up North

9

in any event, if Punk was already old news. She'd never get away with it in a confined space.

Each passenger's face displayed revulsion, arms were folded, while the conductor reared a ready-to-rebuke finger. Except my grom beat him to it. 'Do you mind,' she pronounced, getting to her feet, 'there's ladies present.'

She re-sat to deafening applause of the silent variety, before re-placing her arm through her grandson's, and leaning my way: ''Gettin' worse, the foul mouthed bleeders.'

It must have depended on the particular words, I told myself.

Whatever, no-one appeared to mind us stinking like pickled onions anymore. For Madam Crudity, nothing escaped from her dynamically censured orifice until she alit, and even that was inaudible – though the two fingers she rammed against our window spoke volumes. She couldn't have been a regular.

And so continued my white-knuckle ride, during which my escort pushed me to open my eyes, pointing out each and every hellhole. She quoted its name, depicted its speciality in bloodthirsty detail, and enlightened me on every wretched soul slaving therein, factory, after factory, after...

The district's name was Attercliffe, from 'At the cliff', according to my dad. I'd half lived here as a child.

 In the summer holidays, mum and dad at work, my sister and me would stay at our maternal grandparents', but in those days it was real *Coronation Street* terrain, with as many un-inventible characters. A cousin and me would often be targeted by an elderly, very fit one: Batty, who'd either dye her hair a different colour every day, or all the colours in one day. We'd find her Picasso-like tints too much and yell 'Parrot face' each time she stepped out of her door, provided we'd not strayed too far from ours. Occasionally, she'd catch us out and the only other safe haven would be our toilet, stationed at the far end of the large communal yard. 'Come out, you sods!' she'd shriek, punching the door, leaving us with no option but to shed a tear. It would all finish up in a brawl between Batty and the other neighbours, allowing our naughty-if-desperate selves to sneak out and off.

Funny, how my memories of those days recur in black and white, barring Batty's hairdos...

We'd now coughed onto the old high street, at one time unofficially known as Sheffield's Golden Mile, for its number of pubs. Teddy boys, I was told, would place bets on who could down half a pint in each, from one end to the other, and keep on his feet. It was meant to make a man out of you.

The houses had since been reduced to rubble, as had most of the pubs, only to be unearthed one *per* mile if you knew where to look. Shift workers no doubt maintained the profits in most, though the prime clientele of a few were the second generation Teddy boys, who maybe felt more at home down here, and less like living anachronisms.

The real remnants of those bygone days were the factories, some so sinister-looking they gave me nightmares...

''Dancin' Friday?' my grom nudged. If I'd passed out, this was the question to revive me. I felt half-alive – hopeful. 'Watch this old feller get on here,' she said, the question a mere ruse to get my attention. She nodded to where he'd sit: side-seat facing the driver and they'd idly chat. She spoke of the years he'd been using this... terror truck, and praised the good Lord for keeping the 'lucky ol' soul' in the same job, current work-climate and all. Before her voice, once again, waned, withered into the distance...

... except I'd not switched off this time. I aimed a careful eye. He looked somehow wiser than the other commuters, more alert, and neater, like he made a real effort. I asked whether his sandwich box was new...

'He's had it years.'

... and hooked a malodorous thumb between my teeth.

'Now *he* takes pride in his work,' she said. 'That's why he's still...' And then stopped, for a double-take, repeating the single instance she'd glanced my way the whole journey: 'You're lookin' a bit white, 'you alright?'

It was thanks to that same younger son of hers that I'd been allotted five years to make my way in the world, with pewter – that tinny stuff – under the strictest supervision and at this time of year before sunrise and past sunset. The rest of the world, apparently, wasn't so lucky – I'd be a *craftsman* one day! As per an American I met in Worksop, at a record stall...

But then who was to say yon dandy was grateful? Reconciled to his fate, did he put on a show? Or did he look just too... just too hard-nosed for...?

Like *Ebenezer Scrooge* before me, all I saw at present was my ghost of the future.

And I'd make light of it the only way I knew, by badgering my grom: 'How much is a ride on the Ghost Train these days?'
'In Skegness? No idea.'
They could save their money on here, I said.
'And he calls me senile...'
I flew upstairs leaving my grom to her black pudding dessert – she made a great alibi; her eating habits were a fascination for us all. I tore away every last piece of clothing and pressed them into a plastic bag, which still wouldn't prevent their vinegary, industrial reek from uniting with the unflagging tang of my mum's wood polish. I sank onto my bed and hauled up the black leather record box from beneath. Its contents would form my blanket, a blanket of paper and vinyl... my silver and gold. I gazed out to a dark, starless sky.

What price, my weekends? The dedicated nights. My Northern Soul...

\* \* \* \* \*

That was the reason I'd never take my grom's bus home. And why we met in front of the house. As on this Wednesday evening, as if we timed it.
'Nice day at work?' She wouldn't wait for an answer: 'Hey, it's a...'
And I wouldn't wait for that wintry palm of hand. I'd since darted up the path. She ran behind with that hoarse laugh of hers.
We stepped into the steamy kitchen together.
'They're here, the workers,' rang my mum's ever cheery welcome.

## 2

*'Now is the winter of our discontent made…'*


I directed the parka at the cubby hole, otherwise referred to as the 'storm cupboard', beneath the stairs, the place my sister and me had spent many a befuddled night – because we occupied the last house on the block, my dad suffered 'gable-end' attacks, sparked as they were by the slightest weather rumble: 'One strike o' lightnin' in the right place', we could have ended up on the pavement nursing sore heads before the thunder had even clapped. I wedged myself between the table and wall, to my mum's eternal amusement. I once thought of writing to Roy Castle to see if there was a record for the world's smallest kitchen, and this was after my dad's architectural adjustment.

\* \* \* \* \*

One summer's evening he came home from work like he knew something we didn't, *Woodbine* in teeth and lump hammer in hand. A man on a mission, he swaggered through the door, glared at the pantry, and smashed it to smithereens. It was as if the old hole had been picking on him years, as if it could talk but only he could hear it.

''Not laughin' now, you bastard!' I thought I heard him think.

Millie Jackson, a Soul singer with attitude, once boasted of owning a kitchen spectacular enough to blow people's minds. Well, ours was spectacular enough to blow my mum's.

'Pete,' she ventured, 'why didn't you wait till I'd took the food out first?' She wouldn't push it. The whim had no doubt taken hold in the day and that was it...

\* \* \* \* \*

13

I clasped my cutlery and inhaled the vapours. The pressure cooker hissed in sync with my stomach's snarl.

My plate was under my mum's nose by the time she completed her shrewd hint at slipping me a couple of pancakes to keep me going – my dad didn't like anyone pigging other than himself. I submerged them in *Henderson's Relish* – not unlike *Lea and Perrins* but unique to Sheffield: Mr. Henderson refused to sell his recipe – and wolfed them in a manner akin to my grom's offal-gobbling, except I kept my teeth in. It was one of the reasons I took refuge in the kitchen, it being the nearest I got to a conventional starter or dining room. Though there were others.

My dad guzzled in 'the room', crunched up in his armchair in front of the telly. I not only rejected the simulated leather sofa but kept as far away as possible, by burying myself into my miniscule trench, as I saw it, unless I sat on the coalbunker in the yard, but that was more a summer quirk.

Although I'd not yet come to the conclusion my dad's eating practice was an unhealthy one, I was concerned by another destructive force: *Calendar.* That depressing regional news programme with the depressing musical intro. Depressing presenters presenting death and job loss in depressing locations. Depressing meteorologists predicting the depressing weather, who'd slap fragments of magnetic cardboard onto the northern bit of those depressing British Isles. We'd only recently upgraded to a colour television, which somehow managed to enhance the programme's greyness. I had a similar aversion to *The Magic Roundabout.* To tear onto that set and tear out *Zebedee*'s spring: 'Jump now, little shit!'

Thank goodness, then, my grom provided real colour with her nippin' bys. And from my entrenchment I held a bird's-eye view: of the lady herself, who sat on the sofa; and of my dad opposite. My brother Sam, a 'latecomer', cuddled beside his grom and received the same magical goodies treatment I once had, except his thing was *Marvel* comics. My sister Jenny was never home these days, spending more time with the Yorkshire *Rambo* to-be.

While I hated teatime television, I was at least able to laugh at their reactions to it. Or more my dad's reactions to it and my grom's reactions to his. And I shouldn't forget the cat. Unable to concentrate on siestas taken with her silverfish friends by the fireplace, her drowsy eyes would sway from my dad to my grom and back again – to the untrained eye, she looked like she was only lacking the umbrella and strawberries. They were more an old couple than mother and son, a genuine northern *Alf Garnett* and missus.

My mum interred my official pancake-serving beneath a mountain of hash – vaporised chopped-things and meat. I'd first drop in my nose, to scald my cheeks, to cleanse my mind of the day's excrement as with some ancient Chinese remedy.

Sam leaned over the sofa without falling – his grom grasped the waistband of his pants – in response to my mum's worry that I'd end up burning my face off. In response to my dad's suggestion it was possible I'd gone 'doolally', and that *that* was what happened to people who didn't sleep at night, I called him a warthog, without knowing what I meant or caring to. What I knew was that we could talk to each other like that. It was our way of dealing with the banalities of a bleak, industrial-class midweek.

But if my dad had managed to elicit my first verbal response, my mum would be the one to bring the spiritual cleansing to a close. She'd know just what to say: 'So how was work today?' Even my dad deemed it inappropriate, before backpedalling from her glower. My grom then had a go at him, said it was clear for anyone where I got it from.

I didn't need to say much at all to get the ball rolling and keep it rolling. This was the deciding reason for my enduring the culinary-straightjacket. If teatime telly served as a catalyst for riot, my job would involve casting over a modest contribution, a word, a phrase – bait; like I was holding hemp above a lake of famished fish, a tad of which I'd add from time to time... feeding out my line.

The custom had developed over the last year, my having become a worker. I'd say little for an hour and focus on recovering my health.

All the same, I wouldn't get too generous with my frugalities. For when my grom deemed it time to put me back in my place, she'd do so, often with alarming delicacy.

In the intervening moments, I'd tap my usual tap, for reinforcement. And, armed to the hilt, new comic in one hand, well-thumbed ones in the other, Sam sprang over like an Olympic athlete. As he flicked through their vibrant pages, I informed the rest of the house that if they should require my attention from here onward, then they'd do it via my 'intermarry.'

My mum screamed in delighted horror at my semantic error, said there was little wonder I'd 'not got no qualifications. Do you mean intermedrary?'

My dad's correction of her linguistic boob sounded more pessimistic.

What neither of them realised was that my malapropisms were intentional. While they nourished the teatime theatre, they also kept the why-I'd-left-school-with-a-blank-sheet interrogations down to a bearable minimum – what neither of them knew also was that, even back then, I was a regular little wordsmith, albeit a very secret one. You weren't supposed to be clever where I came from...

'That's *Iron Man,'* Sam pointed, peeping up and down again, his finger bent back on the red and yellow fellow.

The lingering quarter of my hash and pancake mash-up had taken on an air of grout, and so I pushed it aside for a rummage through a *Spider Man* mag or two. What *I'd* be likely to marvel at was how the webbed Super Hero's Super Villains in some way resembled a member of our family. *The Lizard* was a dead ringer for our grom – especially when she got caught out in Skeggy; she seemed somehow scared of sun-cream. *Doctor Octopus* was surely my mum's ultimate whimsy – a duster on every arm! But then my Dad wasn't a Super Villain for being every part *The Mighty,* hammer-swinging *Thor.* 'The Pantry Pounder.'

I'd made these observations explicit; Sam's reaction had been to demonstrate authentic signs of respiratory problems. And yet response from the room was inexistent. My requested, if repetitive, *Clangers* impression proved equally ineffective: those funny little creatures on that funny little planet. Not only were they were Sam's favourites but they made up a minority of teatime characters I didn't find so demoralizing – *The Wacky*

*Races* generated the odd smile; *Peter Perfect* and *Penelope Pitstop*. For the impression, I held the page of a comic between my palms and blew against its edge, along to Sam's legs swinging scissor-fashion...

My grom had only waited until I'd done playing with my little whistle. And crooned: 'I see the trains are on strike this Friday', transcending the realms of nonchalance.

I was grateful my mum had none of the same knack. Her nod was too considered: ''Don't suppose Phillip will make Wigan this week, then, eh?' Though she did ask Sam whether the *Clanger* had had enough and gone home.

'Is it still here, Phill?' he whispered.

I ruffled his hair, my relief as firm as the gunk in my gut – my life depended on that Friday Soul train.

Still, revenge would go for less than a song. It was a rule for some and they should have known better. You didn't use ''strike'' as a form of attack in our house, not with my dad about.

He dropped his knife and fork onto an empty plate: 'Wouldn't be surprised. Bleedin' unions.'

And if ever two words made my grom look up, those last two were they: 'Don't start with your "bleedin' unions", Peter!'

'Union' was indeed another of those funny, fish bait words I'd feed out: 'Mam... you know the three pounds I borrow on Wednesdays... till Friday?'

Her eyes narrowed: 'What about 'em?' A purring... catfish.

'Well, if I didn't pay... union money, I'd never need to borrow them in the first place.' It was a naughty thought.

My dad agreed. Why should I have to pay union money?

'To keep his job,' his mum scoffed, smirking at the cat.

'They won't keep his job,' he said, in my defence. 'They've destroyed most of 'em round here' – he'd get all het up and yet he knew I'd have paid the union more to get rid of me.

'Well, Jeff says...'

But she was cut off: 'Jeff ought to know better!' Jeff again, that younger son of hers, my dad's brother. Mr. Chalk and Mr. Cheese – in younger days, Uncle Jeff wouldn't eat bacon on a Sunday if Wednesday had lost and United hadn't, it was a stripes thing. So my dad would taunt him with his extra rashers. He now

17

reminded my grom that Jeff wasn't so pro-union during the "Three-Day Week', when he'd be comin' over here wantin' to borrow pub money. Or can't you remember that far back?' he said.

She put up an index, warned he wasn't too old for a clip yet. She was always threatening to hit him.

He'd carry on regardless: 'No coal. No electricity, no gas.' Closing with the soft and piteous 'nowt.' He regretted not voting for Edward Heath.

My grom then reminded him that he'd once said he'd 'punch the "big teethed" so-and-so on the jaw if ever he came to Sheffield. Or can't you remember that far back?'

And there he appeared to drift elsewhere.

Meanwhile, my mum went puce. 'You're not votin' for her, Pete,' she part-enquired, part-ordered. 'The cow stopped our kids' free school milk...'

He then reminded *her* of the nights he'd grafted whilst the rest of the mill snoozed.

''Your own silly bloody fault,' thought my grom.

'They'd all brought their sleepin' bags...'

He ought to have done the same, she said. He might not be such a miserable sod.

'Whenever any got caught, that was it.' He really did look like he was wearing blinkers at that point, refusing to acknowledge my grom's very existence. Then came the pause, for the sake of emphasis: '... all-out strike.'

She couldn't see what his problem was: 'Jeff would've lent you one.'

'Lent him what, Edith?' asked my mum.

'A sleeping bag.'

'Don't talk to me about unions. I don't know who said the workin' man's his own worst enemy, but, Labour? Never again.'

To place the lid on it, she urged him to put his head in a bucket of water.

And when my mum asked me if I was proud of myself, for having 'set him off again', I blamed *them*, for bringing the subject up. Their reaction was simultaneous clamour, the one sounding like Bob's knackered stallion down the shire, the other like Stan's knackered Cortina four doors down, both now agape.

18

'Watch out,' cried Sam, overjoyed at the chance to use his favourite big brother-line, 'there's a bus comin'!'

Of course, our haughtiness wouldn't live so long. My grom didn't settle for defeats.

Having disposed of her son with ease, not that he'd noticed, she began to fiddle with that ever captivating bag. 'To think I'd brought you a treat,' she said.

I looked over my shoulder. Before Sam egged me on: 'Go and get it.'

I was led by forces recognisable – I told myself such, hoisting Sam to a shoulder; I just can't help it, I said. And once we'd positioned ourselves at either side of our grom – my spot had a defunct towel my mum had placed in preparation – I expressed our mutual regret.

We were exonerated in no time. 'They're for you,' she sighed, as if on some *After Eights* advert, tendering me a bag of broken biscuits from the market – I suspected she knew I wasn't keen on broken biscuits, and that I didn't like saying so. She just couldn't resist...

'Look what you nearly missed,' my mum whistled. 'Do you want a cup of tea with 'em?'

As a lad, one of the films they'd taken me to see at our local pictures was *Billy Liar,* with Tom Courtenay, about a character appearing to have created his own little world. During a scene, he stood shaving in front of a wall-mirror while his mum nagged him for what I couldn't remember. All I'd recorded was how he turned and machine-gunned her to bits, after which 'reality' resumed. I'd do likewise with my mum, mostly when she questioned me about work.

This also was one of those moments.

I declined the tea and, from a second-hand paper bag, rooted out two, formerly pink, wafers, a sort no less soggy than the rest but which I could just about stomach. Sam took the fearful remains into the kitchen, acquainted as he roughly was with the ritual. I promised to feast on them later – there was more chance of my dad voting Conservative and I didn't believe him for a minute. All the time, I couldn't help thinking that had she spent that penny more, she might have managed a packet edible to humans.

That was my final conscious thought, for a while; the after-tea wave had drawn me under. Hardly surprising considering I hadn't slept for the last two years, at night at any rate, and had just bolted my way through a dish fit for six pigs.

The last thing I heard was Sam's thin voice, from a faraway kitchen: 'Are we givin' these biscuits to the birds like last time?'

3

*'When beggars die, there are no comets seen.'*

And so back to my recurring dream, the one I was woken from on my 49 bus, by the rare attraction in the coat. I'd have it again just after my tea. To a musical backing of Mr. J's *I Only Get This Feeling,* it went like this:

*'That's how to spill coke down your shirt,' Jed laughed.*

*But some things were worth it, I supposed, if very few. 'On my way,' I promised, to the one Soul brother who'd understand me like no other.*

*Willing witness to an imminent miracle* (me going about 'my thing'), *he returned my fervour with an incredulous nod, gilded in that three gold-buttoned, black box blazer, five-inch side-vents* – I never let on, but Jed was a real life miracle all of his own. *Tonight* – this morning, whichever way you looked at it – *he modelled a sky-blue Fred Perry shirt, virgin-white skinners* (straight-leg trousers); *the scorched-earth loafers. All was topped with that French crop, its burned-in parting reminding me of Moses.*

*We chorused with our black American hero* – one of, though they none came more heroic – *to a backbeat of handclaps and an already swirling, intoxicating odour of sweat and cheap fragrances.*

*'I can feel it comin'.'*

*Jed's head bobbed at a hallucinatory rate, the edgy guffaw: 'Let me have it!'*

*My dance space was diminishing, the crowd looking to be seen around me, No 1 – 'Jed...?' Upward glance, priming myself for an acrobatic feat our dreamland had yet to behold, I caught him leaning over the balcony, directly above, for perfect view. I raised the clenched fist...*

21

*... while he cupped his hands and yelled: 'Stop', in an outlandish voice: '... stop... stop...'*

The trouble was I never got any further, if ever I got that far...

'Stop it, Peter,' griped my grom. 'Does he ever *stop*!'

Out-and-out liars, he decreed. And this without first consulting my mum, without knowing whether *Fairy Liquid* did or did not make your hands feel as soft as your face. Coupling her whisper with a sympathetic nudge, my grom asked if I was back in the land of the living. I'd just been there, I said. Not that he'd suffer my daggers.

It was venting-spleen-on-adverts time and he went about it like an honest politician.

As we had neither the money nor the space for a three-piece, my mum sat on the arm of my dad's chair whenever we entertained. She told me I talked in my sleep.

'I... didn't swear, did I?'

Sam, who was by now on my lap, also looked curious, but all he wanted to know was if I'd fancy my chances against *Iron Man,* when meows at the back door diverted matters. My dad bumped my mum with the side of his head, indicating she should glide from the chair's half-mooned arm and let the cat out.

'Why not, tho'?' Sam insisted.

If I'd forgotten the question, my mum wouldn't allow Sam time to repeat it, for erupting in the kitchen, evoking the pressure cooker's performance: ''Cos he's a *poof*!'

Nor would I allow her time to defend this latest eccentricity, since we were all interrupted by a venting-spleen classic:

The poise was chocolate box, robed in mystique like so much black silk. Knife glinting between brilliant white, flawlessly symmetrical teeth. Plummet pending and... perfectly performed into, undoubtedly, piranha-infested waters. Mountainous terrain gracefully scaled, turret-window effortlessly penetrated. Shadow-like glide in and out of her momentarily unoccupied bedroom, and our mysterious man of delivery had accomplished another day's errand of the essence. And thanks only to a particular woman's yen for a particular brand of chocolate...

'Liars,' my dad fired again. 'He's not got a bloody hair out o' place!'

My grom couldn't believe it: 'Peter, it's an advert.'

And there'd be plenty more where that came from:

'... *A first class* d*icket to* D*ottingham,* b*lease'* – or something like that...

'*Where's that, sir?'*

'D*ottingham.'*

'*Sorry, sir, but I think you need these.'*

'*Ah...* D*unes!'*

Judging by the following day, it sounded like they'd worked, 't*icket',* 'N*ottingham',* 'p*lease'* and 'T*unes'* all present, correct and breathing more easily – or something like that...

I'd have wagered neither of those two had attained so much as a second-class ticket to Stratford-on-Avon, though my dad's criticism was still melodramatic. He should have practised yoga. Instead, he produced bile: 'Have you ever seen anything like that silly lookin'' – partially whispered – 'gett!?' His use of "gett", as opposed to 'git', denoted he was ready to muffle something stronger, which none of us would quite grasp. And he did.

'What did you say?' asked my mum.

'Well,' he groaned, and afforded us one of his idiolectic descriptions of how it was enough to make him vomit that which he'd never consumed.

We were thankful for Orff's *Carmina Burana,* rolling seas and a flaxen surf-man.

Back on land, the latter massaged his chin, allowing we, the enraptured or envious viewer, with no required input of our own, to comprehend his subsequent design: 'Now I'm going to show that Raquel Welch stand-in how to...'

My dad directed a self-assured grin toward his youngest.

But Sam was puzzled, a finger eclipsing *Thor'*s silver-winged casque. Once I'd clarified his dad didn't wreck kitchens for a living, he said: 'He swims more like The Chocolate Man.' He meant the *Milk Tray* man and he had a point – he didn't *surf* like the other, not in Skegness. It was just that my dad wore *Old Spice* and didn't waste beer money on *Milk Tray.* If he nurtured a partiality for the product, he let the advert off. And if he didn't...

To conclude the slot, we were blessed with an advert my dad at least found bearable, due this time to Sam and me having developed the routine of adding a forceful 'Liars' on to the closing line, about *Opal Fruits,* sweets conceived to actually quench your thirst. It was a family effort, and again, true to form, my dad's eyes shone our way. Sam squeezed my arm like he'd waited for this one all evening, like every evening.

Although my dad had a bit of an *Alf Garnett* streak, he didn't resemble him physically – though my grom was the spitting image of Missus *Garnett.* He looked more like Richard Bradford in his silver-headed *Man in a Suitcase* days. He dressed like him, too. While in the '60s many a young man was dyeing his hair grey, my dad had grown his own. The *Alf Garnett* thing derived from his having spent most of his adulthood, as far back as I could remember, being unable to get to grips with what he deemed as life's injustices. But no, he wasn't a misery. He simply allowed things to affect him more than they should, right down to an advert and its 'immoral' means of persuasion. Why, then, didn't we keep the television off? He paid a license fee so it was bloody well going to stay on. Yes, the fee lined only the BBC's coffers, but they didn't have adverts to go at.

The good to come out of it was that it rendered him a real-life character. And I was sure he knew; he'd often laugh at himself. Crowds smothered him up in our local, my friends included, since he'd recount a tale like no other; spice it with a unique passion. And never would he let one of those "injustices" go by if he believed there existed a solution. Although the consequences weren't always favourable, they made for an extensive repertoire.

\* \* \* \* \*

For instance, a good ten summers previous, my mum, Jenny and me were engaged in a spot of castle-building on the beach – by then my dad had christened Skegness our 'second home'. He was out in our wave-less Wash, attempting an *Old Spice* impression before the advert had been on telly. Without warning, a commotion arose: a rumble of engines, screams, chased by a mass gathering of people. Designating a zone of beach to serve

24

as their no-man's land, space: one groyne to another, the Mods and Rockers lined up, faced each other and growled. We happened to be slap in the middle.

As the other, normal parents grasped their offspring by whatever came first, grappled with whatever else and took flight, we stayed put. Reason being my dad cherished his hard-earned one-week-a-year by the sea with his family, and if taking that lot on was the extra price to pay, so be it. In Neptune-like emergence, he seized the first deckchair and waded in.

He turned out to be the most violent person on the beach. Worse, due to his duck's arse and Tony Curtis quiff, the Rockers believed he was one of theirs, as if his time 'surfing' had been some sort of reconnaissance mission. In awe, they left him to it.

He created a following. And would have gotten himself arrested but for having his wife and children with him.

\* \* \* \* \*

On another outing, circa 73, to Bramall Lane, United's home, he instructed me to place myself on a step against a wall, to get a grandstand view of a spectacle about to unfold *out*side the ground, minutes after the final whistle.

It had been United v Arsenal and we were heading back to our bus stop, until my dad's absorption got the best of him. The Arsenal supporters vacating the ground's away end didn't look too appreciative of a chant laid on by the United devotees at the other end of the street —one line only, repeated throughout: *You're going home in a fuckin' ambulance.* Yet another opportunity for a lesson in how not to behave in polite society.

What maybe my dad hadn't counted on was the particularly large North Londoner, who, as soon as things had gotten antisocial, made a lunge for my scarf, as in a trophy for his much wider neck. But then maybe the ruffian also hadn't counted on breaking his nose against my dad's forehead.

When PC Flustered turned up, he was greeted by a *Man in a Suitcase* look-alike, a look-alike looking like he was experiencing some sort of spasm: the winking eye, the tilting head, twitching thumb – never *say*ing ''Just lookin' after the lad.'

25

Young Flustered still got it right. With six or seven arms wrapped around his own neck.

Through a mouthful of that evening's egg and chips, my dad said he thought the aggro was worsening, and that: 'We ought to think about kicking it in the head.'

When we quit the matches it was more down to awful football than anything else...

\* \* \* \* \*

Recently, though, the old comedian had become irascible – the lion was now an angry lion, that's how I saw it. He was unhappy at work, felt exploited, not so much by his bosses but by his self-labelled 'comrades'. Steel hardening in '78 should have been gruelling enough. He was conscientious; they weren't.

All would have been difficult to establish at half-past six in the morning, on the other hand, where he carried himself like a Taoist emperor.

And then there was the strain only time would heal: the memory of 16th August 1977.

\* \* \* \* \*

That summer, the second scorcher in a row – the previous had been a record-breaker – I'd go on holiday with my parents for what I expected to be the last time, having turned sixteen. They'd granted me the choice of destination: anywhere within a hundred and fifty mile radius, sufficient to keep up with The Martins down the road. I elected Cleethorpes. Some big holiday camp beginning with 'B', boasting on-site entertainment.

On arrival, we were quick to learn the town had succumbed to two mass invasions. One had painted the totality of the beach red. The other had painted the rest of the place all the colours under the sun.

For the former, nothing had changed regarding the sea, so we were told: it resided around Holland, Germany and Denmark. But there appeared to be no beach either. A compact mass of ladybirds had concealed it – ''Should've seen 'em the year afore,' reckoned some old-timer, head tied in a hanky, 'I got 'em in my ice-cream...'

For the latter, the more diversely coloured, swarmed compact masses of Teds and Punks. From afar, discriminating between the two tribes proved entertaining and challenging, as each resembled a swaggering, grunting pack of deckchairs – I should have taken that one as a bad omen. Drawing nearer, the difficulty decreased and I won more ten pence pieces from my dad than vice versa. The giveaway was face upward, the top bit, which was either black and greasy or like that of an Attercliffe character from my distant past. What with remnants of the Silver Jubilee festivities visible, it made for a gaudy town.

Beach out of bounds, Ted-Punk street clashes appertained at regular intervals, which would have been fine as a spectator sport but both sides picked on me, too, for holding my nose in the air walking by them. I couldn't help it. And I was now at an age to be thumped for it.

Nor did I help, then, when hearing The Trammps' *Hold Back The Night* streaming out of some promenade bar I proceeded to complement it with my dreamy thing, exaggerating the slightest gesticulation, convinced I was creating a new martial art.

It was evident from his frequent nods my dad was enjoying my ballet, if clearer still from his alternating head-swivels that he wasn't too impressed with my audience. But then he'd never been keen: Punks were 'vulgar little wimps' while Teds were, well, not real Teds but 'young imitators of an old look' – if some weren't that young.

Deeming things could turn nasty, I abandoned the Shaolin Soul spectacle once my grom pitched in her Dickey Bird's worth: '*Pe*ter, silly mare, you're worse than *them*!'

16th August was punch-up free though far from banal. It pampered the supernatural.

That morning, half six-ish, I lay awake bothered by the idea that any other week would have had me tumbling about a number 49 in a coma.

No better reason for seeing the day, I decided. And so I squeezed my head into the other bedroom, tapped my dad's shoulder and asked if he wanted a *Daily Mirror*. He looked as if he'd just seen a burglar, warning me not to wake the 'little un'; *he* wasn't nocturnal like some of us. I considered splashing him with cold water. Time was he'd have done the same: 'Come on, it's a lovely day, no wastin' it...' But I thought again peering over at Sam, who occupied a side-bed at the caravan's other end, reliving the day before, I bet, and things enchanting only his eyes could see. My grom lay opposite: a toothless, roasted lizard by morn... clutching the arm of the granddad I'd never known? Some promenade arcade? Sweating for two fat ladies on the blue line...

I planted my feet on the steps and shut the surfboard-like portal of what otherwise conjured up a pink and white spaceship. Eyes closed, I was conveyed to an enchanting world of my own, by those, ordinarily so elusive, perfumes of the past. The heady scent of morning dew, sprinkled over freshly chopped grass, was swept along by a hypnotic salt breeze. The tormenting aroma of eggs and bacon on some long-ago morning fluttered its impatient wings. The punch of an evening's newspaper-draped fish and chips thumped me drunk; and the breathtaking vapours of a bygone gaslight in a bygone caravan all but sobered me up. With alacrity it was lit, by the one person permitted the act: my dad, post-a swift thumbnail flick against an ever re-productive *Swann Vesta* match, singled out from the hanky pocket of that glorious 'Italian boy' jacket. I tasted the beer on his breath, heard a meek, red and cream *Philips* wireless jingle a synthesis of ethereal tunes:

Labi Siffre's ghostly acoustics. Val Doonican's *Elusive Butterflies* – was that its name? *He* once even had his own Saturday night show, Aran knit and rocky chair all in... And *El Condor Pasa*. Another too apt a title for one more too haunting an echo. My dad accompanied them between Lincoln ale philosophies. Except is *Woodbine* throat would never allow him to compete with the raucous rage of Barry Maguire, a man envisaging desolation if we didn't play our cards right. An accompanying, harmonious 'Man with no name'-type whistle was, thus, the key for our poet protestor. And would Jenny hear her Fab Four's *Michelle*? Would the roof hold out to this rain? Just how tough was that transparent bit (the plastic opening my grom had had me believe was a flap for families with flying cats)? And all was safe, snug, and I opened my eyes...

On my return to a more tangible environment, I couldn't see beyond my nose for another invasion: a woolly kind, a sleeping kind. I felt its weight in hands which, when held to my face, looked as if they belonged to someone else.

I stretched out my arms, scraped my feet along the ground to distinguish the gravelled path leading to the site's shop. Distinguished, I dropped to knees in acknowledgement of muscles I never knew I owned, refuting the idea nerves had anything to do with it.

I then remembered paths tended to lead two ways.

Indeed, one thing led to another. Before long, a bedraggled, ripened soul materialized before me and evaporated behind me at about the same time, oblivious to the mist and to my person, weeping into her tabloid. And so I renounced the *Dalek* sink plunger-technique for fear my plungers plunge something I wouldn't want to see once the rest of me got there.

The newspaper shop emerged as a gigantesque lantern suspended in a white void. Inside, everyone looked to be experiencing waterworks complications.

Below the window an array of placards read identically: THE KING IS DEAD!

I took that one as a cue to lie down, apparition number two distracting me just in time, in matching undies and the single bedroom slipper: 'Irene, is it true?'

Irene rushed out of the shop: 'Sandra, my young Sandy, how's Roger taken it?'

'Oh, he's still pissed,' she panted.

No sooner had young Sandy gotten her breath back, than they burst into *Are You Lonesome Tonight*; to begin with, it was just the two of them, like the very birth of a craze. And then folks of all ages, tugging at their drawers, hopping out of the haze; a hoary-headed woman in, patently, someone else's long johns – even the newsagent bounded over his counter... up to the sun's cracking of the clouds, dissolving our stupor and cotton-steel air, and doubly exposing Sandy's baked nudity.

'Come on,' they now bade the semi-slipper-less rock 'n' roller, advising that, if she didn't, she'd catch her death. Her inferiors followed suit.

I came across her missing footwear on my nervy route back, prior to a helicopter propeller's prying swish seeming to read my thoughts, causing the slipper to fall back onto horizontally-swept grass and yours truly to flee like a naughty schoolboy.

At the caravan, I was surprised to see everyone up and ready for the off. 'Elvis is dead,' I announced, wrist-flicking the rag to my dad, who was sitting on my grom's then side-bed now everybody's side-sofa. It landed on his knees via a glance off Sam's head.

He pushed the paper aside: 'We've heard.'

At a loss, I flung my pooped self onto the side-sofa opposite.

'Half o' the camp's been singin' about it,' said my mum.

'I bet none were fans,' said my dad, like it was her fault.

A deflated bearer of news, and yet being so dampened any ridiculous notion that might have otherwise developed. I recalled the abuse from the Teds. My dad's reaction was a tad cold but not hypocritical. I therefore decided to leave out the part I'd played in the tearful rude awakening. I'd only participated for the sexual experience anyway, I told myself.

'Anyhow, come on,' said my dad, 'we're goin' for a helicopter ride.'

'They're givin' goes for a fiver,' said my mum, cleaning down the draining board.

Not for the first time, my grom was adamant: 'I'm not goin' up *there,* Pete!'

She kept a distance. The rest of us were the first in the queue.

To the unpromising accompaniment of a youthful David Bowie droning from an untidy dashboard, my dad and me settled for the rear while my mum and Sam sat beside the long-legged pilot. My mum nodded to the sole cassette's broken container: 'I believe he's actually from Yorkshire, you know', attempting her best accent.

The pilot looked disinterested, what with a pending day of *Space Oddity* on loop, perhaps.

My grom became the size of a stick insect, amid a multitude of stick insects awaiting their own bird's-eye trip, and my dad wondered how seagulls never mistook her for a lobster.

But our apparatus seemed to lack a sense of humour, and, as from an abrupt outburst, as a would-be Yorkshire Bowie moaned about his own dodgy circuitry, fleetingly turned everything on its head, causing my body's upper half, unrestrained by the waist belt, to lurch forward and my folded arms to unfold and fly back. If my dad, as a consequence, became the victim of a thump to the chest, if smoke wheedled its way into the vehicle, if we span and span, his eyes remained fixed on our guide…

The pilot managed to regain some form of control and so plonk the contraption right side up with hard-hitting recoils on rough terrain just outside the camp. Should the thing explode, he then thrust open his door – which dropped off – and made a run for it: *'Get out!'* Back still turned at two hundred paces.

My mum wrestled her own way out of the fuming cockpit, kicking and shoving, Sam in an arm, finally prompting my dad to take the opposite direction. And prompting me to fiddle with a strap that didn't want to part company. Or was I not putting in enough effort? I felt a comfort I'd never known...

Only my dad's urgent turn and gaze would jolt me back. That ever engrained gaze.

Like a bird takes a worm, his hand snatched my neck, elevated me from the belt and pitched me out somewhere. With the collar of my shirt, he whisked me to a secure distance as the summer's scorched earth whizzed beneath my feet.

There was no explosion, just the pilot's head popping up mongoose fashion, which we all saw as a sign to do likewise.

Hands were shaken, little was said. Things needed time to sink in.

The gathering was euphoric, save my grom. Her reaction was red-eyed, as if we'd done something very wrong. She returned to base.

The holidaymakers bestowed semi-star treatment on us for the rest of the day; we lacked only the journalists, what with the death of a king. By evening, things were back to how the day had started… sort of.

Downing our pints, my dad let go with *Love Me Tender*. I understood the second he wrapped one of those arms about my shoulders, reminding me we could have joined the singer today. 'I'm just glad we're all here,' he said.

Once we'd fought our way out of the pub, we proceeded along the promenade to the ubiquitous echo of bewailing Teddy girls and boys, some in search of a consoling ocean, when a policeman barred our route. I panicked, imagined my dad was about to be arrested, not for some drunk and disorderly offence, that would have meant arresting half the town, but for saturating his underage son with ale. The sergeant approached: 'Where you been, lads?'

This time my dad deigned to verbalize: ''Just taken the young mourner for an imbiber, officer', comportment never so steady, diction never so clear.

The taken-aback copper apologised in a tic, sprang back into the beady-eyed, bluebottle-blue battlewagon, and away it, he and they stole.

My dad was focussing on a sea that wasn't there, when I asked what he thought all that was about.

'No idea,' he said, and broke into *Crying In The Chapel*.

I relived the day's events in my dreams, to Jean Michel Jarre's assistance, *Oxygène,* as if the holiday had turned out to be some culturally defective marines' convention. Maybe I'd set my hopes high with Cleethorpes, but I'd had a bellyful of the fights and of, when not reading about The Sex Pistols' antics, dodging Sid and Johnny imitators to-and-fro. And of suffering Elvis howlers from that morning onwards.

It was my dad's turn to experience the fidgets the following dawn, though he returned from the paper shop without his usual, said he'd bought a local one. He first pointed to the front page's bottom right corner, reading: *'Two Teddy boys rob bank',* under which the article painted the lads in question, a picture not unlike my dad and me. But if it now made sense, why the police had pulled us up last night, I wouldn't skid into a wardrobe crisis just yet, because my dad was in distress. Unfolding the paper, bending a finger over its headline of *'Pilot saves family in horror crash',* his voice quavered: 'And what about that?'

My 'Bastards!' was tailed by my mum's disapproval and little Sam's not knowing what to do.

'Leave him,' said my dad. And told us not to worry, with a wink, that we'd 'get 'em.'

We didn't.

Instead, thanks to the holiday ranch management, we learned how a couple of unknowns had ridden into town from another called Nowhere on their knackered stallion, hoping to make a quick buck before the sheriff had time to get his boots on.

Weeks later, my dad managed to hunt down the company from which our wandering *bandidos* had strayed, and sent a threatening word, which was returned with scorn and realism. There'd be no *High Noon*: my dad wasn't big enough. Having borne the dread of his family being blown to bits in a fell swoop of greed and indifference, he not only ended up with his face in the dust, but rubbed into the old beast's faeces for good measure.

I wished I'd chosen Bridlington.

\* \* \* \* \*

At home, life carried on as usual. We didn't have time for broken eggshells in our house. Without August '77, my dad would have had his targets: unions, Teds and Punks, Arsenal. Mick Jagger, Eartha Kitt. Georgie Fame, Mike & Bernie Winters – the huge grinners. *Top of the Pops* for doing away with Pans People – Legs & Co couldn't cut it without Dee Dee. The adverts, as well as something chasing our recent slot this evening: a trailer for *Crossroads*.

Before *Benny* could mumble a half-witted line, my dad caught any button his fist landed on. Not easy with just two other stations to go at.

I was shot down asking my mum to spare me a bath: I'd had one last weekend and would want another come Friday; it cost a 'bloody fortune to heat up that boiler!' Saving grace being we *all* must have stunk.

Well I wouldn't stay in.

At a certain hour, ITV reeled them off on the run: *Tetley Bitter Men*. Freddie Truman coming up a mineshaft, coughing fire for a pint of *Webster's*. Men carping about a thirst hastened by a *John Smith's*-less week down south...

My final crisis loomed as large as yesterday's: the daily expedition; the winter visit to the old 'lav'. Once more, I'd remind myself that Sheffield steel men built empires, and that I should at least possess scraps of such mettle.

On my signal, Sam slipped from my knees and hopped onto his dad's. I then went forth, claimed the North American parka from the Northern English cubby hole, turned, and uttered someone else's immortal words: 'I'm just going outside and may be some time.'

4

*'There's nowt as queer as folk.'*

Settled and only partly numb, I gained a sense of pleasure and achievement. It was more the idea that grieved me. It was degrading, unique – although I considered myself different to everyone on the block, I'd have yielded to the convention of a porch. And it did nothing for the ego, when some delicate creature put the question: 'How do you cope goin' to the bog outside?' It was fine for Jed, he lived over the newer part of the estate. His toilet was neither outside nor in a porch, but inside the house.

What, then, might I have found agreeable? Well, I could keep the door open with the light off – it hardly meant letting out heat – granting myself an impression of freedom as I looked to trees entangled with a starry evening sky and... imagined (a vigilant Sam saved me from Captain Oates' fate the last time I dropped off, the other two thought I'd gone out; my mum had gotten fresh with the shammy while my dad had shipped off to his own fantasy island with Louise English, one of Benny Hill's *Angels*).

I'd recall the series *The Adventures of Black Beauty*. Or more the steed's stable hand – she'd played havoc with my newly baked hormones. I got a semi-naked-in-the-fields feel, as it were.

Ours being the end house, it had land attached until the next block. As kids we called it 'The Wood', where sexual exploits were rife: the initial touching of tails to girls showing up and showing us what they were for (not that I ever pulled that one off, as tonight would demonstrate. Never so unsuspectingly I'd spend the coming hours up yonder, with one of the opposite sex, following which nothing would ever be quite the same).

Alas, this seating's reminiscence was pulverised.

It was a paradox ice cream vans reminded me of winter. But of course they didn't drive about so much in summertime, pumping out their *Greensleeves,* because people went to them. I knew they had a business to run but couldn't get why they didn't play Marvin Gaye.

It was for the same reason I loathed *The Magic Roundabout:* it had a similar kind of tune, an English winter Sunday-like tune, the day the vanguard came out in force, as did all things evil, on Sundays. English winter Sundays...

I gave up on God and Heaven in the traditional sense after *Songs of Praise.* Those decrepit, wide-mouthed weirdoes. My dad watched it so he could call them hypocrites. As for Nicholas Parsons' *Sale of the Century,* he watched that one simply because the studio was in Norwich – he liked Norwich. That programme reeked of old people. Not like my grom but those I imagined bought *Shackleton's chairs.* Then there was Radio Two's *Sing Something Simple*, following Radio One's current national Top Twenty at seven o'clock as the stations joined forces. Jenny and me once waited not quite an hour to hear The Supremes' *Stoned Love.* But no sooner had we recognised the merits of ex-Beatle Harrison's solo number one, than *they* started: more wide-mouthed – I visualized – freaky-voiced freaks, with what must have pre-dated World War One and must have sounded freaky even then. Already having renamed the thing "Sing Something Suicidal", we scampered out to play.

Again my fingers leapt to my ears for our rascal raspberry-ripple squirter, except this time I was stymied by a frozen-handed slap on the back of my neck, delicate labour seen off in a jiffy. I opened my eyes to my grom's ripened mug, inches from my own; she was side-lit by the kitchen light, the other side by the full moon.

'I've said goodnight four times,' she estimated, before pardoning me for my unstructured response. I shouldn't worry, she said, she'd heard worse at work. Tearing off down the road, she made sure to call back they'd not known she was there either. 'Oh, and don't go giving them biscuits to the birds anymore...'

My mum scrutinized my stance as I faltered in relating my painful pickle. But then she'd been acting queer all evening, I reported, only for her to sing out that it took one to know one.

'Who's that?' my dad wondered, on the doorknocker's knock,

deeming the rest of us had X-ray vision.

'Jed,' my mum revealed, back through the door, arms crossed, lacking only the three Ogdon-esque ducks on the wall.

My dad ordered her to show him in, to not leave him out on the cold step.

My best friend's cherry leather trench coat creaked in concert with the groaning door. He nudged my dad's shoulder and pinched Sam's nose.

'Look at all my comics, Jed.'

When my dad signalled sitting-space, I said we were heading upstairs, forcing my mum's gruff flinch, which covered an end of the two-piece to the other. It wasn't as if she didn't know I'd need to get my kit off before getting out, except tonight she appeared to pass out at the thought.

'Joan, what is it?' asked my dad.

'Nowt,' she said, patting her hair.

And so to the perpetual plea: 'If you've got somethin' to say...'

On that note, Jed afforded him a grin while my mum reverted to happy-families: my grom had had a bingo-win and left me a fiver.

'It's under your nose,' my dad nodded. 'No, you're gettin' colder...'

Sam singled it out beneath an old Three-Day Week friend: 'Under the candle stick.'

We were at the bottom of the stairs for my mum's threat of 'Don't mucky that floor.'

Jed had taken his shoes off, I told her, which he appeared to take as a dare to keep them on, while looking a tad perplexed. Not to worry, I said, she was possibly on drugs.

Then again, she wasn't the only one.

## 5

*'Beauty is the wonder of wonders. It is only the shallow people*
*who do not judge by appearances.'*

He first dissected his reflection in the long dressing table mirror. My jealous mission was to keep him on his toes with whatever I could invent, say, a speck on a buffed loafer. I wouldn't point 'it' out directly of course, and so his eyes would cling to my lopsided pauses along the way. From a pounce, he seized Jenny's blanket and eliminated what was never there: 'I'll be listening to Black Sabbath next.'

His next concern was the record box, where again I'd play a quiet-but-commanding role, if only a while. Keeping an ear open for my endorsement, he'd herald our evening's potential esoteric openers based on the Laurence Olivier, 'Exeter, Warwick and Talbot' model, from a film we'd seen at school, which was a much welcomed break from *Kes*. Example: 'Jackie Lee's *Oh – 'that we now had here' – My Darlin'*, darling?'

Except I'd decline everything belonging to American import format.

Thus my chum disputed: 'But this tune shall be rememberèd piece,

By we who are never abed.'

He was articulate with his record lists, Jed, post-*Henry V*, but then he'd had lots of practice. The more I rejected his claims, though, and the rattier and redder he became. In time, he'd make false accusations about my collection and its buried away oddities, like Mary Poppins' *A Spoonful of Sugar*. Or Clive Dunn's *Granddad*.

His problem lay in the fact that, as Northern Soul was black American, the imported singles had no middles to them, and so a 'bit' was used: a small, flattish, circular object which, when placed at the turntable's centre, filled the missing space; an adaptor of sorts. And while there existed British re-issues of some of our favourite American recordings, on more conservative looking labels, we'd strive to obtain the colourful and costly originals. Although I happened to have lost my bit, I'd grasped the knack of placing the disc onto the moving turntable in a swift motion and obliquely pointing my index to its axis, preventing the likes of Major Lance from sounding like one of the regulars up in The Grouse on a Sunday evening talent night. Whereas Jed, never having grasped said knack, hence his histrionics, would retreat as in some sudden religious conversion, now judging I 'possessereth much unequalled poppycock.'

He didn't keep records at home because his parents were old and lived in a quieter part of the estate, not when he had a Soul brother who lived 10 minutes over the other side. What he bought he'd call round and listen to, just never enough, evidently. His choice of opener, Garnet Mimms' *Looking For You,* which had cost me eight pounds, was a sort of homemade or pirate thing with a ready-made middle – I couldn't afford the original. It was one of the rare moments I could hold him hostage, by brandishing the likes of Tammi Terrell's *This Old Heart Of Mine* under his nose, on its original navy, middle-less *Motown*. Which he'd snub, with some improvised yarn about Garnet Mimms being Curtis Mayfield's brother – 'Mimms' was only his stage name.' It had nothing to do with my copy of Mayfield's *Move On Up* being British.

And then my time was over, the second he raised himself for a virtuoso exhibition in front of Jenny's dressing table mirror. This evening's faultless impersonation was of your narrator. I recognised tics I hoped looked better on me. He could do that, take off anyone on any dance floor and yet couldn't dance himself – *he* was the only person he couldn't imitate.

However ticklish my torture, all was brought to an untimely end by an unlikely tap at the door. Jed was lightning incarnate kicking off his shoes. He stuffed them under his coat and lay on the freshly polished blanket, fearing that fastidious cleaning lady. 'Oh, you never know,' she said, in answer to my asking why she'd felt the need to knock. She picked up a duster that wasn't there when we walked in, brushed something in passing, and closed the door behind her.

'Do you think she spotted 'em?' said Jed.

My dad's visit wasn't unexpected. He'd forever feel the need to show my mates, especially Jed, who was more like family, what a cool dad he thought he was; or rather how "on it" and "tuned in" he thought he was. He rubbed his hands: 'What's this one, lads? I like this one – Nice shoes, Jed.'

Who slipped a foot back into one and pulled the other from under his coat.

'He's slacking a bit, mind you,' I said. ''Had to clean one on our Jenny's bed', provoking a screech from the other bedroom, the whole house seeming to bend double.

'He's jokin',' my dad reassured, nervous titter.

My mum's hygiene routine made her cock of the estate, a status not so easily earned, there were some bona fide battlers, in-built grubby net-curtain detectors all. But how many had trained their cat to moult outside?

'Garnet Mimms,' I replied, to my dad's initial question, in wait of some witty remark.

'Aye, I like that one, aye… aye... Garland What?'

'It's 'Garnet', Pete,' corrected the re-loafered peacock.

'"Garnet"? As in *Alf* Garnet?'

'Garnet Mimms,' I reiterated, reminding myself of the sergeant in *Zulu*.

''Sounds like cheap jewellery,' he jibed, for his ever appreciative one-man audience. 'Or a dodgy drink. Imagine, Jed, if his second name were Garnet?' He wielded his hands in a name-in-lights fashion: 'Tonight, The Alhambra proudly presents… Garnet... Garnet.'

I'd try to keep my mouth shut at these moments, or I tended to get tongue-tied with the two of them, ask my dad something silly, like what was so clever about the name Billy Fury – Billy Fury, Gary Angry, sounded bloody stupid! Only for them to laugh at rather than with me. And so I gave up, good-humouredly vanquished...

As the poignant echo of Mimms' frantic quest faded, I deemed it time to give thought to the sartorial magic trick, by tugging at a stiff-hinged door belonging to the divided wardrobe.

It was tough sharing a bedroom with my sister at seventeen, sole plus being the dressing table mirror, where I'd spend many an hour either in adoration or frustration, depending on the flawless or not quite the case fit. Then there were the moves, which I'd analyse by plonking the *Dansette* on Jenny's bed, considering how difficult it was to step away from my reflection between tunes.

Other than the table, it was all negative. Like Jenny bringing back her *Rambo*-to-be and playing my records, hence my hiding the bit and losing it. Or the more obvious hitch for a seventeen year old male: the bed-scratching, my five evenings at home – she may have been rarely here but could still catch me out. Or my immediate problem. 'That's pretty,' said my dad, 'put that on', singling out a vividly visible summer dress.

Exasperation, compounded by the knowledge my passion for attire had stemmed from the very man. If Jed's brother Steve had groomed the plant into glorious bloom, my dad had sewn the actual seed. The hours I'd gazed at photos dating from '55 to '65, of himself with his mates or my mum. Without exception, he epitomized the modern jazzy Italian, that late '50s model – Albert Finney/*Arthur Seaton* in *Saturday Night and Sunday Morning,* like him. 'Christ, it's your dad!' someone always said, whenever that film was on telly.

And then there was the music. His heroes were more Nat King Cole and Ray Charles than Bill Haley. Not forgetting Sam Cooke, who made me cry before my dad had even explained the words to *A Change Is Gonna Come*. Billy Fury was more his style guru, and who could blame him?

But if we had no time for Teds and Punks, our gang owed them thanks, for clearing the high streets' shelves of flared trousers. Meaning we'd be no longer obliged to rummage about second-hand market stalls and the obscure little '50s specialist boutiques in Manchester, Leeds and Nottingham. The downside was that it put a lid on the double takes. We believed our detractors as incapable of understanding us as we were them, and with more than dedication we followed a universal, unwritten code, if each of us had our own adaptation of that code. There was nothing like being a dyed-in-the-wool individualist.

Unlike my dad, I disliked Jed's hair. Only because I'd have died for it. Where his grew biologically into an early Rod Stewart piece, mine, left un-flattered for more than five minutes, had me looking crossbred between Nana Mouskouri and Mary Hopkins. My reply was to wear it at a decent length on top and achieve a clear-cut flick-up at the front – a quiff, for all intents and purposes, but I'd never call it that. It was a delicate procedure, which Jed called 'Operation Brian Setzer', and was facilitated by a furtive helping of hairspray – there were things I couldn't even tell my best friend. No surreptitious moment at hand, the hand made do with the comb, three minutes out of the five. For the remaining two, it gripped round the tool's sweaty spine in my trouser pocket. I'd have sympathised with that Narcissus fellow if I'd known who he was. Then again, Jed and co, who'd all call by to use the dressing table mirror, probably didn't know who he was either.

For Steve, an unwritten book of short stories was his most influential hand-me-down. There was something mysterious about a word he'd use, succinct yet suggestive, exclusive-sounding: 'Mod'. I'd once spent a whole afternoon in a Hunstanton promenade gents' rooted to my seat, facing the term's acutely carved plural on my cubicle's wooden door. I all but grieved years on, discovering the doors had been replaced.

This was before the coming of the young 'revivalists' – or in Jed's undying words, 'the half-baked, face-*less,* uncomprehendin' green hordes'; he was such a snob... – who were waiting just around the corner.

As for now, he, my best friend, had placed his Curtis Mayfield on the deck.

And I, with a defeated smile and slacks, made off to the infinitesimal sink opposite, in a damper corner of the other, sun-barred bedroom.

At the top of the stairs, I spotted my mum through the quarter-open door, forever at odds, it seemed, like she had a point to prove to the varnish. Until Sam came to my aid with a flustered cry: 'There's some people on the telly kissin'. Shall I turn it over?'

She'd forgotten about our Sam, she confessed, darting past and down.

Once young *Aramis* had splashed to my excruciating rescue, ravaging the memory of the soap's marble-brown cracks, I stole a lustrous, silky black dress and knocked ahead of re-opening my bedroom's door, to find my dad flicking through the records and Jed shoeless again. On my asking whether they thought it – the frilly item my mum couldn't have worn outdoors, I'd never seen it before – went with the trousers, my dad left, leaving the door ajar.

But then he never could fathom why I'd put myself through the next test on the evening's schedule, my bathe-substitute, soon as having thrust my shoeless buddy up the bed and wedged myself between his legs, ever shirtless and chilled.

Jed prodded where none-else would.

From our school days, fleck sighted, he'd go at it like my dad went at the pantry, hammer-less yet as if besieged by the same persuasive force: squeezed, wiped, hunt for the clone. And while I believed he was sick, his wacky blackhead love affair did have its uses... as when, in some nightclub, I fired the intoxicated lines – 'Of course I like Barry Manilow' – and Jed erased two zits on the opposite side of my neck, the girl none the wiser.

He was ever so quick: 'Look at the size o' that beauty.'

'Careful, you're hurtin'.'

Just not quick enough this evening to prevent my mum's shot. '*Aahhhhh*!' she screamed. 'You're dis*gu*stin', you are!'

I'd get it cleaned, I told her – the dress. There was no need to 'have a dickey.'

'*Me* have a dickey? Where I'm standin'...' But that was as far as she got, and why we'd never know what she meant.

'I think it's me, Phill,' Jed nudged. 'I'm not hurtin' him, Joan, he asks me to do it.'

'Well you ought to say 'No'!'

My dad called the 'noisy sod' to come down, said she shouldn't have been here in the first place, not while we were 'busy.'

Gaze at sea, she made her most impressive exit to date.

''See what you mean,' said Jed, focussing on an awkward little blighter. 'What's she takin' for it?'

Like from Morecambe's two-handed slap at either side of Wise's lovable grin, as my mum pushed open the door at the bottom of the stairs, that exultant audience laughed wholly again, and we with them, as if seated front row.

43

Job done, Jed pushed the record box back under the bed and pulled his shoes from the knickers drawer, before joining my dad in ogling the latest crumbly bombshell for *Cadbury's Flake* – my dad's principles went right out of the window whenever she was on. Sam's 'smacker' soaked my cheek and earlobe.

'You stink,' he said, pulling a face.

'You do realise you look like the Gestapo in them coats,' his dad laughed.

Only because he wouldn't recognise style if it bit him 'on the arse,' I told him, to my mum's alarm, Sam's face hitting the sofa so hard he'd have been safer laughing out loud.

'Anyhow,' she said, 'don't you normally go dancin' in Rotherham on Wednesdays?'

I described how the self-labelled 'East Dean Mafia' was becoming unkind to the garb. As if my dad would ever let it go.

'What are they, so-called Teds?' he scoffed, Rotherham being a Ted stronghold.

My retort was a brisk 'No', should he make next week's trip.

'Give 'em a good hiding, you're like a set of...'

'Well...' my mum coughed.

'Well, what?' he checked.

'You can't surf like The Aftershave Man,' Sam told him, tardily...

As we strutted down the path on that snappy, almost icy evening, my dad saluted us with 'Heil Hitler!' And summoned Jed back.

I marvelled at how delightful life was at these moments, blowing rings with the winter air I exhaled, anticipating the return of that unique chortle...

I'd no idea this would be the night. A change *was* gonna come... somehow.

'Sam wanted to know if I could fight *Iron Man,*' Jed reported.

'So what did you say?'

'I said: "Yeah".'

I was sure I'd said I couldn't...

*'... his addiction was to courses vain,*
*His companies unlettered, rude, and shallow,*
*His hours filled up with riots, banquets and...*
*... never noted in him any study.'*

I'd tell Sam I met *Iron Man* in the pub car park and flattened him...

My deliberation was fractured by Jed's dig: ''Lucky bastard, you.' He looked ahead. 'Do you know?'

I responded in a style befitting the moment: 'What?'

'Well... your dad...'

Did he mean the man who let *Cadbury's* get his goat?

'He's funny. And little Sam...'

I wasn't having that one either. Not after the broken biscuits cock-up.

'And your grom...'

He doted on her most. Then again he didn't suffer the hand-slaps.

A potential remedy to Jed's sober façade, which was getting a bit embarrassing, presented itself in the form of two young senoritas, who, although occupying the street-end's bus shelter, weren't waiting for a bus. 'This man is a sexual tyrannosaurus,' I declared.

But as it appeared zilch would be forthcoming by way of a verbal response – they produced the Presley upper-lips; blew bigger bubblegum bubbles, that sort of thing – we moved on, to a part-whispered backing of 'More like a diplodocus...'

Jed flung open The Grouse's swinging doors, where I was barred by a trembling hand belonging to 'Frail ol' Jim'. 'You'll be the end of me,' he threatened, 'comin' in like that. You bring back too many memories.'

''Remind you o' the good ol' days?' I said.

'The bad uns, more like, I keep thinkin' it's the SS walkin' in.'

I was rescued by The Detroit Emeralds' *Feel The Need In Me,* its speedy ascent above the geriatric uproar and Jed's more youthful guffaw. Our thirty-something landlady, Marlene, pulled the pints and placed her elbows on the bar, tendered me that ever inscrutable stare, as I shuffled on up...

... back, and on up again...

The groove went skew-whiff from strain more than anything else – my grom supplied the y-fronts and they'd have tested Houdini; I'd yet to make the connection between such negligence and the lack of real sex...

... – all during which Marlene's husband Frank, or 'Brick Shit House' among crossed customers, had passed his enormous head through to our side, still standing in the other. 'Do you ever find, Phillip,' he said, to more pensioner approval, 'that your beer's lost its charm by the time you get it?' I told him his wife was worth every flat mouthful, but rather than quash me he looked guilty himself. ''Hope so,' he cleared his throat, 'it's gone up today.'

'What's the damage, then?'

''Penny on both: Magnet and Bitter. Oh, and two on the lager.'

The big softy at heart knew I wasn't old enough to drink; and probably that I'd have surrendered my wages just to hold his wife's hand. She was a woman. I was seventeen and she was... thirty-one? The kind of thing Bobby Golsboro songs were made of... *But,* while ever her husband imparted the wherewithal to conceal my lusty thoughts, I'd play the game. And so I staged an Olivier-type exhortation of my own, Jed – who'd already been taken by another World War Two discourse – not so much lending a hand as pushing me on. 'No, felled citizens, ye that held them vasty French fields in a cockpit so he could run this pub!' Phrases of that ilk, to the ancient warriors' tumultuous encouragement. Until I committed the error of alluding to that ever approaching 'pound a pint', when Frank's guise took on a more dour air – there was holding his wife's hand and the serious stuff. I concluded to 'yon valiant countrymen' that 29p was still a long way off that dreaded day.

He shook his head and ordered me into the other side where I belonged, before heaving his top-half back to the same place.

46

I'd have snatched my drink and tagged on, had it not been for The Miracles' *Love Machine.* 'You have,' Marlene insisted, 'you've got ants in your pants.'

If I told her there wasn't room, only by around 3am this coming Saturday, shuffling along to Pat Lewis' *Look At What I Almost Missed,* would I grasp, going by that salacious leer, what she thought I'd implied...

She placed another pint of *Guinness* into Frail ol' Jim's shaky hand. He'd drink half and refill the glass with a *Barley Wine,* one after the other, in that order, all and every evening. The shakes were understandable. That he was still alive was a thriller.

Dropping the coins into the till, she jiggled her hips to a Cliff Noble instrumental, which indicated 'the other four' were already here. ''Came in before you two silly buggers,' she winked.

Jed's escape from Colditz was, as always, by way of an edgy and complex route – he loved the heroic tales. Though this evening he'd have done himself a service holding back that while longer. For when we picked up our glasses... we were foiled by our friends of the flea world.

'In before your crowd,' Marlene thumbed, and pressed a ten-p piece into the palm of my free hand. 'Here,' she said, 'go put some music on.' Free's *Alright Now* wasn't how she defined the word either.

The jukebox became the victim of two disdainful gawks.

Salutations differed according to area. Hefty hisses derived from the 'Hairy Corner' – we sometimes called it the 'Polluted Corner'; we varied it – the place those oily booted, leathery creatures in shrouds of unkempt hair installed themselves six evenings a week. The batting eye-lashes stemmed from the 'Div' girls, middling, and the smirks of odium from their Div boyfriends. It appeared much friendlier in our habitual locality, the bar, Frank incorporated.

The Hairies, or 'Yetis', were in truth an affable bunch, and Jed's main brokers of funny cigarettes. And although we found them unsightly, mutual respect did exist. Like us, they had their scene, their Rock music, and were as devoted to it as we to ours. Theirs was a Sheffield central club, The Wapentake, which also boasted a region-wide clientele. They let us be as we did them, barring the odd joke about the jukebox and personal hygiene, or when they'd 'head bang' and we'd fret about things jumping from those tidal waves of hair. We in fact complemented one another, enhanced the opposite's manner and appearance, each of us striving never to be mistaken for one of those middle-grounders. Conversion either way would have paralleled the Americans going Communist. Yet being poles apart rendered us similar.

The Div, on the other hand, was a different kettle of fish – unless she happened to look like Jane Fonda in *Barbarella,* or Sally Geeson in *Bless This House…* Coined at Wigan Casino, an umbrella term for multifarious subspecies, the Div made up 99.9 percent of the population. Here, they were split into two strains: either working-class and dense, or middle-class and very dense.

For the former, life offered little more than dodgy junctions on the common and Ford Escorts on the never-never, anal sex – didn't need Johnny for that one – and kicking travelling Spurs enthusiasts until eyes hung from sockets. It was all downhill from there.

The latter were Punk rockers, or ex-, homemade orifices outnumbering freckles, jackets on the back of which apple-white paint endorsed a wacky diet of global destruction and intimate relations with Royalty. It was a wonder they had time for a drink at all.

Loathing was shared and tension like the pressure cooker in our kitchen. At best, we were pill-popping homosexuals, proof in the pudding, or refined wear. Or the weekly trans-Pennine trips to a club that opened its doors at midnight, closed them eight hours on, and offered nothing harder than bottled *Coca Cola…* Oh, and, regarding the opposite sex, a club in which we looked but never touched – we didn't have the time…

Yes, I could see their point.

And so we were back where we belonged. Frank was wringing out a drenched bar towel.

I attributed our preference for standing to the long waits outside the headmaster's office, for 'six o' the best', or four in April's case, Macca's other half. Chris and Paul completed 'the gang', a simple title agreed upon at one end of our school's middle floor corridor, during a cigarette break from that lack of education.

Six blank sheets were hardly a true reflection, and my story would have spoken for most.

If I was plagued by numerous events, four were far-reaching, first doling out bewilderment and anger, and then anger, then fear and anger, and more anger, this last one goading me on to rebellion – not to be confused with the "apple-white" variety.

\* \* \* \* \*

Bewilderment was the upshot of a reading exam I took for Mr. Tuffand. Each pupil was made to leave the class and read aloud a sheet of words to a voluptuous lady examiner in the corridor. Keeping an eye on the rest of us, Mr. Tuffand would nip out to see how the examinee was doing. Whizzing through the P-section – '... paraphernalia, parsimonious, promiscuity...' (I could have told her what they meant) – I noticed Mr. Tuffand heading to the door. Better than average in English, I felt a rush of excitement, convinced as I was my auburn muse's tally would knock him sideways. If only. From a thud to the nape, my vision was turned on its head, and while the weapon was a mystery, it was a secondary issue at this point: I'd always believed we were disciplined for doing things wrong. As my classmates fell back from the ceiling to their diminutive wooden stools, my pupils began to focus again, either on their amused or bemused expressions.

'Bloody idiot!' snarled Tuffand, who looked to the examiner as if accounting for himself. 'Ten, he is, with the readin' ability of a sixteen year old...'

I got his point later in life, but was lacking in the capacity required for such an advanced philosophy and methodology at the time.

Anguished but equal in enthusiasm, I analysed each pupil's performance thereafter, hoping those who hadn't shown signs of amusement might fare badly – 'Fluff it, Tracy' – and that those who *had* would hit the jackpot – 'Go on, bastard, 30 out o' 30!' I might also have been enlightened on the identity of my teacher's martial-art object or style of freehand, since everyone in the classroom said it had been too quick to notice.

Alas, every contender in shorts or a skirt suddenly lost their ability to read, due to a fleeting condition known as exam stress. I expected Nicholas Prickett, who, before flooding the corridor, kept one eye on me and bungled every word with the other, to be comforted with tea and biscuits – this same Prickett had since done away with *Beano* and *Dandy* for *Beezer* and *Topper.*

When Tuffand told him 'laugh' didn't have an 'f' in it, well, that was it. I told the rest the temporary illiterate was 'gonna cop it after school.'

He would have, too, had he stood long enough.

I was reproved with the slipper the next morning for having, as per The Pricketts, "beat" their "son black an' blue, all because of his inability to read, as if the affliction's not bad enough in itself." Ludicrous. My slaps must have found their mark one in twenty – the bookworm's dives might have impressed Gordon Banks! The bruising was his own doing, punishment for a horrendous lack of coordination, for which I lost heaps of playground credibility.

The incident began to rotate those wheels of destiny in the wrong direction...

\* \* \* \* \*

A year on, through my abhorrence for the pop group Sweet, I set up my own Slade fan club, of which I was the boss and in which no member was allowed hair longer than a number eight on the clipper-range. Unlike Sweet, Slade represented the masculine – head-shorn virility and not Hairy-fairy. We'd play the straggly 'Sweeties' at football in the playground, and if we lost, fights broke out leaving them wishing they had.

And then the fun was over, the day we learned our headmaster had designated the whole of that spring morning for terror inducing, an extended assembly of sorts, to ensnare the two ringleaders. It worked, too, because after two interminable hours, I deemed the fear of God had started to show... But no sooner had I stood and awarded my cropped-headed chums a thank-you by nod and wink, than Julie Siddall jumped the gun, brown braces contrasting with glorious white chemise, in relief, her doe-like eyes drawn. 'I'm the leader, sir,' she said.

Tracy Woolly was more forceful, two rows in front, tilting before a creaky chair's back: 'I'm the leader, sir.'

'B... No, wha...?' stuttered our headmaster. 'Oh, for heaven's sake, this is *not Spartacus!*'

Pity he was unable to seize the moment's majesty. Instead, a riot blew up behind me; teachers knocked aside my bodyguards like nappies on a washing line. I was apprehended by both ears – my hair had proven a quandary – and dragged out to a bravura snapshot of thirty Skinheads pointing toward Nigel Bottom, the longhaired leader of the 'Sweeties'.

I was neither slippered nor held in detention, but made to return home at the school day's end, to compose a poem about Slade, and to hand it in the following morning. If I couldn't believe my luck, I decided against sisterly aid, judging the work ought to be of an aesthetic nature, rather than based on pure animalistic fanaticism. I only peeped at the plethora of pinups sellotaped to her bedside wall for inspiration, pinups snatched from abundant editions of *Fab 208* and *Jackie*. Fickle, was our Jenny. Within a day, David Cassidy had swung from 'the ultimate shag' to looking like a 'right sissy'.

I entitled the poem *Cum On Feel The Noize,* after one of Slade's many chart-toppers, and its subject reflected what I made of the song: an imaginary party where everyone was having a great time. It consisted of five six-line stanzas, each sixth line repeating the title. I used an AB rhyme and put effort into its meter...

... which all turned out to be a wasted effort. As soon as I handed it to Miss Grimbody, and parked my tiny backside on my tinier allotted chair, she read my work... and as silently left the room for a good ten minutes. During which time raised voices were heard, from inside the headmaster's office, leaving us kids baffled as to their cause.

Grimbody's manner was nervous on her return, as when she ordered me to read the poem aloud. And on the fifth, or sixth, reading, my love of an audience let me down – our headmaster was watching through the window. ''Can't hear a word,' she barked, 'read it again.' And again, provoking that all-important tear – the headmaster took off there and then.

It wasn't a badly written poem, she said at last, 'considering.

Though, on future occasions, you shouldn't solicit parental help.' I was quick to add "solicit" to my extensive mental list of vocabulary – I didn't know what else to do – while her confidence grew: 'It's also a shame your speech impediment prevented anyone else hearing it.'

'I heard every word,' murmured Kay Gosling, poised at the room's opposite end, her umbrella appearing to wilt from her desk's redundant inkwell.

Grimbody preferred to move on, to try and teach us something.

Word never got back as to the severity of Nigel Bottom's punishment. Maybe he just got off with the slipper…

* * * * *

The fear thing transpired five years on. Exam period looming, Jed and me had planned to wag the day in a neighbouring wood with a packet of twenty *No 6*, to try and form a picture of our not too distant future. How did qualifications in a land of unemployment compare with the quarterly rumours of Wigan Casino's imminent closure? Then there was the omnipresent cloud of nuclear war. Without Dave Allen's weekly sketches, *The Daily Something* had warned that lord knows how many Russian missiles were pointing at Sheffield's eastside alone – they were after those factories and I couldn't blame them. It was hardly a toughie, though reassuring to articulate identical attitudes: all-nighter service as usual.

Come lunchtime, we chose to eat instead of depositing our pennies toward new *Fred Perrys*. We'd each buy an uncut loaf from the baker's opposite the school, extract and scoff the middles, and then nip next door and ask the lady behind her lardy, salt-encrusted counter to pack them with chips. Mine was swamped in mushy peas, Jed's in scraps and vinegar.

Bellies stuffed, we realised we were 20p short of our afternoon's nicotine-supply, when Benjamin came strolling by. Except that when Jed requested the money, Benj turned out his pockets with an apology, spittle, halitosis and a jiggery briefcase, before enthusing about a 'cinema afternoon.' He ruled out *Kes* for something to do with 'England at war.'

'Oh, when kings were kings!' cried Jed, all armour, shield and

52

swinging mace. He'd have galloped off for 'Harry, England an' St George' without the sudden drizzle. Benj hadn't dared to tell him it wasn't *Henry V.* I said to sit on the room's opposite side.

It wasn't tricky going by undetected, or it allowed Miss Bland to wait until a more suitable moment, as the curtains were drawn.

I parked directly in front of Elaine 'Beavers' Bennet, since she had the habit of seizing any potential occasion – say, a chemistry experiment where the class needed to lean over one another to see anything – to unzip my fly, get a hand in, and massage her own crotch in synchrony. And it was all serious-ties free. She also had the second largest breasts in the school, after Mr. Tucker, or 'Friar', the physics teacher. Whenever anyone commented on them, she'd play on it, batting her eyelashes, deeming she was the next Jayne Mansfield. She once told our maths teacher, Mr. Benton, during some technical drawing task, that she had bigger measurements to everyone else. 'So I've noticed,' he said, lifting his eyes to the ceiling.

Throughout the endeavour, she'd rest her abnormalities on my shoulders, my head fixed within. But no matter to what lengths she'd go, and how many orgasms *she* put away, I refused to douse my trousers and wrestled against it. She could have milked it till the cows came home, as much as I relished the tease...

Today, she seemed more occupied with the traditional side of classroom activity. 'I can't, Phillip,' she whispered.

It was a documentary-style fiction about a nuclear attack on Britain, a film the powers that be had banned, we soon learned, apart from viewings in 'educational establishments'. Why our so-called educational establishment had felt the need to play the thing, I didn't know, nor did my peers, their parents or mine. 'You should've walked out,' huffed my mum, oblivious to the fact we'd only just walked in. It wasn't as if we were being told anything new, but were forced to observe a future that could have been our own, depending on the same powers that be and whether they decided to fall out with other powers that be abroad.

Elaine clutched my upper arms. Her forehead fell to my shoulder as I witnessed expressions of opened-mouthed dread. If the lads abstained from such, they chewed harder on their no longer cool-serving *Wrigley's.* All except Benjamin, who wept uninhibitedly, eliciting hugs from every girl in the vicinity, before fleeing to the toilet with an upset tummy. It turned out to be my afternoon's sole pleasure, given it was his fault I was there in the first place.

Three or four scenes from our black and white edification kicked me with indelible bruising, scenes supposedly set in places like Rochester, and maybe Canterbury, cities I'd only ever imagined being colourful in a heraldic sort of way. One was of a young boy playing in a garden. When the sirens are sounded, no-one's ready – that was the point: no-one would ever be ready. By the time the parents get out to him, then, the poor lad's already had to deal with the flash and flaming retinas – I did, I saw Sam in Jed's anxious eyes. To this day I can still hear those sirens, the sound of that blast... and that line cutting right through me: *'The blast wave from a thermonuclear explosion has been likened to an enormous door slamming in the depths of Hell.'* It was a war game alright, and they could keep it...

We never uttered a word during our stagger home that evening, when all had been said that morning and confirmed that afternoon…

Essays never scared me, it was the method by which I expressed myself best, irrespective of a teacher's response. And although I believed Miss Bland was taking the Mickey expecting two thousand words beneath the title 'My Response to a Nuclear Attack on Britain – she obviously didn't read *The Daily Something* – I knew I'd get there before my tea. Not that I'd be aspiring to academic recognition, I'd given up on that one, just the right quantity of quality to flatter her, that she leave out the interrogation as to my previous day's half-day absence.

A synopsis:

*My dad wakes us in the middle of the night, gibbering about the oncoming of yet another sadistic storm. As usual, we head for the cubbyhole, and on the way make out one of those sirens. ''Told you it's a bad un,' he says, 'we need a mattress', and disappears.*

*'He doesn't want us all to sleep in here, does he?' says Jenny.*

*'Leave him,' my mum says, 'he knows what he's doin'.'*

*I sense something's wrong and decide to offer a hand. But I lose my balance to a rumbling floor – an ear-splitting rumbling floor...*

*And before I know it, our roller coaster belongs only to Avril and me, on this stirring summer's day* – Avril, my cousin; the girl I'd get locked in the loo with when Batty was on the warpath. *We sigh in unison to our ascents, our descents, chuckle to the Hound Dog-ish gyrations of our train, and, tucked away in our bubbly passion-carriage in the sky, kiss...*

Miss Bland wasn't convinced: 'Any excuse, Rowlings, for hard-core pornography. And whatever did a fairground in Great Yarmouth have to do with the assignment?' Once she'd made herself blush, she hoped to move on.

The thing was that, had I known she was going to accuse me of writing pornography, I would have written pornography – anything to take my mind off that bloody bomb! And besides, I never mentioned Great Yarmouth, she made *that* one up as well... All I was now left with was the 'F' she allocated me for my essay, which I was at least able to return more crudely, my metal-legged chair scraping the tiled floor, knocking a ruler from the desk behind. I walked out right there. And in again the next morning for six to the back of the legs.

What I wouldn't do was yield to banging my head against a wall for good measure.

It was a shame about my English exam, questions set and invigilated by Bland, because I couldn't resist the temptation of publically cutting off my nose to spite my face. That is, when every other scholar proceeded to read questions on, and open their copy of, Jane Austen's *Mansfield Park,* I opened my copy of *Suedehead,* Richard Allen's *Skinhead* sequel, the kind of books we like-minded boys and girls read back then, back when they at least *felt* more relevant.

''Finished already, Rowlings?' Bland enquired, deigning to notice my static state.

''Only just started, Miss.'

Results circulated, we tried to convince our parents 'U' stood for 'unbeatable', and that we'd achieved all seven. My dad was having none of it and learned the printed truth from an O level results league in the local rag – our school had dipped a place to second from bottom. The paper crashed to his knees: 'You should've played football Saturday mornings, you need sport

55

with study!'

'I'd never have got back from Wigan in time.'

That was as far as the argument got.

\* \* \* \* \*

If our "education establishment" had given us anything, we snootily clad six at the bar, it was each other. Though, back then, we were more like work colleagues, models of the same assignments, those of being obliged to stand before assembly as an example of how not to come to school. Whenever we were sent home to get changed, we'd chat so much that we forgot to go back. Records were our key subject, some collections being more sophisticated than others, depending on the older brother influence – I was the odd one out with the older sister, who'd lost all sense of taste by '71. Jed's brother Steve had been the chief authority, given he'd frequented Manchester's Twisted Wheel on a regular basis, as well as taken his record player on his honeymoon to Blackpool.

We were unassailable and nurtured the good judgment, a judgment part-based on that to which we were routinely exposed, like in this pub. *Alright Now*'s wretched conclusion very much resembled its wretched introduction. Jed directed his question toward the Hairy Corner: 'Is that how we define a rock classic?'

'Don't start,' Afghan warned from behind a cloud, 'or I'll put it on again', generating our three or four seconds' wide-eyed hush. Threats didn't come heavier.

Discussion now got underway about Friday, the first of the month, which meant one thing: the Wigan 'oldies' all-nighter. It wasn't as if we hadn't talked about it the evening previous or wouldn't tomorrow, but that the butterflies flapped their wings twofold. Things needed repeating, like the procuring of pills, or 'gear', all throughout Frank's absence in the other side. But then I was a rare participant; staying awake was no task. And on occasions I did take part, I tended to act like Norman Wisdom in frantic search of *Mr. Grimsdale* – 'Christ, take a downer, man!' some brother or sister would advise.

On our landlord's return and Jed's request he refill the glasses, I held my best friend's arm back and waved a couple of pound notes: 'The same again for everybody.'

'Bingo win?' Frank laughed. ''Ought to invite her up here.' He turned for more glass: 'I'm sure she'd be at home with you lot.'

As he shook his massive head, we were joined by Macca's brother, Mick, five years our senior, an ex-Wigan habitué and owner of a vinyl collection and wardrobe to die for. He never entered the room without eliciting a double take, from anybody. 'What's this,' he said, 'an SS convention?'

He worked shifts for the *British Steel Corporation* and was either on nights or mornings. Afternoon shifts meant we didn't see him at all, but when we did he never looked any different. He exploited the locker-and-coat hanger trick to the max, up until Grantham's Ripper tearing along. He also earned a lot more than me. Now was my moment: ''Nearly forgot, do you want one?'

'Bitter please… Rich, are we?'

'His grom gave him a fiver,' said Frank.

There existed people to whom one didn't relate such information, and a style guru was one of them.

Toasts were made first to the lady herself. And then to Stevie Wonder, to Gladys Knight, to Gene Chandler, and to anyone else we could fit in before the beer ran out. Frank drank to Alvin Stardust. The Yetis rose as a unified woof to Led Zeppelin.

I got the next round, too, inviting Frank this time and having one sent round to his missus, insisting she be aware of the dispatcher's identity.

At some point I noted the place had been quiet for a while, but that I'd also begun to lose my clammy grip on Marlene's donated silver. Problem being, these moments could end up in disaster. I likened my fifteen foot journey to walking the plank, prayed my heavy-duty mattress-carrying vessel would be passing below once more. I probed everyone's demeanour: Who had left his/her seat within the last few minutes?

It should have worked in my favour, that the jukebox was inactive. And yet, through nerves, eyes penetrating my back, I'd rest over its roomy glass dome and allow my coin to drop too early, to rattle through its workings like a busy tap dancer. I *then* sought out Marlene's typical first choice, all so blurry by haste – up down, up down, D8. Buttons pushed, I took an understated tipple, before adding the two remaining tunes, as the letter and number-box span its ebullient way along to… B4. It was a mystery how anyone had managed to pre-empt my strike – there was a smaller version attached to the wall at the room's far end but I'd been vigilant. The truth gleamed in orange and green.

The sniggers were punctual – Travolta and Newton-John weren't even allowed time to reflect upon recent aestival romance. I heard talk of Showaddywaddy, and that if I was looking for *Happy Days,* that one was taken off last year.

The mockery's core source was a spiky blond whose plastic jacket still read *White Riot,* another Nigel. Of course, his faction whooped it up, until my sweaty clenched-fist smashed the glass. I'd give the disc a spin alright, it'd play far better to Nigel's slit jugular…

*Billy Liar* moment ended, I promised my warped gawp that our time would come.

'I didn't ask for this,' Marlene complained, peeping in.

Mick wasn't impressed either: 'Did you put this on?' Though he did instruct Nigel to shut his mouth, who'd comply without complaint, all the way up to tomorrow, same time and place, when and where we'd start over…

Last orders been and gone, our evening had passed like any other. Or so I thought. It wasn't over yet.

'Can we have your drinks off, please?' hovered the line.

On someone's reckoning it had been off all evening, our landlord wondered what that made him, the someone, if he'd been drinking it all evening

Proposals were submitted, each answer barely meriting a post-card, with Jed's clear-cut 'A cretin for shouting the same thing every night' coming off the winner.

And with panache, this ostentation of peacocks quit the establishment.

I patted the jukebox's shoulder *en route…*

## 7

*'Vows are but Breath, and Breath a Vapour is.'*

The unofficial earthquake was on time. The ground trembled to the thunder reverberating from the Grouse's car park, over and beneath which Jed pleaded that I escort him to the fish and chip shop just over, and join him in a 'Coronation Butty.'

Amazed I was still full from my tea, Mick asked for my mum's recipe, said he'd save on the shopping. As he made off, one hand in a trouser pocket, the other clicking along to some unheard tune, that mohair ensemble modified itself, in sync with the changing traffic lights at our frosty crossroads.

We then witnessed the arrival of the fifteen engines, their riders yielding to red, their motors snarling like Jed's *'greyhounds in the slips'*; Mick was to play hare. Green or thereabouts, 'Armageddon' sawed the junction in two, abandoning the rest of his raggedy faction to whistles and vain attempts to catch up. Target attained, he sounded the Red Indian war cry. Mick replied with a V sign.

I told Jed to repeat his last line.

'I said,' he said: '"Think about it, a thick fishcake covered in mushy peas between a breadcake"...'

April had heard enough: 'Get to the chippy with him, you're like a pair o' women.' She was one of the boys, our April, but a real girl. 'And the night after next it's Wigan, gentlemen,' she reminded, executing a black-fisted salute with a chilly looking white hand.

The chippy was on mine and Jed's route only, 200 yards from which I'd be transported to a gastronomic heaven.

Fearing a vinegary counter, I stood upright-to-arc-like, prompting my dad's comedic partner of the same name to ask what the hell I'd been drinking – each Pete used the other as his stooge in The Grouse, save evenings my dad played team snooker for the Working Men's Club next door. Their audience called them 'The Two Petes'. And since this Pete's laugh was as infectious as *my* best mate's, we soon drowned out the deep fat fryers' sizzle. Patti Smith might have done the job on her own, rasping a prophetic *Because The Night,* had she not been swimming against the tide as the fat-encrusted radio lost the station in waves.

'Big Mavis', who allegedly lived off the remains of the day, presented Pete with a wrapped serving for the family – he was allowed out every evening on that basis. Looking Jed's way, she said: ''Usual, Rod?'

The grin was pert: 'With a handful o' chips.'

She knew his proper name, she was his next-door neighbour, but insisted he was Rod 'The Mod' Stewart's love-child. 'Salt 'n' vinegar, darlin'?'

'Give me all you got, Maggie Mave!'

She had a bit of a crush on Jed. The operative word, according to Pete, who, candid as ever, said she'd break every bone in the poor lad's body. Our queen of toilet humour promised she'd 'let him lay on top', wiggling her hefty hips to A Taste Of Honey's *Boogie oogie* doodah – Frank and Marlene must have heard her resulting shriek. Once she'd doused the butty and chips in vinegar, Jed snatched the bottle and helped himself to a real portion.

Husband Colin, whose head didn't reach the counter, hadn't uttered a word but gone about his business, tossing and stirring fish and chips in the big metal baskets inside the fryers. It was common knowledge who was boss in that household. Jed would recount many a yarn having held a glass against his bedroom wall a night previous.

'Poor bastard,' thought Pete, post-our 'Goodnight's.

'Poor what?' said Jed. 'He groans more than her...'

But Pete had since become engrossed in Jed's extraordinary vinegar intake, while Jed had become too engrossed to notice. By a streetlight, Jed held up a chip and informed us United had got Brighton this Saturday, proof of which we read in reverse, from one end of the chip to the other. It was mind-blowing the ink had survived at all, I said.

I could only imagine what we looked and sounded like that black-icy evening, slipping and sliding along to a series of one-liners: a trio of *Little Demon* bangers in motion, with an endless stream of gunpowder…

At Pete's turnoff, he warned us against any more 'arm-in-arm malarkey crossin' the road' – Jed's habitual dragging me over to the chippy. 'I mean, what would your dad say?'

And as he sprinted off like a hungry teenager, to disentangle his steaming sack, a chain of the evening's events, from waking on the bus to leaving the house, flashed in front of my eyes. While 'Uncle Pete' was unravelling his five portions of fish, chips and mushy peas, I'd begun to unscramble my mum's abrupt, bizarre behaviour. I sat on a patch of grass…

That was prior to the burning sensation trickling down my thighs.

Having shaped his paper spout – something he'd perfected studying episodes of *Vision On,* however much he refuted the idea – with which Jed would wolf down his lime-striped residue, he poured it, the residue, over my legs and squinted into the distance.

I was caught mid-curse by a couple's tumble to our right, wife acting as crutches, challenging evening in The Grouse per chance. In vain, I felt awful about the bad language.

'Don't worry about it now,' pledged the husband, in what I would one day learn to be a Galway accent, 'I can do a lot fuckin' better than that, so I can...'

'Be Jesus, listen t' him now!' bade the wife, lugging his arm. 'The lad was tryin' to be polite, you gret big heap of a shit...' Despondent, 'I'm the one who's sorry,' she said, 'I can't take him anywhere...'

Despite my bottom-half, they made me smile. Good omen: I'd be seeing more of those two…

Jed brought me back, with 'It's them two birds.'

'Birds?'

'That ptero-wotsit and her friend. She was across the road. She shouted to the other one an' ran back into the bus shelter.' His eyes widened: 'They're waiting for us.'

Not this weather, it was −1°c. They must have been desperate.

'What do you mean, ''desperate''?'

'Just watch your Soul strut,' I instructed.

He said I was addressing the master. I was also wiping peas from my cheeks, having shot the rest over the wall, a place I hoped would serve as a sexual refuge in the coming moments. I urged Jed to let me do the talking.

'No, you did that comin' up and failed like a waz.'

I hadn't failed, I said, I was just messing. And besides, he'd believed himself above them.

Well, he said, he'd not had a drink yet and so probably was.

To be sure they were here for our benefit, we played disinterested, taking only the craftiest of snaps by the shelter... before trading glares of disbelief. 'They didn't look that good walkin' up,' I thought I heard Jed think.

Our near walking backwards may well have bolstered their titters, but we'd need something more positive, something earnest and intelligent to...

'So, how's it going, diplodoco?'

Something like that. And if I looked anything like Jed, we both looked a little obvious.

I made it clear I'd been joking, that: 'You look more like Raquel Welch in *One Million Years BC*. And you,' I said, pointing to her bubblegum friend, 'you're the spit of Victoria Vetri in *When Dinosaurs Ruled The Earth*... just a bit darker.'

Again it wasn't the reaction I'd anticipated – I could never fathom whether John Smith was my friend or not. Victoria wasn't: ''Bit of a dinosaur nerd, then?'

I didn't answer. Or rather, I answered, but with a question of my own, by asking if she'd like to come and play with my triceratops. I also asked Jed how he viewed the matter, except he was too interested in Victoria's reply, to answer...

'Mime artists and dinosaur nerds,' she smirked. 'Congrats on the *Bill and Ben* impression, by the way, walking down. Any chance of an autograph?'

The other two now gazed in my direction before Raquel's hair could catch up.

Except I'd play for time, that I might un-nest some protective muse from the bleary depths of my cudgelled brain, like a three-inch thick, Sheffield steel shield for this young lady. I was rescued, voice shilly-shally, by one of my dad's predilections, it being that I'd got a soft spot for her. And as things stood, I'd make sure to thank him in the morning.

She sounded comically cynical: 'Oh yeah?'

'Yeah. A little swamp on Bolshoi Road.'

'"Bolshoi Road"? Exotica. Then you must take me and show me,' she said, tilting her head, her bobbed hair falling away from unquestionably brown eyes. My stipulation was that she donate a bubblegum, at which she nitpicked with *'Juicy Fruit',* and apologised for using them up waiting for us.

I'd be quick to jump on that admission...!

'Do get on with it,' said Raquel, seeming to wake, before forming a very pretty smile of her own. 'I mean, it's obvious you fancy each other stupid... Shall we leave them to it, Jed?'

'Err... yeah. Keep the faith, Soul brother,' he winked.

As they strolled away, I observed how Raquel placed an arm through Jed's, like she'd known him years but not seen him for years. I'd no idea what he said but saw her gaze up to him and laugh, how her head fell onto his shoulder in a state of complicity, as if they knew something we didn't, had planned it all along. What I knew was that they were happy. As was Victoria. However brief this bliss, it would for all time spin its merry way back round, like the letter-and-number box on our favourite record machine... and not a second of it would be wasted. Such were our viewpoints and values founded during those wagged school days. It was easy for us: we were invincible... weren't we?

The question now was, would she mind sharing her last *Wrigley's*.

'I've been chewing it,' she said, and half-dared a 'Or is that...?' Pressing the gum to the fore with her tongue, she produced a faint clacking sound pulling a piece away, to Jed and Raquel's last, light cry, their cheery landscape fading into the late evening's icy air. What I couldn't work out was how she managed to blow bubbles with them, until she explained, in a whisper: 'I'm gifted with my mouth.'

And so I squeezed my clammy comb with a surely visible shudder, gaped to the bounds of a throbbing heart. Fluids were shared and foreplay had never been so stimulating... despite the fear I should reach the finish line before running the race.

'Where are we going?' she said, in a more distinct accent, as I yanked her to The Wood, behind the houses.

We were already by my favourite tree.

My spine bumped against its mammoth trunk. Our mouths locked in a muffled clink. Fingers a riot, we collapsed to the grass in rime-coated abandon, where she purred and writhed like a back-scratching black cat on a sundrenched pavement, at odds with the pulled-and-pushed skimpy Scots skirt. Disengaging for a lungful, I flung the coat behind me and made for my fly. But I didn't need her help... if saying so was difficult, in a delectable sort of way. Her hand ceased the sorceries only when, in semi-sleep-like concern, she wondered whether my old briefs actually caused me pain, which sprang away before my rip and toss. Sliding her top-half down, she arched her back. A breeze sufficed.

'No,' I begged, and maybe told her I loved her in the same steamy breath.

Drawing her turtleneck top above a white cotton bra, she guided my juddering person through winter night's pant, and revelled in the flood... ahead of delivering a scandalous smile: 'I won't ask if you always shoot that fast, but do you always shoot that much? I mean, how often do you bring yourself off?'

Bring myself off? I'd never heard it put like that before.

''Better being a girl.' She placed a kiss on my belly: 'Would you like to do it for me now?'

She was convincing, I'd give her that. And although I declined, I didn't run away. Instead, I sat beside her and covered us with my coat, where, beneath a full moon, above the houses at the foot of the banking, we viewed a Sheffield-by-night shimmering in the distance...

She broke the calm-instilling silence, with 'So what's your name?'

'Err... Phillip... Yeah, it's Phill.'

'Are you not sure?'

'Yeah, Phill... double l.'

'And I look like Victoria who, then?'

'Vetri... but not really...'

'You mean you were bullshitting me?'

'And your accent?'

'Oh, we just hate having been taught to speak properly. It stunts your growth,' she said. 'So where do you live?'

'Down there,' I nodded, releasing my free arm, flicking my fingers as if splashing off water. Truthful with my name, I couldn't be precise with the aim and point out the end block house, about 200 yards from our feet. 'And you?'

'The private houses opposite the shelter. We moved in a few months ago. 'Seen you and Jed walk by most evenings, and tonight, well, we thought we'd go for it.' Her glistening black eyes peered up: 'We don't half laugh when you come back down. Those strange dances of his, in the middle of the road. You just sit on the pavement in hysterics.'

'Yeah... he's wapped. So where do you work?'

''See, most kids at our school would have said something dull like 'bonkers' or 'nuts'.'

'School?'

'We're doing our A-levels at St Michael's at the top of the street, and Denise is staying at ours until they're over; we wanted to stay together. You look amazing,' she said. And: 'I love Soul but Denise and I are more into Rod Stewart. 'Been to Wigan, once, it shattered me. I don't know how they do it every week – Well, I do, but it's illegal.'

She huddled into my chest when I said I'd never get how anyone could 'be turned on by a cockney jock in tights'; she rammed my coat collar to her mouth, to prevent waking the sleepers in the bedrooms below.

And as I uncovered midnight eyes from midnight hair, she smiled: 'Do you understand why we love to be around lads like you?' She talked of 'spoilt, punky brats' at school or on the avenue, of 'middle-class arses.'

'Well, I'd prefer my kids to go to a Catholic school,' I argued, squinting at steel city lights. 'And maybe keep 'em out these shit holes, if you'll pardon my French.'

'It's okay,' she said, like she didn't agree. 'I'm doing French A-level.'

Maybe she didn't agree, but I doubted she'd ever made use of a lavatory in the kind of Siberian conditions my home boasted. 'Oh, I'm half French. 'Just hate speakin' it.'

*'Mais vas-y, tu pourrais m'aider avec mes études.'*

Indubitably, she was gifted with that tongue: *'Oui.'*
*'Tu n'aimes pas parler français à ce point?'*
But she'd be wasting her time this time: *'Oui.'*
*'Qu'est-ce...* Can I smell bullshit again?'
*'Oui.'* It was time to change the subject. She must have had a favourite Soul tune?

It wasn't that she avoided questions, more she didn't hear them: 'We've been watching films of a movement called *La Nouvelle Vague,* from the late fifties...'

And I wouldn't be patronised or condescended to.

'Listen,' she said, sitting up, to surrender a miscellany of Gallic sounds I presumed to be film titles or artists, culminating in an Anglo-Saxon 'You're hard again, aren't you...' Removing her hand to click her fingers, she found 'Jean-Luc Goddard, *A Bout De Souffle',* paused... and allowed a capital P to all but mistily shape before her glassy lips, in 'Paris. '59, I think.' The best tagged on: 'I couldn't help thinking of you – You just have to see what's-her-name-Seberg. Naughty short hair. That gutsy gamine thing. Suedehead...'

It being how my mum bought me in a sale from 'Marks An' Sparks', I had her know. *'Abercrombie* all in.' But I should have quit while I was ahead, refrained from taking a stab at the filmmaker's name: 'Joan Luke God... waaa..?'

'You're funny,' she said, rubbing her nose into my neck, to then reel off a list of Soul classics: *'If You Loved Me*, Peggy March. Anything by Edwin Starr – Dave's always called him 'Our Elvis'. *What Can I Do,* Lorraine Chandler', like she'd acknowledged my question after all, just put it on hold: *'Be Young Be Foolish Be Happy,* The Tams. *Baby Do The Phillydog,* The Olympics – I love Phillip Mitchell's *Winner Takes All*, do you?' On, she went: 'Brenda Holloway's *Just Look What You Done* – Oh, and Junior Walker's *Take Me Girl I'm Ready.* Denise and I don't half dance around the bedroom to that one – That saxophone, wow!'

Lost in an abyss of tedium, she was a passionate girl seeking passion.

And as long as she understood things be of a fleeting nature, she'd come to the right place. If Marvin Gaye had stood Jed and me in good stead with *Wherever I lay My Hat,* The Fantastic

Johnny C had confirmed all with *Don't Depend On Me*. And if it was good enough for Marvin and Johnny, then it was good enough for us. In the interim, I'd need to know: 'Do you dance to Junior Walker... in your uniforms?'

''Depends.' She broke off to put a finger to her nose: 'Why does my hand smell of vinegar? It depends whether we've just got home from...'

But how did she know all this stuff?

'Well, my brother, Dave, went to The Twisted Wheel in Manchester – We're from Cheshire. And others like Va-Va's in Bolton and... Up The Junction? In Crewe? 'Did The Torch in Stoke-on-Trent, too – Our Mr. B wrote a song for him.'

'What?'

'The forever-young Marc Bolan, *Dandy in the Underworld*? I could have loved him, she sighed, with a wink, 'if Rod hadn't gotten in the way. Anyhow, we got to know Sheffield through his visits to Samantha's. He loved the place. 'Took me to Wigan about a year ago, without my parents knowing – 'Bit of a rebel, you know. He's just got divorced. Though, Catholic, he's not supposed... – You are, you're hard again. The smell's not becoming, mind you, do you wear it a lot?'

She looked puzzled on my asking if she'd heard of *'our* Mr. J'. I followed up with 'Chuck Jackson?'

In place of a direct answer this time, she readdressed her posture. And, after something of a timid throat-clearing, as I took in the city's full moon, she went into song. Our very own *I've Got The Need*. I'd never heard anything like it. Bound by my own fascination...

So what was the Rod Stewart thing about? I asked her in time.

Now she was direct: 'He's a sex god.' As direct as she was with her next piece, opening air modesty conquered. That there *I Was Only Joking*.

Another apt piece; I'd never listened to the lyrics before, but then I'd also never had it sung expressly for me. And all I could think was that she was casting a spell. Had the *Juicy Fruit* been part of some elaborate plot? She played violin to boot, she told me...

Undaunted, I called her a 'darling.'

'And,' she beamed, *'Men who are dandies and women who are darlings rule the world.''*

'Where did you get that from?'

'Oh, just some book I'm reading.'

It was through deference I took her hand and lead her back to the oak, that I might somehow make amends for my earlier performance, be *her* Frenchman for the night, more *Cyrano* without the nose than a *Flintstone* without a club, coat serving as cape. And while she wasn't impressed with my pointing out the notches above my head, I made clear they signalled the times I'd fallen from the tree and broken my arm.

'You're wapped,' she whispered. But my dad's latest number was mistimed. She peered down the banking: 'Someone's come out of that house, into the back yard.'

''Somebody lettin' a cat out,' I said. 'Or in.'

She gave a full running commentary: 'He's opened another door. He's put on a light... and closed the door...' – why he hadn't made do with the upstairs bucket was a mystery. The moment the flush reverberated like Niagara Falls, she all but burst into tears: 'Those poor souls.' Like I was to blame: 'Why hasn't someone welcomed them into the 20th century?' Before I led her away, she was about to go down and *invite* him to that hundred year leap, I was sure of it. 'Can I see you again?'

I asked whether she'd get into trouble.

'No,' she smiled, between ardent kisses, and that they both had keys. Releasing herself from the cape, she crossed the road like a model on a frosty catwalk. 'Anyhow, we don't have lessons till tomorrow afternoon.'

'What's your name?'

'Victoria.'

'Really?'

She blew a joy-peppered kiss and disappeared behind a front garden's privet hedge, from where I heard 'It's Nathalie. With an 'h'', like I'd know where it went. 'After the 't'. It's French. Goodnight, Phillip-with-a-double-l.'

I was in no rush to get home. I craved a cigarette but had run out in The Grouse. For it to hang from the side of my mouth, half-smoked, ash holding on. A *Gauloise* would have been just right. To lean against that lamppost like Joan Luke Godwar... –

I'd have wagered he smoked *Gauloises* in his films. Hands in pockets, collar erect, I longed for Shirecliffe Hill's antenna to be the Eiffel Tower. To break the news to myself, tough-world-out-here nod, that another ship... – no, a horse-powered car, that was it, one of those French things – had passed in the night, offhand flick of unfinished, un-tipped cigarette to the... 'sidewalk'...

Fag-ash-Jed was never around when I needed him. But then I could always sing.

Yet I knew my delirium wasn't based solely on an ever nearing Friday, or its alcohol mix. I was acquainted with that cocktail...

''*Oy*!' Stan bawled, quietly – he could do that – squeezing his head through the bottom quarter of a rotting sash window – the damp and ice made them stick. 'Cut it out, I've got to be up in an hour...'

I was pushing my luck asking if I looked like Alain Delon.

'More like *Andy Capp*!' He threatened to give me a 'bloody pastin'', shook his space-limited head.

I completed my remaining yards on tiptoes, and was welcomed home by the cat, Brainy, a title bestowed on her by Sam: for him all she did was eat and sleep. Forever in high spirits at this time of night, she'd purr and raise her back in frequent jerks against my calves. At my most attentive, I'd even allow her to spring onto a mohair knee.

she clearly wasn't one for the more acidic odours, all the same.

I flung all but the trench coat at the laundry basket in the kitchen – or at least that was my aim; the shot-slung sweatshirt misfired. But I wouldn't take time to see where it landed for being distracted by my leg-tops: I'd lost all visible trace of y-front seam indentations.

Between the sheets, without delay, I grabbed the transistor from under my bed. It was tuned into Radio Hallam, a station offering a melodically inclined and, after mid-night, advert-free programme; songs back to back but for the odd romantic request.

The Devil had ordered them: Blue Mink's *Stay With Me*. A certain Sylvia's *Pillow Talk*. Even when The White Plains upped the tempo with *My Baby Loves Love,* Nathalie's supernatural lips filtered into every refrain. I ached for three minutes of the cockney jock himself, as per a request by some mysterious female caller... until the dog-tired batteries gave up on me.

And so I sang myself a lullaby: I don't remember the words exactly, from that there *Only Joking* number, but they had something to do with my dad telling us how stupidly we dressed. Oh, and not that it prevented us being proper heart-breakers...

## 8

*'Deal mildly with his youth,*
*For young, hot colts being raged do rage the more.'*

Cue music: *'Junior Walker's Take Me Girl I'm Ready. Denise and I don't half dance around the bedroom to that one – That saxophone, wow!'*

These, my sunrise sessions. Maybe less predictable than the sunsetters, the dreams were no less intense. The tactile kind. The one you're woken from having just dropped off through exhaustion – I *had* just dropped off; I *was* exhausted...

*... St Michael's bottle-green. Badge, some sort of phallic emblem. And whatever were they doing with that violin...*
*'Think about it,' said Jed, 'a nice young banana between a freshly baked breadcake...'*
*While Sam advised there was another bus on its way.*
*But this rug, the lush; the lustre – this middle-class rug! Silver without the fish...*
*Oh – 'No,' I said, and maybe that I was 'comin'' in the same confused breath...*

'Aye,' my mum clarified, 'you've been sayin' that for the last five minutes and you've not budged...'

*... and that sorting out Jed's banana might also...*

'Not bloody likely, get out o' bed!'
She was either too early or too late, if all I captured from a blind peek were nebulous impressions of a night no more. Again I thought of Jed, the skilled indoor tile fitter who only turned up

when his boss said he should – when there was work – lost in a duvet...

I scampered to the other room, empty barring a lightly snoring Sam, and dried more thanks to speed than congealed cloth.

I scurried back with another predicament: my last pair of y-fronts had gone to the wild. I flicked through Jenny's dressing table drawer with a teeth-rattling tremor.

''You up yet?' my mum kept on, at the stairs' midway point.

My response was audible only to myself, I thought.

'That's naughty,' said Sam. 'Phill's bum's in the air – I can see his willy. He's playin' with Jenny's knickers.'

Needs did must.

I clutched my brother by the nape and hoisted him from the floor, akin to how my dad might once have saved my life.

My mum asked what I was up to. But at that point I wasn't sure.

'Makin' me laugh,' Sam said.

I wondered if she might 'throw up my clobber, before *I* clobber him...'

'Aye, and I'll clobber you,' she pointed.

'Can I eat my breakfast in peace?' ascended the appeal, serene by comparison.

'Which clobber do you want? That in the kitchen, or that on the grandfather clock?'

'What do you mean, "that on..."?'

'Dad, I saw Phillip's bum.'

'Joan, come down, please, you're starting to give me indigestion.'

'What *are* you wearing...?'

'Joan...'

She retreated.

'Lend some o' my pants,' said my little brother, knocking the wind out of my sails. 'Maybe Father Christmas could bring you some new ones.'

To be or not to be angry with the lad, at this perplexing hour.

''Don't like your willy anyway, 'got hairs on it. Ask Santa for a new one of them as well.'

Clobber tossed, I began to make my way down, not yet into the dominion of Hades, more into the mire of my dad's early morning doctrines and my mum's admonitions for another nightly transgression... or two. I plummeted to the sofa and laid my head on a pillow.

'Morning, Phillip,' welcomed my dad, gnawing on burnt toast, eyes beyond the cobalt flames of a battling coal fire – just where remained his secret. Reading the zeros on a Pools cheque?

But as nothing induced contemplation like glints in an old fire-place, I'd send out a search party, there casting these dead beat eyes of mine. And as with those of a dying man, my life flashed before them. Or at least a medley of the more recent bits: '*... one o' these days, you'll have to take me to that place you dream about...*'

'*... 'Bit of a dinosaur nerd, then?...*'

'*... Do you mean intermedrary?...*'

'*... I don't know how they do it every week – Well, I do, but it's illegal...*'

'*... No coal, no electricity, no gas...*'

It was on '*"Lucky bastard, you*' that I snatched them back, to where my mum was brandishing a bed sheet.

'Do you want toast? What's wrong with this? It was clean on yesterday!' Three octaves in one breath – and she couldn't half get round the house at 5:45 of a morning.

Steadily drawing his eyes from the flickering coal, 'What have you done to the sheet?' my dad asked me.

I didn't get it. I'd known the Pools Man not dare to walk up the path amid one of his advert harangues. And it was the same fire in the evening. 'I peed the bed,' I lied.

'"Peed the bed"?' crooned they, one in bass baritone sporting an ironic grin, the other in soprano resembling Béla Lugosi in drag.

My dad assured my mum I wasn't a freak, that I'd 'just had a little accident.'

'I've never known him do it afore.'

'He's at that age, Joan, leave it. But you're going to work,' he said, 'before you start. I told you when you were at school, to get some qualifications, to avoid them holes, but no, you'd rather go dancin'.' And so to Thursday morning's opening unruffled canon: "Made your bed, now lie in it – I'm not sayin' you should soak it through, mind, that's your doing..."

73

'Do you want toast?' asked my mum.

''Depends if it's like wood again.'

'Aye, you can talk.' She suspected my trousers had transformed into wood, lifting them from the washing basket, until the shoes fell out. She squinted at the stains down the front: 'They smell putrid...'

'Jed did it' – that one went down well.

My dad now stated he couldn't wait to get to work, for a bit of sanity. My mum thus hurled the trousers somewhere other than the pile and I realised I'd transcended the boundaries of his patience.

Lecture-time.

'Listen, son' He looked up to the clock like he might not fit the whole speech in. 'You get in at god-knows-what-time. You use the washin' basket as a shoe-rack... – Jesus, it smells like that fish market...'

Guilt creeping in, my mum's glance wasn't as stern, as she plonked two planks of charcoal and a mug of syrup into my lap.

'Then what? You use the grandfather clock as a clothes rail' – the clock was on the wall, above the telly. I'd no idea what he was... 'Yes, that's it, you take a look – Am I right, Joan?'

'Yeah... but it was only a sweatshirt...'

'It's always mohair this an' mohair that. And is that how you thank your mam when she knits your jumpers?'

I was determined not to answer. I'd learned during one of these sermons that you weren't supposed to if the question was rhetorical. And so I munched on my inflexible board, edible only along with copious gulps of the over-brewed tea.

Alas, the *Stanley Ogden* accentuated quotations got me every time: *'How sharper than a serpent's tooth it is t' have a thankless child*!'

He'd not finished either, looking set for some grand finale, when my mum held up a hand: 'No, Pete, leave it now. I said I wouldn't mention that.'

'I'd prefer he did that than pee in the cupboard,' he argued. And looked my way again: 'Why did you pee in the copper bin?'

Right enough, there was an empty space in the fireplace – No, I didn't...

'Shut your mouth,' he said, 'there's a bus comin'.' From a last sip, he deemed it was no good looking at the cat, 'she couldn't have done that lot over four weeks – And she'd have to be a bloody good shot from the mantelpiece...'

My mum now nodded her head back, signalling the sheet: 'But what if he's got a bladder problem?'

I'd have considered living with my grom by this point, had one of her suppers not all but put me in hospital on my last stab. Instead, I surrendered my cup and plate to the kitchen table, snatched my coat from you-know-where and got out into the yard for a nose-blow.

Still, I was able to console myself in the fact the old man left out 1956–'58, his National Service years. They were hard work.

My mum demonstrated further signs of compassion with a tentative wink, at the other side of the window, until I kicked over a copper bin's worth of disinfectant and hot water, which must have been heard in Rotherham once it struck the coalbunker. I never remembered those peeing offences...

She met me back in the kitchen with an old bread bag of sandwiches: 'Your favourites, bananas on breadcakes.' She raised an eyebrow. ''Hear they're Jed's favourites as well.'

It was a little too early for theatrical conundrums.

My dad was waiting by the front door, stroking an inactive Brainy. 'She's not very lively this morning,' he said.

'Who in their right mind would be at this hour?' My question was rhetorical.

'Have a nice day, loves,' wished my mum, skipping over to the threshold.

9

> *'Now, soldiers, march away:*
> *And how thou pleasest, God, dispose the day!'*

'It's a lovely day, boys,' Stan reported from a floating milk float, returning to song: a new rendition of an old Tams' masterpiece.

'Not for some,' my dad retorted, and muttered that if that man was right in the head, then *he* knew where there was a houseful. I deemed it only natural our milkman should croon on by, he'd be finished in an hour. Though I wouldn't fathom where he'd picked up the Tams' refrain. Nor would my dad: 'It's one o' yours, that.' He scratched his chin: ''Always imagined him to be into Peters an' Lee.'

Like clockwork, we reached our stop with the bus' glaring beams at those crossroads, this side of The Grouse, allowing my dad just enough time to take account of the shelter's present condition: 'Can't the kids pick these *Wrigley's* packets up?'

There was never room on the bottom deck, and at the top of the stairs we were accosted by the scheduled glut of toxic chemicals. We parked down to the effortless cries, the instinctive pleas, the rasps of phlegm and tar. I'd never smoke again, and I meant it...

*'Jenny gobled me here,'* read the back of the seat in front, a provisional eye-opener.

''Not ours,' I said.

Only for my dad to concern himself more with the author's spelling. And from a second's pause for reflection, however symbolic, we became old mates armed with a to-hell-with-it tone, off to do battle against a greater force, and hopelessly shed tears of utter joy. No two men had ever been closer.

The packet of *Player's No 10* he held up to my watery eyes was dishevelled. ''Choke to death if you don't,' he said.

76

About half of our route was one long roller coaster ride of the same Bolshoi Road (or at least that's what my dad and me called it), with the "little swamp" to its credit, evoking recollections of what felt like a dream...

'Snorer,' came my dad's prod to the ribs. His ash plummeted into my lap: 'Quick.'

I almost didn't make it: my black-fisted salute to the white-walled, green-shuttered façade, or legendary, now derelict, King Mojo Club, one of the places it had all started for we Steel City Soul types; Pete Stringfellow's original venue. It was our policy to acknowledge the consecrated concrete with a reverence otherwise reserved for Wigan's Casino Club. Too young, we'd still understood what the Mojo was about. Though it was coming to something when my dad had to remind me.

'And rather than do it on the sheets,' he leaned down and whispered, in preparation for his drop-off, 'you ought to try a dirty sock. I did... till I got called up. Then I got bromide in my tea. See you later.'

It was lovely to see the old fighter laugh at this cruel hour, to see him peer up as the rest of our regiment pulled away, eyes visible thanks to the vehicle's lighting. He'd never fail to fit '56–'58 in there somewhere.

My stop fell soon after, as with my Victorian gates into Anguish, where I was greeted by the habitual question put forward by the caretaker: 'Mornin', Phillip, how are you?'

I offered my habitual reply: 'Fine, are you?'

McGoohan, by sharp contrast, or Patrick, knowing him as well as I did, a habitual hallucination, never posed stupid questions. Indeed, he never spoke, but, inclined against the clocking in/out machine, stared; raised that sardonic eyebrow...

No sooner would I snatch my allocated card from the wall, however, produce the ominous clink, than the stabbing eye would recede into the dark... if the undying questions remained: Was Patrick right to stalk me this way? Was I a *Prisoner*? Would I be bereft of a number claiming social security...?

Making across the yard, I sensed the study of the caretaker's own cynical eye, heard his whistled rendition of *Born Free*, and ascended my 6 flights. On the top floor, I was welcomed by the cell chief – who never let us listen to the radio either side of

Simon Bates' erudite slot – all the way to the last... captive, why not!

To the industrious hum, I went about my business, which meant bending numerous sheets of metal around a hefty iron wedge, creating even joints to be soldered together with amalgamated strips of tin and lead... having popped the latter into tiny pots of spirit and resin... from time to time, which... facilitated the task when... placed beneath my soldering lamp's flame... about chest height. The flame could be adjust... adjust... ad...

*Brenda Holloway's Just Look What You've Done, of course, an apt backing for another involuntary slumber* – these dreamy sunup-sessions differed also in that they could be life-threatening; my hair was on fire, according to Mr. Alcrap.

'Your hair's on fire,' he came running, 'what are you doin', lad?' He slapped my head with a workman's apron, workman still attached, and repeated: 'What are you doin', lad? Other than makin' everyone piss themselves?' He suggested I should be more careful, or I'd end up with third degree burns.

'Wednesday Keith', who lived and breathed Sheffield Wednesday, as soon pronounced more dissatisfaction with affairs over in Hillsborough, said 'that shower' had had the same, sleepy effect on him two nights back.

I wished his apron a speedy recovery. Simon Bates hadn't even taken the helm yet...

The highlight of the day was late afternoon and my grom's 'Just nippin' by to see the lads' performance.

'Now then, Edith,' each and everyone returned.

'Wigan Pier for this one tomorrow,' she boasted.

'If he carries on the way he's goin',' warned Cedric Alcrap, 'it'll be The Infirmary or The Northern General.' He told her it was like working with a 'spontaneous combuster', that even if the River Don was just below our window, I'd 'die o' poisonin' either way.'

'He'd still make Wigan Pier either way,' said my grom. 'Wild horses wouldn't stop him.'

78

Glancing over an ancient pair of black, horn-rimmed spectacles, my boss looked at a loss. 'Go on,' he urged, 'take him with you. I'll have one o' the lads clock him out.' He said he'd see me bright and early tomorrow morning.

Although I made a run for it, fearing a seafood aperitif invitation, I didn't half wish my guardian Hell's Angel, as I thought of her, were coming home again this evening...

Getting back an hour earlier, I was able to dictate what Sam could and couldn't watch on telly – though he did make the point that if Jed had been around I'd have been powerless: *he* could fight *Iron Man*. I devoured my egg and chips, for which *Henderson's* was surely invented, with as many slices of *Sunblest* necessary before my dad got home. And I devoted more time to steam-pressing the slacks, wet tea-towel in one hand, Victorian iron piece in the other – I was going to buy my mum a new iron this Christmas, or split the cost. She loved the fact I did my own trousers, there existed a real camaraderie between us at such moments.

It just didn't last long enough. 'Nice day at work?' she asked...

## 10

*'Man can believe the impossible, but man can never believe the improbable.'*

My mum deduced I was heading out earlier than usual, going by my nifty endeavour with the iron. I wouldn't refer to the something taking place in the pit of my stomach, the something she may have sensed. She kept at it: ''Not fighting with your dad over *Top of the Pops*?' Prior to a knock at the door.

Determining 'they' at *Tomorrow's World* couldn't even look after this one, an opinion founded on a flick over to the BBC and back again, my dad made an educated guess at the Pools Man's Thursday evening visit: *'He*'s early as well.'

It was more by way of telepathy than x-ray vision that I believed he was wrong. But rather than let Jed in, I zipped up my fly and zoomed out to meet him.

We turned left out of the gate, as opposed to our traditional right, and up via The Wood leading to the next street, where I stopped for a breather and Jed for a *Capstan Full Strength*. As neither of us had uttered a word, I nudged his shoulder: 'Good night, then?'

'Four times,' he blew, from an almighty puff, and shook his head and said it again, like he couldn't believe it himself.

My very own Rod Stewart doppelganger. It was a wonder she ever let him go.

As pride of friendship fought head-to-head with a jealous pang the size of a table tennis bat, I considered equalizing the odds with a 'Same here'. Instead I went for the jugular: 'She made Gladys Knight sound like Siouxie and them Banshees.' Yet all I got for my attempt at casualness, staring out at that same vista, was the beat of my heart; saying I couldn't remember her name looked to impress him more. I made my mark telling him what I thought of his allowing 'a 4-up Stewart fanatic' to know where he lived.

He agreed, steam-training a trail of smoke against the fresh breeze, before proffering me a drag of his *Capston.* 'They're calling for us at eight,' he coughed.

Did he mean down at his house?

'At yours.' He watched me choke on the cigarette. 'She interrogated me.'

Once I'd gotten my breath back, my criticism was abrasive: he was no less than a 'disgrace to The Fantastic Johnny C.' So this was the reason we'd taken the banking.

*He* reckoned he'd followed me.

But I'd leave it there; I had been in a bit of hurry to get out myself. And besides, they'd soon get the message, call once, twice at the most.

Jed then resumed talk of manly conquest with a boyish grin: ''Covered every season.'

'She ripped my pants off,' I said, groan of the martyr.

At which he snorted: 'I can see 'em from here', applying a three-quarter burnt *Capston* for guidance. 'Next to that tree.' He said it was a good job I never got knocked down in them.

They turned out to be my answer to the giant lust-bruise decorating his neck, something he'd have shielded from my mum with his *Harrington* jacket-collar had he stepped in.

It was a different story in The Grouse, of course, where he placed himself below the bar's brightest light and leaned his head at 90 degrees the 'wrong' way. The thing glared like those y-fronts.

Frank was impressed. 'What's had a go at you,' he asked, pointing over to the Yetis, 'one o' them? Marlene, quick, come an' look at this!'

'Give over, Frank,' April winked, 'he's embarrassed enough.'

Too overcome to grasp the irony, he noted that if my best friend pulled his jacket down any lower, 'we'll see his nipples – Marlene, come here!'

Marlene first wondered who'd chosen our latest musical offering: Tommy Hunt's *Loving On The Losing Side.* I said I'd dance to it if she'd join me... only it wasn't my moment.

'Never mind him,' Frank elbowed, 'it's this dirty sod you want to look at...'

'Paul Schofield,' Macca nodded, displaying four fingers, '*A Man for All Seasons*' – which happened to be his dad's second favourite film, after *Carry On Camping*.

Jed had, by now, begun to blend in with the tomato juices at the back of the bar. 'Aye,' he huffed, hoisting a thumb back, 'while he was singin' with one o' Gladys Knight's Pips.'

''Black, yours?' asked Paul.

'Closing my eyes, yeah,' I said, but knew I was wasting my time. Wigan a night away, we were all too giddy to make any kind of sense.

All the same, during the odd pause throughout the evening, I hoped Jed might make more reference to my latest conquest. He never did, but then that could have been due to my 'voice of a black angel' claims. Maybe he believed I'd wanted to do one better.

'Can we do it four times, one night?' April sighed, as if considering putting down Bristol Rovers to draw with Torquay United, except she was caressing the lapels of Macca's blazer.

'Now look what you've done,' said Marlene.

What about me? I heard myself cry.....

## 11

*'Time eases all things.'*

My dad was impotent on Fridays.

What's more, the flames no longer shimmered in shy blue; they danced, leapt, hopped and somersaulted from brick to brick, as in cadenced approval Friday had at last returned.

Set for the ad hoc interjections, the first ever spluttering of rap being spluttered in our house, I launched in where Stan had left off yesterday morning, with The Tams' old *Be Young Be Foolish Be Happy* number.

The first bit couldn't be denied, my dad, indeed, interjected, eyes rapt beyond the hearth, about me being young. As for the second bit, oh, I was certainly living up to that one! And as for the third, well, if I wasn't, then it was all my "bloody doing", since happiness was staring me in the face.

It was odd to think Stan could feel this way each morning. A Tams connoisseur with a milk round. The man was blessed...

Anxious we shouldn't wake Sam, my mum broke up the improvised duet on top of wondering why *I* couldn't be like this each morning. ''Not grumbling,' she appeared to tell herself, like she'd decided on a long weekend. ''Just wish he'd keep his gob down.'

'If you ask me,' my dad started and stopped, realising he'd done that one. He was in a bit of a tiz following last night's "performance". He deemed there was something not right with my head. 'It's bloody daft...'

'Well,' said my mum, dragging the word out, handing me my toast and tea, 'I have been saying.' And took off back to the kitchen.

He couldn't get over how 'politely' and 'graciously' the two lady-callers had carried themselves, 'considering...' After I'd congratulated my mum on the toast, which she said was no different from yesterday's, he looked to her and lauded their 'breeding.'

She was more intrigued by my muddy trousers, in the fruit bowl.

Sam now slid himself round the door, claimed he enjoyed being woken by the singing, as it meant I was off to 'Wigan Pier' tonight – or rather he had no school in the morning. He lay across my legs.

''Came down the banking, that's why,' grunted his dad – hence the mud; how was I to know it had been raining? 'Oh, give over,' he said; he wasn't born yesterday. ''Came down the banking to avoid them poor souls.' It was, in fact, those last two words that forced his list of titles – 'Silly bleeder, The Mohair kid...' – to flicker into the distance...

It was, in fact, those last two words that incited my question of whether either of the "young belters" – as he described them – had used the toilet during their visit.

'I don't know!' he snapped, wishing he were twenty years younger.

''Ought to,' called a voice from the kitchen, 'you never took your eyes off 'em.'

As any sane male would, he whispered under his breath. 'He's wapped.'

And suddenly, vividly, I saw the girl whose name I'd forgotten, that blissful chuckle. Her head fell against my chest; those jet black eyes peered up. And I said something like: ''Forgot to mention, my dad's a bit of an old charmer.'

Except the toilet thing took a determined grip. I asked my mum this time.

'She went, didn't she, Pete? Nathalie?'

'She did, aye, now I think – Isn't she beautiful, her, though! I had her in stitches half o' the night, I did – 'Know where I'd like to have her...'

'Peter, calm your...'

'Where's that, Dad?' said Sam.

'Never you mind, he's bein' naughty.'

More than that, he'd given up on me. Or I thought he had. I'd need only to push my mum on how my dad's latest muse had taken to an outside bathroom and he subjected me to sermonic prose the length of my arm: 'She's refined, not like the rest o' that crowd that think they are – Workin' class snobs, there's nowt worse. It's them you let frighten you. The likes o' which bugger off to Minorca every year so they can tell the rest of us where they've been. Not a word o' Spanish – apart from 'Avey vous une bon vino roco?' – and wouldn't know a red if they drowned in it. Allus goin' on about how cheap it is – 'Be a lot cheaper for the locals, I bet, hah! Feed 'em any old crap and tell 'em it's a local speciality. Half of 'em come home with food poisonin' and still don't get it.' He laughed again: 'The Deigos must think all their birthdays have come at once when they see them daft sods gettin' off the plane – Refined? About as refined as our Aunt Fanny's pigeon loft...'

He was convincing for a man whose bashful feet had crept no further than the perimeters of our green and pleasant land.

But we didn't have an Auntie Fanny, Sam pointed out. Or a pigeon loft.

'Exactly,' pronounced his dad. Not that Sam looked any wiser. Or as if he cared for a longer explanation, like maybe two words.

They couldn't all have been working-class with money, though, could they? How did he then see the 'the proper uns', I asked him. The real Middle Classes?

If he hesitated, his reply was categorical: 'They're just dead.' More to the point, Nathalie was unclassifiable, and my coming down the banking was an act of cowardice – *'Oh, what a tangled web we weave...'* Any other morning, that last one would have had me in tears.

For it was a Wigan Friday – That today would jump aside and let me into tonight!

'If you two don't get a spurt on,' my mum warned, 'you'll miss that bus.'

Stan was at it again when we got outside, belting out The Tams.

'Now, if you'd come down the banking to avoid him, I might've understood.'

I wielded the Soul fist as the *chanteur*'s chinking white bottles once more floated unto the late black night.

*'... neither a borrower nor a lender be!'*

It was a wait, but when it went, it could have been Junior Walker's very own.

'There she blows,' Alcrap would still authenticate, as the weighty door near came off in my hand. 'Another week over and another one soon to... – Jeez, y' only see him move like that on a Friday!' He asked whether I'd be wiping my hands now that I'd washed them. And did I have my wages? 'And don't forget we're stocktaking Monday – Have a nice...'

I lunged down the ex-murderous steps like my life-sentence had been annulled, bumping into the grimy bunch locking up the workshops beneath. Ancient Betty, the sheet-metal stamper, had become so fond of her bump that she stood face-turned. 'God bless ya, lad!' she said, paying me a semi-toothless grin as I clung to the lapels of her colour-drained hopsack. Her associates screamed with delight.

I masked something similar spotting Jed in the factory yard, astride the midnight-blue *Vespa*. Another Steve-hand-me-down, she purred below Friday's busy beat. 'Heyup, lad,' hooted her rider, reflecting my approval. He said he was in this neck of the woods and thought he'd hang around, meaning he'd called in on a West Indian connection to purchase his amphetamine order for the coming night, though which should keep him 'up' until Thursday.

Betty looked cheeky and indebted when I asked if she'd mind clocking me out, straight after which Jed mumbled something about me being spoilt for birds. I ordered him through the gates for fear I should wake from another dreamy tease. With a ready rev, he contemplated picking up my grom *en route...*

Bolshoi Road scooter-style had to be the nearest thing to a fairground ride outside a fairground. And what with Jed's Jenny

Hanley predicament – he might at least make the tail end of *Magpie* – I felt like I'd only just got on getting off outside the barber's...

'Ka chang,' rang the bulky door's bell.

'Now then, Phill...'

'Hiya, Geoff,' I said, faintly, without knowing why, as the evocative tang of lacquer jived about my tongue. Coat hung, I sat in 'my' seat and began the token rummage through the pseudo-journalistic refuse, placed pell-mell on the glass coffee table, I assumed, to add to the shop's sense of motion.

Geoff had only one helper per go, someone he'd ask to take a break from the catwalk, or so it looked, otherwise he worked alone. It meant there'd never be more than two out of the three, giant, diversely shaped mirrors being utilised at any given time. And yet it would always be a guess as to which he'd be taking advantage of. 'Today, Phillip,' I'd hear him say, 'we're going to take a peek through theeee... hexagon mirror.' Had I been in his place, I'd have spent most of my day in this seat, faking reads of the pseudo-journalistic refuse, peeping over its pages at the latest angelic apprentice, as I did as a customer – weren't barbershops supposed to be a male thing? And why were all his girls called Angela? Did he hide the medallion until that last ka-chang and drawing of the...?

'Jed was in earlier,' he chirped, breaking my trance. ''Dancing' tonight, I hear?'

'Of course, Geoff.'

'This is the other dancer Jed talked about,' he said, astute on distinction.

Angela peeped through the middle mirror: 'Oh, hiya.'

It turned out that Angela had cut Jed's hair – high honour, but then he did appear to be at some hormonal peak; that he'd put the French crop at risk so she'd utilize his shoulders as breast-rests. All the same, as I wouldn't have him getting one over me, I decided she'd get my twenty-five pence tip as well. Geoff was clearly doing alright for himself... Meanwhile, I got my head down and feigned a read of an article dedicating itself to The Grantham Ripper's favourite pastime, like it wasn't clear to everyone around me...

'He'll need a nape-scrape,' the boss advised in due course, 'so careful with that cutthroat.'

'Righto,' said Angela, with a mirrored smile.

'Oh, and you see the mole on the back of his neck, darlin'? Try and keep it on. 'Part from that, he wants a trim.'

He was a wit, was our moustachioed Oliver Tobias.

During the procedure, an ex-teacher-turned-high-pitched-whiner whined about one of his ex-pupils getting a little too near, from out the back of the lacquer-loaded wireless.

''Like this one,' she waggled, wielding the medieval piece.

Last scare aside, I agreed she'd done a fine job, to the point of asking Geoff if I should get my hair cut on a weekly basis. He wasn't convinced; you were supposed to lose your hair as you got older, not grow more. Yes, he was doing alright for himself...

My last port of call before home was the shoe shop. Or not a shoe shop exactly, though the footwear was very specific. I required a pair of tenpin bowling shoes.

The inventor of these sensitive soles must have spun in his grave the instant they were robbed for such a soulless sport, hence my lack of remorse snatching a pair back, persuaded as I was I was returning them to one of their rightful owners. I also saw each success as a vengeful prize for every time Jed and me, not so long ago, had been made to walk the disheartening winter streets for not spending enough dough; for not achieving 'strikes' beneath the guiding wings of a geek. We did tend to hog the pinball machine, true enough, get excited about replays, but it was the place's single form of entertainment. I'd have snatched them had they been available to buy or borrow.

The jumpy part wasn't so much the idea of getting caught, more of failing to obtain the shoes. That ballerina's tutu. That goalkeeper's pair of gloves; that extra serving of confidence and grace – the umbrella in the cocktail. I wouldn't have missed my night in Wigan without them, but they did render the experience even greater than it already was.

I faced 28 echoic, beaten-yet-buoyant lanes, studied to a setting of strewn skittles, while an unfortunate David Soul insisted his baby didn't give up on the two.

The job had to be a swift one, given that, amid my secret scan, beneath and on top of every chair at our end of every lane, I'd be obliged to look interested in the games – why else would I be

88

here? Added to which, that rancorous old manager still manned the helm, fixed and foreboding behind the central control counter, like he lived there. I threw up my hands in anticipation, dropped them as that last skittle weebled, wobbled... but wouldn't fall down. And I imagined that, had our contemptible crowd rolled copies of Mr. Soul's lamentable attempt at music down those isles, instead of hurling these digit-splitting, primeval balls, the skittles would have dispersed as easily. Silly game either way...

At last, from beneath an unwieldy plastic chair, the black magical 8s pounced, producing a chiaroscuro effect when I blinked. Parka pockets were invented for this pastime.

I thrust open the swinging glass doors to lightening blue neon. I skipped and hopped, trotted, like the flames in our fireplace just this morning. And I ran and laughed, and ran and laughed, as the bracing horn section of a certain George Clinton's *Please Don't Run* – now, wasn't *that* ironic! – replaced the rolls of thunder. On, I chased, riddled with that of which I wanted more. There was something in the air, I could smell it, taste it.

And the estate I was carving aside seemed like a different place...

## 13

*'All the world's a stage,*
*And all the men and women merely players...'*

My grom alerted Sam that if he kept picking his nose it would have stretched to either side of his face by the time he was my age. His innocent response was to ask if that was what had happened to her. She deserved it. She'd say the same to me, while my mum's mum warned me never to swallow apple pips, or a tree would grow in my belly and its branches out of my ears. The nightmares could have explained my not being a keen sleeper.

My mum's just-in-case caution came by way of a hissed 'Don't be smutty', in line with my own innocent response to having got my hands on a real-fine pair o' beauties. It was bad enough me being a thief, and I should hurry up with that iron, I'd been at it an hour already. The electric bill was due – we were always forced to go steady just before the bill.

'Let him be smutty,' huffed my dad, 'he wouldn't know what to do with a real bird.'

I was bailed out by the telly, or someone reckoning she'd asked ten people to try out...

'Liars!' my dad barked.

'I use *Omo,* Peter,' my mum confessed, 'and I can't complain...'

His grumble was more to do with the 'dopey clock' of the woman singing its – *Omo*'s – praises. He alternated his gripes between the telly and me: I'd not taken proper advantage of Nathalie, or rather 'the spit out o' Dee Dee's mouth.'

I tried diverting his attention: Was *Z Cars* on later? Or *Kojak*?

Except my mum said I was making things worse: one had finished and the other was on different nights.

To compound matters, the real red rag was waved before the

bull: Arthur, King of The Miners.

'They would, they'd follow a donkey if it were wearin' red... – You want see his house!' He pointed a thumb like King Arthur lived down our street. 'His garden's bigger than this estate...'

Peppered with this itchy sense of supremacy, I felt sorry for him at that point. 'Come on, Dad,' I said, 'it's Friday.' I reminded him of what Ronnie Barker's *Fletcher* had advised the other week, about not letting the 'bar stewards' grind you down.

'Aye, but he was talking about his bosses,' he now all but whispered. 'Not his so-called workmates. Besides, they're not grinding me down. They've never done a day's grind in their lives.'

It seemed the more time my dad had to grumble about the likes, the more he would. Come Monday morning, and he'd just get on with it.

King Arthur didn't get to say much anyhow: the box was right-jabbed back to BBC1.

My grom was as forceful with her interjection: 'He does right.' But not until her 'He's only seventeen', would any of us realise she was talking about me, in reply to the Dee Dee look-alike thing. 'He's got the world at his feet.'

'Almost,' I said: my pair o' beauties was in fact sitting by the fireplace, symmetrical to Brainy's streamlined splendour. And by the time I'd slipped into the iron-hot slacks, even my mum recognised I'd been putting off the taut, end of week debate: to wear or not to wear the shoes *en route*. I leaned against the mantelpiece. ''Practically brand new.'

'They soon won't be,' said my mum. 'When have you been to Wigan and it's not rained in Manchester?'

My grom agreed: 'What are the odds it won't rain in Manchester tonight?' Neither of them looked for an answer.

'They're right, Phill,' said little Sam. 'Manchester's rainy.'

'You risk getting caught every week,' stated the last in line, to close a lid on it, 'and they get half wrecked by rain walking through Manchester...'

Once more, consensus sat on the multi-badged bowling bag, bowling shoes nestled within. And once more, I wouldn't listen. For while ever their clichés rattled my cage, as well as the nag there was no straight-through train, I'd look up and raise the two figurative fingers like my figurative hand were no longer my own, and put on the shoes from the outset.

My dad couldn't believe his eyes, asked why I wanted an opinion in the first place, week in week out, if I'd no intention of taking any notice.

'Because he's young and we're not,' his mum told him. 'He got all he wanted to know.'

'Shut your mouth, there's a bus comin'!' Sam signalled, with a fall into his grom's side.

'I'm only forty.'

Then he needed to start acting it, she said. She only wished she were coming with me; she'd maybe snatch some shoes herself for the next one. It wouldn't be the first time she'd had to pinch, so her kids 'didn't starve, by Christ. Coal from the train-carriages, potatoes – I remember both wars; you and your National-bloody-Service!' she scoffed, foregoing the glance. 'Who was it came to see you all in camp? Shirley Anne Field? 'Bet you weren't complaining then' – she bet it was the bromide that did all the complaining. Like she'd stored it up for the end of the week: 'I wouldn't mind but you were only in Aldershot.'

My dad was less pushy: 'I might've gone to Korea.' It wasn't his fault it was cancelled.

She scoffed at that one, too: he'd never known hard times, he wasn't old enough. He was only forty.

'I've just said that.'

I'd since stolen away for a peep in the dressing table mirror. I left the *Dansette*'s arm up, on repeat:

Anything looked good to Dobie Gray's *The In-Crowd.* Had me reaching for the black and white Polka Dot every go, my super silk accessory, which only ever felt cold around my neck in this bedroom. It would step in and out of the reefer jacket more times before midnight than a bee carrying honey to a hive…

I'd not heard the door open, when Nathalie said: 'You look amazing.' And: 'Wow, dazzling number 8s, you naughty boy – Hey, I *love* your dressing table!'

Her ironic eyes trapped me through the long mirror, planted pulses in my face. I babbled, gabbled, all was gobbledygook, until she placed an index to my lips, one arm hidden beneath folded blue denim: ''Been here about fifteen minutes, nattering to your dad – I know where you get it from now. He talks to me in this strange accent, a kind of cross between John Gielgud and *Len Fairclough.*' She looked happy: 'And your mum keeps fretting about the cleaning, like I'm some sort of health inspector. Sam's cute – He looks like you. It's your gran, as well, isn't it? She was eating something behind her hand, it looked like raw...'

*'Foie gras,'* I shot in, like I knew what it was. ''Buys it from a specialist.'

'Oh. She said something about... ''black dag''?'

'It's what the French call it.'

'She's funny,' she laughed, as if reliving the moment. 'Every time your dad spoke, she kept looking at me, shaking her head. The humour must run in the family.' And then she slowed down a notch: 'All I want to know is whether you'd like to see me again.'

All I knew was that I wanted to pass out. 'Where's Raquel?'

'Denise? She went to Jed's place – You look wonderful.'

She had a knack with that one, mind you. And I imagined what she must have looked like in that flame-stitched *Levi's* piece, before she'd taken it off downstairs, that cherry-red tab resting curvaceously on... If anything, she was the darling, I told her.

'Thanks,' she smiled, as if in need of validation, of all the people. 'You won't forget what I told you, then.'

I hadn't a clue what she was talking about and so used the moment to place Dobie Gray's *The In Crowd* back in its home.

She said I was like her brother, that she loved my record player, and how fortunate I was having two beds – 'Lucky you. Does Sam sleep in here?'

'Yeah,' I coughed, considering the tangled web's growth. 'With my sister.'

'Of course, it's Jenny, isn't it? Your dad was telling...'

'What?'

'That you had a sister.' She pointed in the direction of The Northern General: 'The bovine maternity ward's that way... – You know? As in 'Don't have a cow'?'

'Where d' you learn that?'

'Our music teacher said it to Denise. She kept messing up the same note on the violin and began to stamp her feet – Funny...'

No, I didn't like that idea. They weren't supposed to be funny at her school, according to the other night.

'He *is* the headmaster.'

She then let me do the talking, had me feel like I was auditioning for her school's Christmas pantomime: *I* slept in one of the *two* back bedrooms, a bigger one, with my own stereo, but, you know, lumbered with so many records, I'd needed to split them up... – lies, lies, webs, tangles, I couldn't stop... till she placed that same digit on these same lips, jet-black eyes drinking me in as before. 'Can I smell bullshit?' I thought I heard.

Maybe ours was just a hammy family.

No sooner had she removed the edible finger than I tugged my eyes away, laid them anywhere, anywhere but, and suggested we make our way downstairs. Jed and me, we were off to Wigan.

It didn't stop me pulling up midpoint, all the same, at a time I'd normally want to embrace the world, to ask myself just what I was so embarrassed about. Everything, came the reply. Or everything barring a box of records and I'd even lied about those...

Other than the advert for an up-and-coming Mike Yarwood Christmas Special, it was quiet at the other side of the door – strange, Yarwood was on my dad's hit-list; anyone could have worn a wig and done that! – until Jed spoke up: ''Nearly gave you a lift home tonight, Edith.' He blamed me for not doing so.

'Yeah, he's gettin' like that morbid mare' – my dad.

Jed laughed as predictably as the rest followed on, Nathalie included, which may have influenced my not showing her out, my not bogusly arranging another get-together. Instead, I pushed open the front-room door. It turned out to be a blessing in disguise, as my craving for a haven reminded me to pick up the small tub of *Johnson's Baby Powder* in the bathroom, through the kitchen. I couldn't leave without that: 'The talc... the talc.'

If I avoided Jed's eyes, I'd have been blind not to notice the standing poise against a look-enhancing backdrop of faded beige, velveteen curtains. One loafer lay sideways on the other; his hands rested on the back of my dad's chair.

My mum was semi-curled around an armchair arm, hands wrapping a knee. I caught *her* eyes. Either Nathalie had

94

complimented her on the house's cleanliness or she, my mum, had progressed to some new theatre practice approach.

At least our newborn's smile hadn't moved on to something less legible: our nappy-clad friend on the talc-tub, on whose sprinklings I demanded to give everything I'd got. Nothing stepped in the way of that.

'Do sit down, Nathalie,' said my mum, tapping the sofa's shoulder, as I heard. 'Don't worry, the seat's spotless – Phillip, darling, don't mess up the baaathroom, hi've done this house four times today. 'E's a devil for leavin' a black ring around the baaath, you know...'

She was marrying me off. And it sounded imminent.

'I'm sure she doesn't want to know that,' tittered my dad, and wondered whether my future bride might be feeling partial to a glass of wine, like we'd have any.

If his performance was the more convincing, two very wrongs didn't make a right.

'I forgot to put it in the shoppin' chariot,' my mum groaned. Silly her.

'"Chariot??"' my grom repeated. Chariot? When neither of them could have distinguished 'a Bordox from a sherry.' But it was more in reaction to my mum's 'huncouth' rebuke that she let go: Jed and Nathalie were 'laughin' their bleedin' heads off – And the little un!'

Sam had retired to the kitchen, strewn best he could across the rubbed out rag, or once red rug, this side of the bathroom door, should he freeze on the oilcloth. Gazing up in search of supporting glee, he was the sole member of the family keeping me sane.

I considered my escape, by squeezing through the diminutive, damp-decayed bathroom window, which I'd thrust open for oxygen. It was just that, when my mum, our would-be Margaret Lockwood, said how delighted she'd been this week, to meet my nice young 'laaady friend', well, I'd have never lived with my conscience.

'Do you want a bag o' broken gingerbreads for the trip?'

No, grom, I said. And that I'd prefer to be run over by the train.

'Smart boys, don't you think?' my dad tried again, appearing anxious to both boast his natural and adopted sons' finer points and keep his wife and mother quiet.

'A real pair of dandies,' thought Nathalie...

... and there the line came home. Like I'd written it myself: *"Men who are dandies and women who are darlings rule the world."*

Dandies and darlings. And here she was again, right now, playing her part to perfection. Rugby-top, black and gold – Blackburn Rovers-ish but clingy. Black slacks. Black, black, black – that impishly erotic Mod thing, she'd have jazzily snapped! But oh to cite dandies and darlings myself, that would have been something; tell them I'd gotten it from some book I was reading, sly wink...

No. For one, the forty-year-old might have fallen unconscious in his chair. And, well, then there was Jed...

My dad apologised for the broken biscuits malarkey, gaily decorating the threshold: 'She's old, you know.' Though he hadn't anticipated the response.

'I like gingerbreads, Peter,' Nathalie told him, with a peck on the cheek.

'Inclement weather.' It was on my informing him *Shylock* was on the warpath that the register slipped. He sought to make amends with 'Blimey! Dear me! Heavens! Goodness...!'

I'd never understood why my dad called our unfailing Friday evening visitor a weird name like *Shylock,* but then I'd never asked. And I'd known early on it wasn't his real name, hearing my dad address him as Jack – he addressed everyone as Jack whose name he didn't know: the rag-an'-bone man, the dandelion an' burdock man, even women on occasions, when a Yorkshire 'love' or 'flower' felt inappropriate.

Nathalie was intrigued by the name, too.

'Oh, it's just the rent man.'

Who happened to be making his way down one of the resonant arched entrances to our right. 'Aye, they're never fuckin' in!' he spat.

She did find it all very amusing...

At the shelter, I asked Jed to chase on up and order two for the road, which at first he set off to do, I'd assumed. But then he halted after about 150 yards, knuckles like paws beneath the three-gold-buttoned blazer, as if holding a box to his waist. My favourite bit was the severed parting, how his hair kissed his eyebrows from time to time. Had I not known those colours out of sepia, I'd have believed him a ghost from my dad's Box Brownie collection.

Nathalie re-emphasised the Rod Stewart thing, before turning her head back. 'It's lovely to have met your gran now,' she said. 'She's funny. I'll have to meet your sister.'

Ever the enthusiast, she was close to adding something else, when Jed cut in. 'Don't forget The Fantastic Johnny C,' he called down. 'Ask if she can sing that.'

Furrowing her brow, she accused me of betraying our 'sexy Soul session' – she'd hoped I'd keep that one our little secret; 'Boys!' Which was fine by me... except I knew there'd be no pulling the Soul code over her eyes. It didn't take long: 'So Johnny C's his favourite?'

'He's wapped.'

Dave's 'Northern collection' contained a number of Johnny Cs – not that I'd heard of any others – including one she was ready to pounce on: *Don't Depend On Me,* a Dave fave. 'So that's your code?' she said. 'Your vision, maxim? I'm to be someone you had along the way?' She curled that potent lip: 'I mean, have you ever thought of reading another book?'

It was a crazy moment, this one, it really was – it was wapped; things, as well as people, could be wapped. Because my Nathalie was no Grimbody. And this here sense of belittlement was actually – feverishly, yep, feverishly – ripping me apart. Should I look away? No, no way, I didn't want to look away! Should I then drag her and her mixed metaphors back into The Wood and make up for a lost day? As madly timed as it felt, I recalled Dinah Sheridan ticking off her railway children down at our pictures over yonder. *'Isn't she marvellous when she's angry!'* blew young Peter...

Instead of taking her hand, in answer to her question, I summoned what I'd always deemed up until now to be a simple truth: that after *Black Echoes* and *Blues & Soul,* nought else merited opening its pages.

She came back with ease: ''Some act, yours. And you think you're the kings of the stage?'

'No' – yes, my dad's rhetoric teachings went right down the pan with her.

'And for your girls, do you both award each other a *Blue Peter* badge per conquest?'

Faced with her unmistakable, unending glare of disappointment, I could but marvel at how she remained so... superior: 'No.'

'And have you ever thought of thinking for yourself?'

I didn't mean to say 'No' a third time, it just spurted out.

'And here was I, believing you all set to be my own seven day lover – *Seven Day Lover,* the title of a rather expensive number by James Fountain; yes, it came at a price alright! From a silent pause, she glanced up the street and assured me Jed need never worry about Denise again, either, that I'd have done better asking for the *Blue Peter* badge back. The sigh was almost conclusive: 'Strange, how he who abides by such a rule happens to be so first-night-shy, going on reports.' Her last line was the clinical one: 'You're going to fall flat on your face.'

'Snob!' I said, and that she should get back where she came from... but meant none of it. And so I caught up with Jed, for his 'Big gob!'

He judged I'd done the deed in style – he was proud. Feigning a grimace, he bent to look into my eyes: 'There'll be plenty more Gladys Knights to conquer yet, boy.'

The argument, if at all it was an argument, went no further than that. It wasn't long before I began to feel daft – Whatever had gotten into me!

Still, I couldn't help noting my armour had acquired a heavy dent...

## 14

*'The road of excess leads to the palace of wisdom.'*

'A new pair!' gasped an awe-struck Marlene, squeezing the toe-end of my stretchy leg on the bar. She couldn't work out why I never thought of doing one big raid. And looked a little tense when Jed asked would she mind hiding the haul in the pub's cellar.

Although he didn't care for bowling shoes, Jed relished anything with a sense of danger, hence his allowing the ex-commandos to talk his hind legs off. There was no appeal in getting away with the odd pair, but the buzz of a raid; everything he was set to achieve in around a couple of hours and the 'gear gobbling' session.

Marlene had pulled the four pints: two we'd biff back in the entrance bar and the two she'd take through, in a sign we'd arrived.

No sooner had she made her move, than it appeared a drinking competition had gotten under way. Jed confirmed my suspicion by grappling with a beer towel and thrusting it beneath his chin. As there were no other towels free, save those pinned by thick, green glass, magnet printed ashtrays, I arched my body and threw my legs apart. Irish Danny deemed I'd 'turned into a friggin' teapot', setting off old Seth for what could have been the rest of the evening, who profited just as colourfully from Marlene's temporary absence.

Lip-smack victorious, Jed laid the beer towel back onto the bar and smacked the empty glass down on top of it. My own landed a good one and a half seconds on, to my humiliation before military's finest. Following which their champion begged opinion on the state of his collar – shirt, jacket, he didn't say, but was its label tucked inside? We then headed off...

Smokey, his Miracles, their *Going to a Go-Go*: our made-in-heaven entrances. Proffering the jukebox an approving wink, we ground invisible *Wrigley's* in simultaneous precision.

Afghan howled between chokes. His breath split clouds to unveil un-tended hair, hair veiling, at a guess, an un-tended face – I couldn't remember ever seeing it. For courtesy's sake, he asked whether we ladies were dancing tonight.

Macca took the volley, asked whether Afghan had come straight from work.

But April believed her man merciless, and prodded: 'Don't, he's unemployed.'

''No harm done,' assured Marlene, directing us to the beers. 'He's proud of it. 'Reckon he suffers from that disease.' She clicked her fingers: 'What's it called, the fear o' work?'

'My dad says I've got diurnal ergophobia,' I pronounced, eliciting the odd glance, as well as Macca's end-of-week emancipation from an invisible straightjacket, onward and upward, stage bound. Smokey Robinson had no need for big words.

April's eager beaver, his eyes looked fashioned for lunging down those same bowling lanes, like he'd misread the prescription, sliced into the second ration, necked a double-dosage. He'd never accept the accusation. Putting princes to shame, he felt wiser than any king; route beckoning to the Temple of Soul, he basked in the knowledge and peak of it, and rose from an artful bow in recognition of the polluted standing ovation.

The Divs were contemplating a dare, the upshot of how much *Skol* it took. To gravitate or not to gravitate next door. To the Working Men's Club. To scribble their initials with a scrap of chalk on the snooker board players' list; to allow their lady friends a sober scream at a 'full house'.

For Nigel and his latest female peculiarity, I'd no idea of their plans and didn't care for one.

Without the Yetis' Saturday *Wapentake* outing and the estate's acting a collective involuntary witness to their deafening departures, we'd have sworn they lived in that corner...

Smokey's harmonics had attained their untimely end. Macca waited impatiently.

100

Marlene, meanwhile, on apparent impulse, inclined herself forward and, going by Afghan's "ladies" comment, asked: 'Does Macca wear makeup, then?'

'*He* shouts that,' Jed wanted the world to know, 'cos *he* looks like Fagin!'

It was clear she'd hoped to be as selective about who should hear her next line, that Macca 'surely wears eyeliner', but Jed had proven a hard act to follow. This second standing ovation emptied every seat in the room. She thrust a hand to her mouth: 'My big gob.' Before manoeuvring it like a horizontal windscreen wiper: 'Sit down or I'll bar you all!'

If Macca wore eyeliner, I couldn't help guessing April put it on for him, to enhance that self-assured look. Either way, he treasured every second, fitted every part, reciprocated each kiss his audience blew, while his girl, pacing stage-end to stage-end, preferred he quit the all-too-fervent flight and land back onto a firmer terra firma, into her selfish arms.

But then she could always rely on our style-less swanker, Nigel, who again pushed his luck: ''Can't tell which one's the fella!'

All heads turned to Macca for first reaction, which was to produce the largest eye-whites I'd ever seen either side of a human nose, as he witnessed Armageddon rise from his broken chair and raise Nigel to a couple of feet from the ceiling. It was a steady sort of snarl: 'That's April you've just insulted.'

At that moment Frank came moaning about how sick he was of holding the fort in the other side: 'Get back in here!' And produced the widest open mouth I'd ever seen be*low* a human nose – I couldn't resist Sam's 'approaching bus' line but he possibly didn't hear. 'What's he doin' on the ceiling?' he asked.

''Being vulgar to April,' said Marlene, filing her nails.

On Frank's nod, Geddon tossed Nigel through the front door; the peculiarity tiptoed after.

Recalling an order from the other side, our landlord then knelt and pulled three packets of cheese and onion crisps from a cardboard box. ''Never liked the little shit anyway,' I thought I heard. ''Be surprised if he's old enough...'

Macca, still agog on our departure, called Geddon 'The Mighty Geddon'. April tugged that bit harder.

Almost outdoors, Jed and me performed an Egyptian-style teapot dance for the commandos, who couldn't have displayed more generosity of spirit. Outdoors, Chris brought about a kop-style surge to the bus stop, with 'It's here.'

'Flash a bit o' leg!' someone shouted.

Maybe someone hadn't noticed April was wearing trousers. Not that she'd need to flash anything to pull a bus over. 'Thank you, Mister Driver,' she said. 'We're going to Wigan.'

I was at our line's tail-end as we corkscrewed the stairs like a new Alton Towers ride, and so the only one to snatch Mister Driver's reaction, which was a timid plea she take him with her.

Contrary to how our deft driver gobbled up the roller coaster dips, the eventual clatter of clumsily carried feet signalled the arrival of a bus conductor's drained ascent. April lay in front with boyish beam resumption, the impassive sigh. 'Two please,' she requested. And, following the tiniest hiatus, the tinny instrument rattled thus. It worked every time and she knew its rewards: more cigarettes to go round. Ten pence may have been the price of a no-boundaries-in-Sheffield ticket for adults, but not if you were under sixteen again. April brandished a bright orange ticket to prove it.

'Two please.'

'Two please…'

It was like the tapping out of each one-inch by one-inch pressed against a raw nerve, and on the sixth rang the objection: 'Lyin' on the seats doesn't make you look any younger!'

We cast the confused glances, as tedious as the tactic had become.

All it then took was a united salute to King Mojo, and our conductor, who hadn't received the attention he'd expected, appeared to just give in, to the point of sitting amongst us, on the backseat. ''Wouldn't mind,' he said, 'but they're the cheapest fares in the country – *I* know, I'm from Chesterfield! An' they won't be much longer, if she gets in, the way things are goin' with these unions – Nobody wants work!' Once he'd realised he was only talking to himself, with a whimper, he said: 'Aye. The Mojo, eh…' And when one of us asked whether he'd been a regular, he came back a different character, eyes outwardly wistful: *'God,* aye!' He reckoned he could tell us a story or two.

'Go on, then,' Macca sprang, eyes just outward.

'Where you off to?' he first hoped Macca might clarify, accusing him of having started too early wherever it was; he couldn't have weighed more than Twiggy already, 'wet through.' And in time, our conductor escaped from a straightjacket of his own, nine or ten hours old, I'd have estimated, with the odd break for a sandwich and a smoke. He didn't so much burst out as slipped from it with technique and thought, scooting off to a memory or three: 'The two clubs were The Dungeon in Notts an' The Mojo in Sheff. Around twenty of us came over to see Edwin Starr first off.' He said our Mojo was Edwin's first ever English venue: 'He didn't know what hit him, the euphoria!'

Again I peered into our raconteur's eyes, and this time guessed the straightjacket was older than my original calculation...

And yet I'd drift at the odd juncture, glance at my window's reflection. Or rather at a face in my mind's eye. The face of a darling. *"Dave's always called him 'Our Elvis',"* she winked, as if sitting right beside me...

I returned amid a list of artists he'd seen at the venerated club in its heyday, many I'd never heard of: '...The Alan Brown Set, Amen Corner, The Small Faces, Root and Jenny Jackson....' He mixed them up, too, got confused with his Dungeon, as anyone over thirty might: '... Chris Farlowe, Zoot Money – Hey, she was good, Julie Driscol! Who else? Inez and Charlie Fox.' With our repeated exclamations, he looked like he was conducting some fanatical Yorkshire choir: 'Willie Mitchell. The Contours – Wilson Picket.' He built up one act as having 'set the place on fire with that saxophone.' And by the time Junior Walker leapt from his tongue, he'd already blown us away...

... or perhaps I was *half* blown away. These bewildering butterflies. Where did I really want to be? Down here at King Mojo with our once King Mod serving aperitifs for the big un? Or lush-carpet frolicking with a barmy brown-eyed beatnik in St Michael's bottle-green? Did quandaries come more beautiful, I could but wonder? It was a rhetorical wonder. And I felt a warmth I'd never known nor would ever forget...

'... Brenda Holloway – Oh, and Georgie Fame and his Blue Notes...'

'Him that sits back-to-back with Alan Price and grins wider than his keyboard?' said Jed.

'*Hey*, he was blacker than the black uns!' chortled our narrator of nocturnal triumphs, with a double-take. He accused my best friend of bringing to mind a funny story. 'As true as I'm sat here, we were in a pub, long since closed, Nottingham – We were doin' The Dungeon that night – and who walks in?'

'Who?' Macca pressed, like he might throttle him for the answer.

'Rod Stewart,' he said, like Macca should have known. He was with Long John Baldry – 'You know, him an' his Hoochie Coochie Men? Anyway, a bit later, Baldry had this stain on his trousers – Cream trousers, bloody massive! He'd just come out o' the toilet. Rod Stewart didn't half take the... – Oh, pardon my French, duck.' And as tears from a yesteryear flowed freely down his cheeks, we laughed along with him, seventeen and supreme together, in some long-since closed Notts pub, knocking 'em back with Rod The Mod and Long John Baldry...

At the mere mention of Little Stevie Wonder, April tapped twelve knees in succession, making more than the narrator's evening, anxious as she was to shower us with her passion, reminding me of a raring-to-go relay racer I'd seen in some long-gone Olympic games – 'Little Stevie, at The Mojo, imagine! Did he do *Uptight*? And *Fingertips*?'

We'd never know.

Smashing up the narrative with a screech and a skid, our driver reached the top of the stairs as keenly, because 'most o' the passengers have been on and got off free o' charge.' And it wasn't their fault, 'not if there was no conductor...'

Much to his bewilderment, the conductor remained unruffled: 'Alright, misery.' In fact, it made for great amusement, until Macca pointed out we were in Abbeydale. As our heads hit the roof, Paul complained we were supposed to get off just after what was known as 'the hole in the road', a bit of an underground.

'We did that one a while back,' said the driver. 'He should've said where to get off...'

April ran down the deck and near punched him in the face: 'We know where to get off – This wonderful man's seen Stevie

Wonder, I'll have you know!' He couldn't care less. It was more her checking his competence that did him, when she said he was supposed to *stop* at the hole in the road, 'not fly over the bleedin' thing!'

'Woah, woah!' he insisted. 'Hold your horses. I *did* stop, for ten minutes, if my watch serves me right...'

'Have a dance for me,' was the last I heard, flying over the driver as deftly as he'd flown over the rest of the city. We got back into town as fast as our fretful feet could carry us.

Macca requested 'a one-way ticket to The Heart of Soul', in exchange for the £4:67p he let drop into her metal tray, a way of expressing his desire the night should never end. Sliding him his red and white return-ticket, the silver haired lady donated her residential smirk.

Evening-light-robbery. No-one behind these miniature glasshouses could have known what they were doing.

'Have a dance for me,' wished my ticket supplier, like someone we'd recently met, if with a little less yearn, for the sake of being sociable... perhaps.

We then winged over the station's wrought-iron bridge, to allay fears circulating among the rest of The Sheffield Posse they might be heading out west without us.

We signalled our arrival with click-clacks all the way, emitting the odd *Blakey's*-spark. Bowling shoes-clad, and so playing no part in the audible confirmation, I suddenly felt that, as if by design, I was witnessing a scene from the greatest film never made, from within, quietly mingling amongst its characters.

Greetings sang in sweet cacophony. Hands were shaken, shoulders patted, apparel was envied with stolen looks. Bags claimed conquests back to The Twisted Wheel and The Torch... But this station scent. Not just the diesel, more its blend with the evening air; the post-ale panting, smouldering tobacco, *Charlie* – the Soul girls and the smell of them! A glossy singles-box swung on a *Harrington*-sleeved arm; the other hand flicked away a done-with cigarette, which bounced onto our track, and then slept, and awoke, and trotted off as readily as one and all were ready, backed by a fresh south-easterly breeze.

An incandescent glow.

And I recalled our sixties Soul mate, how *we'd* awoken *him*; just what he'd have given to be here at this moment. No, I thought, rubbing my sweaty palms, I wouldn't be going in for any of that growing up nonsense. I rubbed and squeezed, and rubbed, and gripped on to this dear, dear youth of mine for dear life.

I learned a lot on buses, I told myself, as our Soul train pulled away. Meeting our Mojo man had been for a reason. I just couldn't help wondering if he was still sitting there...

15

*'Silence is the perfectest herald of joy'*

Piccadilly ahoy, I tucked up the shoes beneath the jacket, at either side of the prized white powder – a voice proposed gondolas for our Lancastrian Venice; he'd be writing to the town council first thing Monday morning. I wasn't in the mood tonight, for shunning puddles like pools of pestilence until Victoria.

But then no-one had expected Macca to have a taxi by his feet: "Take six?'

'Where y' off to?'

'Wigan.'

The cabby rubbed his hands.

April arched herself on Macca's knees, while Paul, foreseeing jetlag, gripped on to a door handle. I wasn't alone in thinking our driver would be dropping us off on platform two, prior to the abrupt left skid away. Jed did the honours: clarified that, yes, we were Wigan bound, but via a train from Victoria Station. We were as soon dumped back onto the pavement to a string of Mancunian accentuated epithets, regarding the trade he was missing out on.

As I slipped back into the number 8s, April sent the 'foul-mouthed gett' on his way, how my grom might have done – she had that same appalled look.

And bopping along our Victorian platform earlier than usual, awaiting the bulk of our, by now drenched, Posse, I peeped up and caught an eidetic glimpse of my guardian Hell's Angel, looking downward as she would.

*'He's got the world at his feet,'* she said, like through a tannoy.

'Another return to Wigan for a disco dancer!' our skew-capped, sunny ticket-puncher, Black Beam, roared for all, each time as if at last enlightened on our club's true identity. It wasn't

107

a casino, no, and none of these baggy-panted, badged-up, pilled-up youths had robbed the gas meter hoping to make it rich on an all-night, all-or-nothing bet. He punched a hole in my leaf and held it high, that every bulging eye should take note; he smiled that toothless smile. I'd passed the test before Heaven's gates and the cheers ensued.

'Gear?' pounced Gear, by nickname and nature. My natural pre-emption was a negative.

In explanation, Black Beam, whose moniker reflected his denture-less orifice, a title he assumed with pride – it made him feel part of our young cognoscenti – well, he formed half of a double act, with Gear, if only half-knowingly. Beam's act, the more pantomime of the two, was to go about his ticket-punching with a difference: whenever he picked out a ticket reading Wigan Wallgate, he'd cry out the "disco dancer!" thing, raise a thumb and ignite. As the months and years had come and gone, he'd created a following, no longer cheering alone but with an ever increasing number post-Victoria. When he came across a ticket reading other than Wigan Wallgate, he'd holler: 'A single to Suicide Street!'

'Where's that?' we'd play along, like on a junior school outing.

'Hindley,' he'd laugh. 'Who the bloody hell lives in Hindley!?'

Urged to turn his life around, *now,* while he had the chance, our scorned commuter would respond with a sporting smile, to humour the old fool; that he might move on more quickly.

As for Gear, or when spoken of, Last Resort – no-one knew his real name either – the other half of the duo, his act was more of the magic trick kind. He made things-pharmaceutical appear and disappear at the blink of an eye. Where these things came from and returned to was anyone's guess. He didn't carry a wand but everything else.

It wasn't difficult picking out Soul boys and girls from the dead commuters, though handy for our magician when informed of potential buyers to have escaped his notice, say, three or four carriages down the train. And thanks to the old thumbs-up-or-down routine, Black Beam could just as unwittingly reveal a pair of drug squaddies, who, ticket-less and irked, would stick out like sore thumbs, leaving Beam's thumb in a quandary, everyone else's flicking back the last 'bluey', and Last Resort doing whatever he did with his. Our underprivileged pair would have spent a lot of time observing the latter's shadow-like antics, in wait of the perfect moment, yet would never be quick enough – 'Who's payin' that toothless Arthur Askey!?' I imagined them cursing together afterward. Escorted to an adjacent rocking and rolling water closet, Oxford bags dropped on order, Last Resort would be forced to bend double and touch his brogue-ends by our single-minded, plain-clothed, plainly impotent couple. They looked everywhere.

* * * * *

Too frustrated to consider the consequences, they once rummaged beneath his moustache.

''You got a crush on me?' he asked, moustache readjusted.

They got off at whichever, I was convinced, the next stop happened to be. Westhoughton, as per Black Beam, who, deeming he'd just seen off two non-paying local hooligans, waved a thumb down with 'Who the bloody hell lives in…!?'

* * * * *

Before Westhoughton this time round, we were again in Bolton, signalled by Beam's sketch of 'Home o' the weary.' However long the stop took in reality, I couldn't even welcome Jed's altruistic effort of *Good Things Come To Those Who Wait* – another Mr. J number…

And for Westhoughton, April didn't get how anyone could be so awkward as to live in such a place.

Hindley proved too much for some, going by the nervous bellowing a carriage back.

And then Ince.

Noting Macca about to throw up his beer, I leaned forward and promised him it was our turn next.

Finally, I allowed my twenty-to-midnight panic-attack to riddle where it would. I pulled out the Polka Dot, or put it back, and kept this whole delicious response to myself, until my best friend mirrored all. We didn't utter a word: we didn't need to...

Thinking about it, if anyone lived here, in Ince – maybe *he* did, down yonder, the man about to walk through some underpass – would he do so without ever learning that the most exciting section of the world's most exciting ride began right in the heart of his town?

# 16

*'... Yet every step leaves there behind,*
*A something, in thy dance,*
*That serves to tangle up my mind,*
*And all my soul entrance...'*

April rested a forearm on Black Beam's shoulder, invited him to come dancing.

With a flush, he said he'd wait till he'd been down the local bowling alley. He worked the captivating thumb one last time.

I stayed put with ''left my fags' and 'stupid me.' Door fallen shut, I'd now dare to close my eyes, as in weekly defiance of another recurring dream: *the door's in fact jammed, the only door. I'm forgotten. And as the happy hordes skip the virtually vertical stairway, the train begins to creep off, return journey. Old Beam reappears, looks on, thumbs down, like I lived in Westhoughton or...*

The invention was on time; the train gave a cough, my heart skipped its beat and, unlocking my eyes to the opening door, I met Jed's slack-jawed bemusement: 'What are you doing??'

'Exorcising.' From a step down and a pat on his back, I told him I loved him.

He said he loved me, too, scrum-grasping my waist, but thought I chose the oddest time and place to exercise, when we'd 'got a whopping dance floor to go at – These stairs for starters!' Which he'd been up already. He still appeared to view them as for the first time...

On his sergeant-like instruction, we fell in around the back of what made up the friendliest army in history. And considering we debarked on this, our sacred turf from towns foreign, amid the violent 1970s, Wigan's civvies proved as affable. Like all, they thought us 'fuckin' daft' and never held back the sentiment, but we knew better.

'Casino Club,' the sky at last read, red on white, with a lump to the throat. Seating space was full to capacity on the low lying wall opposite; eyes reflected neon night like searchlights through chatty cloudbursts of early winter. Girls screamed at the appearance of a Leicester face – he'd not been over for a while. Hugs were delivered, anecdotes exchanged; spirits rebounded group to group as in friendly fire returned, an extension of the original jest, source unknown to most, like anybody cared. The Temple of Soul would open its doors in a minute's time, and we were standing right outside.

Jed managed to ingratiate us into our enormous queue's front bit, before an entrance no wider than a Sheffield storm cupboard. A big game with a little turnstile. I not only felt thinner through the lines but everyone looked thinner.

'Bovine' – again when speaking *of* him – averted a disaster on a weekly basis, our resonant doorman, who, some said, mooed before he'd had time to open the doors: *'Moooooooooove back!'* There'd be plenty more of that to come.

Jed clung to an arm I believed he believed was mine, as I detected a wave that should sweep Bovine away for a brief moment and... we were in. He didn't like it either, our doorman, from what I heard.

The two flights of stairs passed by inconsequentially.

If I squeezed the talc any more I'd start a snow storm, Jed warned, removing my coat as I might little Sam's, prior to shooting up another flight and handing it in with his own at fifteen pence a go. He'd pay, I'd get extra cokes; a ritual developed from my over-enthusiasm.

Over the balcony, I caught Macca below, an unleashed hound upon the longest beach, accompaniment: these here rhythmic contagions. He didn't so much run as jostle between fitful drops and a surplus of sporadic spins, as in flighty chase of his own tail, or in search of a bone buried a week gone. Owing to the UV strip hanging above the stage – our lightshow in its entirety – his proud and entertained owner flung me a fluorescent beam and an all the darker fisted-salute from the sidelines. She was sitting legs crossed, yoga-like, on one of those inexpressive chairs, which would have creaked without the ricochet of Brenda Holloway's appealing accusations...

112

There was nothing false about this place.

I'd hold on as long as it took, not through lack of oomph for our too short night ahead, more to make the powder last that bit longer, and maybe better my record of fourteen minutes, going by the girl's watch whose wrist I'd rammed to my eyes only last week. I'd have no need for a timepiece this week, to know I was lacking a good ten minutes, as our fussy feet touched down on blessed wood, to Mr. J's *I've Got The Need*...

... and to April's electric-whitened appreciation. It wasn't April's voice I'd hear duet our hero's, all the same, of course it wasn't; as with another's obsidian irises etching themselves upon the walls of my mind... The song had never sounded more significant.

Jed's head bobbed at a hallucinatory rate, the edgy guffaw: 'Let me have it!'

Paul was already delving through 'golden oldies' in what was unofficially known as 'the record bar'. I identified their labels in a squint: *Brunswick* – rainbow arrow give-away. *Cameo Parkway* – classy. *Ashford. Atlantic; Okeh* – passionate pink or a prevailing purple, I'd have spotted that one in Ince. The ones I didn't make out may have been demonstration copies: if you got your mittens on those, it was fewer colours for more of your money.

Jed was away the instant Paul wielded the magic *Wand* like a conductor's baton, only to learn it was the right label but the wrong singer: Wally Cox, and not Mr. J.

There was nothing remotely wrong with Wally Cox, even so: Mr. J was another Steve-hand-me-down, this time Steve none the wiser.

\* \* \* \* \*

About four years back, we were lying around the unisex waiting for Jenny to get dressed and out, to put a lid on the glam, a movement she'd embraced literally – *some* of the characters she brought home, or my dad's reactions... The healing process would be quick, as Jed had brought along half of Steve's collection, unbeknown to Steve, and a few bob's worth.

It wasn't like she'd take a hint, my sister, bum-wiggling in bras and panties to the Black Country rhythm as her Solihull superman ripped from *Cos I Luv You* to *Take Me Bak Ome*. She'd delve into detail about the sexual merits of Messrs Holder, Hill, Lee and Powell, all the while unsure of what to wear, a flick through her side of the wardrobe here, another flick there – in truth, Jed didn't mind at bit and it was a good job I was there to protect him.

Rid of the nymph, we got down to some real refrains, which for both of us meant many first-timers. I'd always wondered what it was about Soul music, why I wouldn't settle for anything else – why I felt contempt for everything else. I got my answer that evening.

I'd not yet acquired the finger-straightening knack, and so granted my best friend full – "bit", pre-*Henry V* – honours: 'The Vibrations' *Talkin' 'Bout Love,* The Miracles' *That's What Love Is Made Of,* The Showstoppers' *Ain't Nothing But A House Party.'* In time, he read out the name 'Chuck Jackson' – *he* couldn't have been anything other than a Soul man, could he! *These Chains Of Love.* The instant I, we, heard that voice, well, it all seemed to make sense. That primary point of mutual revelation; the shackles, the burden, those weighty love-chains. It didn't get better than this. Before that fade into anguish, our epiphany...

'He meant that,' one of us said. It didn't matter who.

Within the space of two and a half minutes, Chuck Jackson had endured the load. As had we. He'd no doubt hoped so would the world, but only a few would ever be awarded the privilege. And maybe that was the secret: this real music was meant to be shared amongst the few. We happy few...

Anyhow, Chuck Jackson became our Soul barometer.

Sometime later, via another crushing Casino Club queue without injury, to be hit by a skilfully constructed wall of energy, when our opener span *I Only Get This Feeling,* ours and possibly Wigan's first audition, one of us referred to Chuck as 'Mr.'. The god then became God and the rest was history. We meant it, too. And always would...

\* \* \* \* \*

… here in our reserved utopia at two o'clock in the morning, endeavouring to focus through a head-height haze, beneath which was formed a sea of the deft and devout. To Edward Hamilton's *Baby Don't You Weep*, I visualised an apprehensive raincloud, a cloud too bashful to burst, intimidated by the multitude, splashing off humble blessings like a novice vicar. Rumour had it perspiration was pumped in through the cracks of the throbbing walls. Or maybe one of us had accidently let off a fire hose, I joked, which was met with ''Doubt this dump's got one', from a lad in baggy trousers and a Norfolk accent. He ran along as if his bus was pulling away.

It was from here, as our vessel drifted about an unquestionably snoring universe, my trance would crack its zenith. Emotional fuses were blown, hearts broken, others mended. Lovers loved while cheats cheated; losers lost and winners never quit. The happy were on cloud nine, the sad couldn't go on; men were made blue – why? If only they knew. Fevers were had and minds blown to pieces, to dancers dancing, who wondered if we dug. The Potato was mashed; *Cool Jerk* was cool, to heartfelt horns, synchronised worship, claps, spins, flops, the kung-fu – the ballet and the drug of it!

All else must have slept whilst all this came to pass.

And if ever a being represented ''all this'', that being was to the stage's left, in clinging capped-sleeve, braces, the cropped hair; artistry of another canvas – that gutsy gamine thing, my dear Nathalie would have said. I'd never know the girl's name; never dare to ask – to get near enough to ask. I'd just sit here, or there, and yearn to tell her how she shone. But then, for my consolation, I knew she didn't need to hear it. Some guiding star was clearly doing the job in my place…

Only Charles Mann's *It's All Over* would hint at an ensuing inevitability, as I continued to vacillate between my thing and my daze, whenever my best friend knocked me out of the latter. Room for a however-short rant, he'd also inform me he was adding talc, in bulk, to his next, as yet failed, chemist raid-list. He was kidding, I thought...

And then the early morning light.

'I'll go down with this ship,' Jed promised, one of his more convincing lines, referring to our vessel's last cruise. He'd never elaborate on it, barring vague comments about Wallgate's train track. But there'd be a million more sailings before that dreaded morning; the quarterly rumours had gotten boring. You had to keep the faith in this game, as reminded the Casino's 'Three Before Eight' weekend after weekend: Dean Parish's *I'm On My way,* Toby Legend's *Time Will Pass You By,* and Jimmy Radcliffe's *Long After Tonight Is All Over...* or maybe I missed something.

Whatever, eight o'clock was here.

Post-sub-zero deliberation – I fiddled longer with the Polka Dot – a cold consensus ruled we hang around and do it all again: such opportunities didn't come every weekend. Only the thought of semi-warmth in semi-homely homes proved a semi-temptation. Or rather the warmth and Larry Grayson's latest antics, his and those of 'Slack Alice' and 'Everard'.

And so, with half our Posse ridden away, we gringos stayed put, spat and smoked in every saloon Wigan had to offer. I ate like my horse, to the other five's retching dismay: they purchased what a lingering Last Resort wrenched from who-knows-where.

At least we drank in harmony, ignoring a smoky hole in which a bunch of leather-clad cowgirls caterwauled an hour long to Tom Robinson, coin after coin, as if his band weren't doing the job well enough.

The other slight oddity, for Jed and me, between said sessions and Frank Bough's sinister smile, was learning, via *Dixons'* window down in Wigan Market Place, that United had lost 0:1 to Brighton. It wasn't the predictable result, more how we obtained it. A solitary working television in the shop window at something-to-five – odd in itself for a Saturday, when a third of any English town hoped to use them – forced us to read the result's reflection through the shop doorway's side-window. We actually learned of United's defeat in reverse. And yes, we initially believed we'd won when we'd lost. But when I recalled how we'd first learned of the fixture...

Overall, our sixteen-hour wait sailed smoothly on by, and the night would be as magical as the last... up until the light sneaking in again, through those cracks.

Why did it always do that?

## 17

*'All that glitters is not gold...'*

*Like stocktaking hadn't got me on a knife-edge, Wednesday Keith pulled that face, the fortnightly grin...*

This was a new one on me, by the way.

*And it wasn't as if anyone sympathised, or didn't know what I was going through. Mr. Alcrap was a stickler for uniformity and discipline. He demanded nought but the precise amount of metal stampings, solders, springs and spindles and... spots on the ceiling where possible. He demanded a neat pile of stock cards at arm's length on his work-side, neat print, easy reference to each card's duplicate, according to its printed number, those placed on each neat pile of stock.*

*A hanging offence alone in Alcrap's book, my ball-point pen was leaky. And having bumped into more of the same stock and so scribbled over my original count, or around it, anywhere there was still space, I'd also forgotten to write out two duplicate numbered cards per item: each duplicate denoted something different.*

*For lack of a neat pile to place on Alcrap's uncluttered work-side, I looked to Keith, that we put aside our allegiances, begin over. And maybe start by getting new cards.*

*But his giddy-as-a-blue-tit smile – his team had won away again – informed me I was wasting my time. ''Have to get rid o' the ones you've knackered, first,' he scoffed, thrusting a handful of ink-laden cards between my teeth. And he was serious: 'Eat 'em, it's the only way – Go on, chew... chew...' Like a train, he went on: '... chew...'*

'... chew... chew...'

118

I'd have preferred Alcrap's cosh, to these tenpin eyes, to the ear-splitting cackles...

So just who had done the dirty deed? Who had rifled my pockets as I slept – Who'd rammed my train ticket into my mouth?

'*You*!' said April, with a choke, and depicted how the ticket man had wanted to punch it. 'When you fell into a coma he put it in your gob!'

I tried everything. I threatened British Rail with my pen, I tittered with my mockers. And again recalled how I should keep the faith, in keeping with the bowling bag patches I'd ever read. Except it didn't work. I just hated.

'Jed said: "Chew",' she kept on, 'so you chewed...'

We screeched into Victoria beneath another black mantled sky, soon after which Jed ceased in his efforts to keep by my side. And my feet were drenched.

The Sheffield train couldn't have rattled away fast enough. Melody, so soon, pounced from the track. A girl with no name foot-tapped on my mind's eye, like from a preceding decade. I'd get through the week; I'd done it before.

The rest were still snickering at my chew-chew performance...

I threw myself upfront on our number 49, strewn like I owned it. And when this ticket man requested my fare, eyes telling of Saturday night excess and how he loathed the Sunday shift, I tendered him a ten penny piece; I wasn't expecting change.

It was a drawn out echo, five in all, like the flattest of skimmed pebbles upon the stillest water. And I smiled to think a certain someone wasn't fluttering her eyelashes anymore. I did, I learned a lot on buses...

I was welcomed home as the prodigal son: four *Walls Sausages* end-to-end sliced down their middles, between four slices of *Sunblest* and two fried, runny-yellow eggs, the tin of tomatoes poured within. No sooner had I collapsed into the sofa than Sam whizzed onto my knees for a detailed account of the latest 'Wigan Pier' adventure, 'right from the start!' But all I could muster was how another pair of number 8s had bought it.

My mum now fell by my side, rested her head on my shoulder: 'What's new...'

119

'That's Manchester,' said my dad, between marvelling at how many City supporters had gotten themselves arrested at Aston Villa yesterday, eyes riveted to a *News Of The World* back-page piece: ''N fact, look at this, they didn't do much better at Old Trafford.' And they were only playing Southampton, who'd taken a point, which accounted for it: 'Stretford Enders! Ought to set that Wednesday crowd on 'em...'

'Aye, that'd cure 'em,' my mum nudged, tongue in a cheek.

Recalling how funny the pair had been in my absence, Sam pressed his head into my other side, said his dad had been 'takin' off Larry Grayson and wanted mam to be the Isle o' Sinclair!'

''Had a nice time, mate?' his dad asked me. I sensed my mum might push a little further but his eyes must have cautioned otherwise, telling me what I'd need to know once I looked up again, that he'd understood. 'Go and get some kip, you look worn out.'

The most sensible thing he'd said all week.

My six o'clock call would make its mark like from a blink of an eye, and yet still have me wrestling to work out who and where I was. The ethereal airs gently fluttered their way back, the photo-like images, hope for a corollary, only for the lurking death mobiles to put me fully in the Sunday picture. I knew the score then. They lay in wait, persuaded as I was, on the corner of our badly lit street.

My mum, in fact, shouted up at a minute to go, though I'd wake another minute before, due, I worked out, to a subliminal fear that some such Sunday they'd forget, or decide to let me sleep through. 'Bless him, he must be done in,' I heard one of them say. On that note, I jumped up.

It was time for The Windmill.

The Windmill, part of Rotherham United's football ground, was everything Wigan wasn't: a small, chic club and, without a Nottingham Palais all-dayer, somewhere to end our weekend in style. Along to more blissful tunes, we'd guzzle to our livers' content, although *Mansfield Bitter,* the one my dad referred to as 'loopy liquid' or 'queer beer', could have the strangest effects. The place was in fact sweat-free as it had something called air-conditioning, which meant we'd also wallow in mohair to our legs' content. We looked good at The Windmill, and would this evening, if the young man through Jenny's mirror was anything to go by...

''Want your dinner, love?' my mum tempted.

I leaned against the kitchen sink, viewed the contents of the reheated dish she held under my nose, which had lamented in a cold oven from about two this afternoon – her gravy was thick at the outset. Still, this beggar wouldn't be choosy.

If I was in a hurry, I didn't make The Grouse in record time: the bus shelter seemed to get in the way. I stopped and smoked a cigarette, waited for a bus I wouldn't take. I asked a passer-by the time; shook my arm when my imaginary watch appeared to be on the imaginary blink. I waited for an imaginary Jed – I knew where the real one was, he must have been thirsty. I dropped an imaginary pound note, which took some finding. It was only on my realising the girl in mind had maybe gone to mass at St Michael's opposite our drinking haunt that I made it to The Grouse in what must have been a record time from the shelter.

Pulling another, Marlene was instant in her greeting: how nice it was of the other lot to not wait for her favourite! Inviting me to a drink, she told me not to worry, they weren't worth it – ''Their loss.' And besides, only three had made it: 'April had to take Macca home again!' She asked where they'd been drinking today. But then how was she to know they'd downed more barbiturate in one afternoon than a dying man might in four?

The other three had gone without me.

'Can I have that blazer when you've done with it?'

And it wasn't the first time...

When Johnny Johnson and his Bandwagon broke out of the concert room, I saw it as a sign to break in. No, I didn't need them. And yes, this first pint lived up to its name.

The room was heaving with talent night devotees, players and public. The Yetis, too, turned up in greater numbers on Sundays, though all that mattered was Mick's presence, in surreal incline against the bar. He'd appreciate my company – 'Quick,' he hollered, ''beer mats away, The Phantom Ticket Gobbler's walked in!'

'A bit o' tact,' Frank begged, exemplifying what a nice fellow he was.

I wondered whether Mick was staying around.

'For this?' One more and he was off to work. Handing Frank an empty glass, he wished to buy the 'Wigan boy' a drink.

'Yeah,' I nodded, both for the drink and with an overstated leer about me. 'Nothin' false about that place.' I only hoped he wouldn't be keeping up the smirk until he left.

His glass was half-empty when he placed it back down.

'What's this about Macca?' I asked, for something to say, our silences all too noisy.

''Kill himself,' he replied, as if referring to a complete stranger, and then attacked his pint's second half the way he'd gone about the first. On his way out, he pulled up between myself and the stage, one upon which a sago-coloured pair of pvc boots were about to bear a would-be Nancy Sinatra – who looked more like the dad and sounded like neither – if Frank's un-plugging of the jukebox and the animated glances the resident drummer was hurling about meant anything. Everyone would howl hell-for-leather once she got up there, as would that short husband once they got home, as per her neighbours, where, they said, she went through the routine again, howling being the desired effect. I couldn't work out what the drummer or organ player saw or heard that the rest of us didn't. And they'd been going long before our Windmill Soul nights.

Mick was prevented from saying what he'd possibly forgotten to say for a Wednesday-United mouthing session in the far corner, which had transformed into a scuffle. It didn't last long: on Frank's go-ahead, Geddon hurled them through the door. 'There you go,' chuckled Mick. ''Nothin' false about this place. If so, why are you here? You think that Wigan crowd are wonderful people cos the gear makes 'em that way.' Of course, I'd defend them, us, pushing him to yell out my name with a sympathy I couldn't take; he brought up an LP I'd hoped to borrow – *Chuck Jackson Arrives!* – advising me to play its *Have You Heard About The Fool!*. Speech given, he was off, before popping his head back one last time, with 'Your dad's here.'

I quit the room to Nancy's circular walk, a chorus of yowls and another scuffle, between her husband and some stranger, who'd dropped his trousers on her first line, pulled out his own organ and yelled: 'Aye, I've got this if you want it!' The shrewd husband got stuck in while Gringo's dirty whites were round his ankles.

Geddon waited for the nod.

In the entrance bar, the unofficial act was equally in full swing: The Two Petes always performed here. And as I wouldn't put either off, I got behind the taller provocateurs, who'd push one against the other: 'You tell him, Pete!' You'd never have believed they'd grown up together, until the roar of laughter, which, they said, often put the artists off in the concert room.

In line with what he'd seen on Dickey's *World Of Sport,* my dad alerted Uncle Pete that an up-and-coming boxer, Sugar Ray Leonard, was going take the world by storm. And that Uncle Pete's hero, Roberto Duran, was going get a proper lesson.

Although Uncle Pete was punch-drunk at the idea, all the more when urged by his supporters to defend his crude-if-dynamic champion, he was still able to admit that, 'pound for pound', Sugar Ray was technically a better boxer. Except he shouldn't have put the freshly pulled serving to his lips before saying so, after which he protested a headless pint and the rest a drenching to which he'd been oblivious. It was on those plosives.

My dad wondered if I was ready for another, like he'd known I was here all along, adding that I should fetch him one while I was at it. He was just showing off: neither of them went to the bar during performances, they had lackeys and fans that bought them.

The evening progressed in the same vein. The hangover would return, I knew that, but up to then nothing mattered. They should have been on telly...

'I surrender' should do it, said my dad, on my telling him I was thinking of learning French.

'Look after your old man,' ordered a ravenous Uncle Pete, trotting away from his turnoff, usual deep-fried ration tucked under his arm.

My dad now asked why there was no Rotherham tonight, before the Attercliffe bus – or 'Ted cart' – ground its way on by. 'Rainbow on wheels!' he gasped, the top deck resembling a psychedelic drape with a quiff. I held him further from the question with how I'd never make it tomorrow. 'Phillip,' he whispered, like someone might hear, 'you do realise you'd be the first in the family ever to be on the dole?'

'Times have changed.'

'Aye.' He estimated there'll one day be people in their forties never having worked in their lives, because they'll have constantly screwed the system – 'When you're my age, you'll see. And where's Jed tonight? And where'd Neil' – Macca – 'been drinking today?' He said he'd heard stories plenty. But as nothing was doing, he pulled out the invisible book of quotations: 'Son... *to thine own self be true.*' He looked incredulous when I told him I'd heard that one somewhere before: 'Aye, from me!' He'd got them waiting in the wings, pressing to make an appearance: 'Remember, *All that glisters...*'

I cut him off: 'Do you mean glistens?'

'No, glisters.' And I should think about it: 'It means glistens...'

Unaware I'd halted at the bus stop, he said he loved me from a distance. Though it did seem to make his evening learning I'd wait around for Nathalie – I *wouldn't* surrender to *John Smith's* Complete Works. Despite his ethics, he didn't want to go to work either.

I dropped to leaning position against an inner-side of the wooden shelter. I drew my train-ticket from a pocket – which I'd transfer from trouser to trouser until the next. And out of the subdued sepia, I noted traces where ink and perspiration had run hand in hand, arrested by the odd tooth mark... I shouldn't have reacted so miserably this morning.

I went for a furtive focus over the road, when who should turn up but my best friend, falling from a bus like from one of his raconteurs' Lancaster Bombers. 'Got a date?' he laughed, speeding along to my pardon like only he could. ''Should've seen Macca earlier!'

He also relayed how a certain bouncer at The Windmill had been given the boot. He was referring to a muscle-bound type who'd never gotten to grips with the Sunday Soul crowd, given we never went along with the purpose of thrusting glass across our neighbours' faces – as was the case on Rock n' Roll evenings, or so the boast went. The ogre had broken my top lip only the week previous, looking to toss me out a minute into my stage act – queer beer again. It was a harmless gesture on my

124

part, and I'd no intention of going further than those same y-fronts; our resident spinner's fine-looking wife said she'd never listen to Marvin Gaye's *How Sweet It Is* the same way again. Everyone was happy, barring said bouncer, who must have realised we Soulies weren't as soft as he'd imagined. I had a great viewpoint, albeit a blurred one.

Now he was history. That was good news. Thanks to me... and those pants.

As routine would have it, Jed flew into the middle of the road in imitation of his most recent observations, until a white *Ford Escort* with 'POLICE' across its bonnet called by. And that was no *Scooby Doo* on the backseat.

'Now then, Jed.'

He greeted the two boys in what looked like black at this time of day with either a carefree or careless snigger: ''Teaching the handsome git how to dance.'

They wanted to know if he'd had a 'good one.' And whether he'd 'be needing a lift.'

'How's that for a police escort!' he winked.

All I could think was that it added to the image – I'd already noticed movement behind that privet hedge... or maybe not. And besides, I was too tired to think anything else.

And so I stuck with my whistled rendition of Mr. J's *Have You Heard About The Fool!*. Poor Mick, I thought. He'd be hard at it by now.

On that shivering note, I decided to make my way down home... slowly, just in case.

2

# 18

*'United and unite, and let us all unite,*
*for summer is acome unto day.*
*And whither we are going we will all unite,*
*in the merry morning of May...'*

Confident he wouldn't miss, I gripped Jed's rear end and suffered a judder from my toes to the tips of every sweat-flattened hair on my head, as we obliterated whatever litter the other four let leap from their wagon's rear window.

I'd no idea what we were doing in Grantham – Jed said *he* was following *them.* But by the same token I didn't feel put out. Spring was here and we were returning the gesture with great big smiles of gratitude.

We'd celebrated May's first Saturday in our sharp and judicious fashion. Thanks to Paul, we'd also avoided Manchester's rainy hindrance: he'd passed his driving test first time round two days ago and, by way of reward, had borrowed his dad's car for the weekend. Of course, we'd have all preferred to make the trip in the same vehicle, irrespective of how Jed derided its matt finish, except the *Hillman Imp* wouldn't allow for it.

Scooter to the rescue.

No sooner had our itchy feet perfected those first struttings Lancashire-side than the amphetamine-fuelled word that Lincolnshire would play host to the rest of the weekend's fun and games whizzed from camp to camp. We adhered without a hint of hesitation but with the utmost enthusiasm.

Because I never trusted Paul with vinyl, and so wouldn't his glove-compartment, I had my mum clean the parka for the occasion, should I encounter anything worth picking up, something else for which these mammoth pockets were made. In effect, I possessed two such pick-ups: Mr. J's *Hand It Over* and

Jed's splash-out of *It's Your Voodoo Working*, Charles Sheffield – tough name though link-free; our only recent connection with that place was having scooted over its twin gas-towered Tinsley Viaduct. And even then I was sure there was a quicker way.

At least we had the drapery of sunny Grantham to be thankful for. A mere two days ago again, as if inspired by Paul's achievement, said boxing cheat of an iron variety managed to cast her spell over more than half of Britain, much to the dismay of the enduring less than half. Meaning people like that other fearsome force: my mum. She wasn't giving in on the milk thing. And cared not that I'd been glad to see the back of it.

Or people like my dad, a Labour man despite the threats. His antagonism was directed toward the reasons he believed 'she' had attained such status; at the likes of those comrades he worked with, whilst they still didn't. It didn't stop him having a go at me yesterday morning, all the same, as if I'd voted for her. And at Sam, who couldn't have voted at all.

He was right, of course. Too busy to understand the implications, we six had voted neither for nor against her. We no more than hoped she wouldn't ban Soul music.

My grom hadn't voted either, but then she'd made up for it by offal-gobbling and clattering through the months in her matchless style. 'Are you happy now?' she asked my dad, removing her teeth, passing the message on from Uncle Jeff – one glance at Brainy and I took off upstairs.

I'd go as far as to say she'd excelled herself.

\* \* \* \* \*

A week before Christmas, her workmate, Bertha, had a mishap when her buffing spindle span from its lathe-end and knocked her, Bertha, out for the count. Not knowing where to turn, my grom sped into our shop and yelled for Mr. Alcrap. If she woke me in the process, the anecdote our part-time medic returned with made up for it. On the scene, he told my grom to get a glass of water from the sink in the nearby corner, which she did, before proceeding to the one hundred and one year old sofa, where she sat down, put her up feet, and drank it. She was feeling "a bit queasy".

128

It was around the time she knocked her own self out at home, having fallen from a ladder putting up decorations. Or rather *she* thought she'd knocked herself out, and rang my Uncle Jeff to tell him just that, once she'd hit the deck. "I'm knocked out," she said.

\* \* \* \* \*

Her main feat was getting kicked off the bus with one of her three remaining sisters – my grom was the youngest of eight; four died young and, according to her, 'that's what it was like, then!' Ida, another old survivor, put miners under the table for drink, but never without it leading to some incident my grom would thrill us all with at a later date. One such holiday afternoon-session – just time for a 'quick un'; the hardship of Christmas shopping – had my Aunt Ida plucking her turkey on the top deck of their homeward bound 58 bus, to save messing up the house when she got in – Uncle Jack didn't need help on that front. To break up the monotony, she fuelled her task with a carol: *The Twelve Days of Christmas*. Not amused, my grom reckoned the bald turkey made 'a great thud on every step o' the bleedin' stairway' as Auntie Ida dragged it down by the neck.

\* \* \* \* \*

Sam had spent his new year muffling his laughter. I couldn't remember the last time I'd seen Jenny, if I was still sharing her wardrobe.

For we six – oh – how we'd fared! Come these weekends, come what may, and the days were getting longer. And yet, to a degree, things midweek felt different. Thursday evening cocktails tasted the same and, on Stan's word, so were the effects. I just couldn't put my finger on it. Ever since that weekend last October, if I thought hard enough.

Paul and Chris would forever be Paul and Chris. And likewise could have been said for our foppish fighter Macca, save that he'd become more Macca than ever; he'd become 'Mogga' – from Mogadon. His and April's unable-to-stand-come-Sunday-evening-sessions had by now spilled into midweek. Indeed, April initiated his new pet name during one such session. But then maybe she deemed anything other than to accompany him on that wayward journey would have meant losing him. And it was always at me Marlene would hurl her questions *a propos* their antics; other than for the Two Petes' turns, Mick was no longer to be seen.

And then there was Jed.

Perhaps he, too, ought to have changed his name, for different reasons. Yes, we shared the same laughs, and as for his own pill-popping zaniness, well, it had rarely been a talking point between us from day one; I'd each time blamed the pills and left it at that. But it just didn't seem to work anymore: his behaviour was getting even stranger. It also dawned on me, post-another two of his Sunday police escorts home, that on all three following Monday evenings, he'd made his immediate way up to The Grouse. Whenever I brought up that fact, in 'jest', no-one took any notice.

Another mystery was that he'd had lots of time off work, though was never short of money. Considering it a long shot, I began to wonder whether he owned a sensitive side I'd yet to tap into. Meaning, was he claiming social security, as well as doing the other thing they said you were supposed to do: feeling humiliated?

Or maybe *I* was being the over-sensitive one. After all, I'd need only to confront him in the bedroom. I'd just never work up the courage.

And Nathalie wasn't the cause. For in spite of Jed's clever bops, my fictitious pound notes dropped, my non-existent, blinkered time-piece, my stopping people for a light, directions – this, that – I had never set eyes on her since. Not once. Not once...

On some sad, solitary something past midnight, I sat on our spot and took in a Sheffield-by-night. It didn't help. Only with her had I not wished to be elsewhere. I recalled how cold that night had been, or how warm she'd somehow made it...

I kept my ache to myself. But – oh – those opening stabs of *I've Got The Need*, or anything like it – and Rod hurt just as much. Of late, *Where Did You Go* had latched on to my conscience, to boot me all the more, from the back of my mind's collection; the Four Tops number, ecstasy in any another setting, now agonizing and no coincidence.

My mum's theatrical bouts didn't help, either. ''Thought it might've been Nathalie,' she'd sigh, whenever Jed, her apparent muse, made his slick entrance. Nor did my dad's telly-ogling and the likes of his Louise English – they all resembled her somehow. The one difference being that he never mentioned Nathalie's name again. But I knew what he was getting at.

'Leave him alone, he wants to marry a darky!' was how my grom shut them up.

Yes. Midweek was different...


At least the armour held firm for our weekends. This one came with a bank holiday bonus.

Having left Grantham to wallow in its sunlit draped dreariness, Jed slowed down noticing an approaching police roadblock – I told him not to panic, that he most likely knew them. In a manual fashion, they directed us to pull over while all else sailed through.

It was a scooter thing.

No longer forming a single piece of a modest collective, we now blended in with the green majority. If our manageress' aim was to transform its off-roads into a car park, our green party had transformed its roads into a scooter racetrack. It was all happening so fast...

Messieurs Roadblock grinned: ''Not down here for trouble, then, lads?'

I asked if we looked the part.

'Well,' said the other, 'we've noticed some o' you lot are, 'see.'

I wasn't looking in the wing mirror when Jed spat, and so didn't see his face. What I noted were their impatient looking colleagues growling behind the steel net curtains of a black riot van. 'He's' jokin', Jed.'

'Jed, is it?'

'And do we need to search you, Jed?'

Jed justified his upset by their use of ''you lot'', remonstrated that the price of *Fred Perry*s had gone sky high because of 'that lot!' And demonstrated how to melt the stern features of two cynics in May morning blue. It wasn't difficult to fathom why Sheffield's police force was fighting to give him lifts.

Beaming out of Wainfleet, our chins dropped before Skegness' greenest Scarbrough Avenue, its flora, a *Vespa* of every tint, sun leaping customised-mirror to mirror, chased on by an exuberant azure. A temperate, salt-peppered breeze made down from the pier, tendered a welcomed Hello. There was a young buzz in the air, distant fairground tunes, an odd sea-wave; amused seagulls, a candyfloss of onion laden hotdogs, fish and chips – why, even the downwind of Jed's *Number 6* tickled me up! And all married my four hours old, eight hours worth of sweet Soul music, an echo still beckoning me back. 'Wigan Casino rules OK,' the graphitised tariff board of the Avenue's car park still read...

And then, snail pace braking to a shiver, glare-shielded by a chimney-stacked sun block, my focus told a duller story. A novelty soon worn by spray job braggers, sentry duty disorder. Not a face recognisable but green, green, with arrows, green...

'Let's get to that Jolly Fisherman!' Jed spat again.

The name rang miraculous. A pint of *Courage* and a pose, lewd laughs courting refined looks, panoramic views, a park and a pier – Bier Garten and Wild Mouse in the sky. Come what may, May, come Wigan Casino, come The Jolly Fisherman. Bracing indeed...

Necking back something on his tongue, Jed first hoped to exploit the clock tower for a private merry-go-round, prior to Paul bringing us back with 'Park up, idiot!' Which we did, amid a mottled myriad, an unofficial extension of the fairground's semi-encircling garden – one chap was so big and green I could but wonder whether Lou Ferrigno hadn't 'become a Mod'. Sam would have stared at that *Hulk* all day.

As our front tyre butted the curb, Jed knocked up the stand, slid off his helmet like he would his Breton cap pre-lesson, ran his fingers through his hair and marched away, as if afraid of contracting some style-deficiency disease. I lost sight of the *Imp* until the evening after, though judged they'd managed to park somewhere spotting April and Mogga scuttling over the gardens to their ride of rides. They'd waited long enough.

At the sun-bathed stairway leading to our Jolly Fisherman, unlike any of our previous visits we discerned men indoors forcing themselves against the pub's window, in a bid to break free – when the door was, in effect, open; I'd recall this scene during the film *Salem's Lot,* except the vampire children would be trying to get in, rather than out. The shared psychosis had been brought about by no more than some motorcycle spluttering its way along the promenade, and it was a shame our happy old timer never recognized the popularity he'd pressed; he might have performed a half-twirl round the clock tower and spluttered by again. The lady in the sidecar looked almost too comfortable...

Jed ordered me to take my coat off – another Steve hand-me-down – realising he was having an off day. Just as Sam gained his education from my knees at the end of each weekend, Jed had gained his via mohair happenings at The Twisted Wheel. For him, this green brigade had wagged all existing lessons covering real life.

We were greeted by The Who, who indeed were asking who; as in their *Who Are You.*

You expected to hear this kind of thing smashing out of holes at the town's wrong end, beyond the park, opposite the train station; mean and moody pubs like The... places you kept out of if your definition of life differed to that of their Cro-Magnon clientele – not nice Yetis like ours. The cheers were missing for looks of dense unfamiliarity.

When a possible ex-druid with a guttural voice claimed he'd always been a fan of said interrogators, that he'd had hair down to his breasts up until this year, Jed spat a third time with woven shade. He'd get louder as the day progressed.

I asked our barmaid if she'd put my hat and coat behind the bar, but to be careful as the coat had gold in it, insisting her film star eyes looked trustworthy. Her reaction was a smile at no price at all. And if my dad's early morning instruction was anything to go by, then at least it was my lucky day.

\* \* \* \* \*

'Never trust anybody by their actions,' he warned – he'd had problems finishing some job the previous day's afternoon, when one of his comrades offered to lend an all-rectifying tool, murdering the job and near killing my dad in the process. 'Take 'em on their *re*actions. Like them commies that run off whenever work's mentioned. That way you see the real person, nowt planned...'

I rammed my head back into my cushion.

* * * * *

I pushed my Shakespearian brother in arms to rest his tired heart, bade him courage, for a pint of, with patience, would pursue... once I'd put my dad's theory to the test.

She smiled again on my asking if she'd let me put my head in her sink, what with the all-night dancing, and the helmet.

'''All-night dancing''? Wow!' She told me it looked nice, and raised her voice adding 'hair', catching me looking over my shoulder.

'Two pints o' *Courage*, please.'

''Shame, mind,' she said, 'if you'd come into the shop in Ilkeston, I'd have done a real good job on it. I'm a hair-dresser.' She was then distracted by one of Jed's nemeses, one informing me of her intentions according to him. ''Suppose you're the expert,' she sneered, like she'd done it all before, delivering me enough *Courage* for a short while. I picked up the pints over a bass banging Detroit bawler inviting us all on down, with her *Devil Gate Drive.*

'Keep the change.'

I parked amid our Soul re-congregation on reserved seating at the pub's park end, where we drank, smoked and laughed, where vinyl was displayed for the comprehending and Wigan recalled with amphetamine lucidity. Later arrivals brought newer narrative of an almost coast-to-coast. Paul picked up frothy headed glasses depicting how Mogga and April had 'broke out an' run!' The couple fell in unwell, by and by craving more.

Come half-three and our fairground staged another, first-of-the-season private show. Gate crashed this time, we weren't, barring the odd, audible drifting-in of engines like peas in a tin, or a mass tree-felling frenzy caught on a downward Boston wind.

The afternoon's sole blip was my one burger too many. The churning inclination was part rectified following a Boxing Day Sales-like scrap for The Rockets, whose workings had undergone a sticky brakes abnormality and so churned out a groan of their own. Jed informed Lincolnshire's eastside that said churning reminded him of an exasperated Frankie Howard. There was no concentrating on R. Dean Taylor's haunted house after that. They must have heard us up at Vickers Point...

I spoilt myself with a stiff short, lining for an imminent second bout with the *Courage,* or *Batemans* for the more courageous. Reviewing my chair, a dusky park to behold proved a much-welcomed return to nature, if no time for calm. Smiling-white cast off for moody-night black, my hairdresser with the film star eyes chased my whisky on its firmly booked destination. I picked up my pint.

''Left your coat earlier,' she said, snatched two empty glasses, turned, and turned again: ''Reckon your gold's still there.'

Post-swift council-style debate, April gazed into my eyes. 'We reckon she wants your kit off, young man.'

'Play your cards wight, y' might gerra bed,' Mogga slurred, on some private planet.

Jed roared for 'a bed', his 'kingdom for...'

The trick was to crash April and ex-Macca's guesthouse room – last August they broke their record for life bans. My scariest moment was waking up in their wardrobe one Sunday, upside-down, on the back of my neck. And if the idea of being buried alive wasn't enough, my dad, on our Monday morning's top-deck, reckoned that, well, had I been sick, 'it'd have been Goodnight, Vienna.' Beneath the pier and a winning's skirt was second most popular choice. But yes, a bed would have been nice.

'Can I sit down five minutes?' asked my hopeful. ''Been given a well-earned break.'

Jed told her I liked my eggs fried, before twisting back to conversation of a narcotic nature. Like in sporadic attempts at an itch he couldn't quite reach, he'd turn our way, interject his wit.

And each time my barmaid smiled that smile, her eyes declared I knew her from elsewhere. I'd need to know her name.

'Vicky.'

'Victoria?'

'Well, it wouldn't be Elizabeth, would it?'

'Like Victoria Vetri?'

'Watch him, he's a dinosaur nerd.'

I'd have ruffled Jed's hair at that point, like Ken Dodd's, were it ruffle-able. But then the same could have been said for this here unshakable *Levi's* strain. I'd not yet heard of 'drink provoking the desire while taking away the performance' – my dad would serve it at a later date – though had 'drunkard's droop'. I was a tad too young for that one just yet...

'Beddy Everette, baby!' my best friend reported, to a *Getting Mighty Crowded* backing…

''Think your loud mate's turned Yank,' whispered Vicky, her nose nudging my ear.

And as ale and whisky scrapped it out for a heart, I kissed like I'd otherwise drown in effervescence, cheers and trumpets riotous, and I kissed and kissed… and pulled away, to regain a little discipline.

Poise resumed, faintest flush, she asked if I'd be heading over to Sands, a club doable in that it boasted funkier tunes than your average, and stood below the pier, or a little before it, practical for the average sleeping arrangement.

'She does,' April decided, 'she wants your kit off.'

Vicky tossed my coat and said she'd catch me inside, having once tidied up.

And so off we strutted toward the opalescent exit that was our promenade-end by night, by way of some furious tribal dance our aliens performed free of charge, supported by The Jam's *Strange Town*.

'Leave it, Jed!' someone laughed, before someone else pulled the plug…

# 19

*'Is this the region, this the soil, the clime... this the seat,*
*That we must change for heav'n, this mournful gloom,*
*For that celestial light?'*

April hauled ex-Macca's ex-body, directing our army via the fairground, supposing her beguiling beam would secure that crucial last ride, even if the boys had put the toys away half an hour back. As all but two of us fell for it, it was a sight to behold, evoking flashes of dizzy *Disney* scenes – that our band of tearaways should sprout tails from trench coat vents for their excesses!

Jed was taken more by life on our side of the road, his eyes reflecting a medley of promenade hue. 'Look at this lot,' he said, nipping my question of where on earth Ilkeston was in the bud. 'None of 'em have any convicts of their own.'

'Do you mean convictions?'

He didn't hear. But asked had I noticed how 'Mod' and 'Ted' rhymed. He barred my smirk with a hand: 'Three letters, ending in d...'

The rhetoric was cut short when someone turned to meet us dead on, pressed us in a North-eastern accent to offer our allegiance, until the glaze of anxiety was snuffed by a frothing beer bottle, a stick-grenade of sorts, impacting against his head, granting Jed a light ale-blood facial. The beggar collapsed into my arms. The bottle crashed onto the kerb.

Screams of a different nature rippled like a breeze of bitter change, and yet I couldn't put my finger on its source. Groups silhouetted, an approach, a retreat; a car shunned dug-in feet, the to-ing and fro-ing. And then, in squadron-like re-formation, on a general's growl, all became as plain as a size ten boot: *'Skinhead! Skinhead!'*

There was something malevolent in the way they did that.

Jed yanked my hood as I laid my patient to the ground. He dragged me down a street leading to the park, safest bet, but for a division of our craven copraphagics catching on, screeching forth their personal excreta.

I took the knee-high wall Red Rum-style, only to recognise that one of us had committed an error of judgement: a step, a day out-stepped, my grand-national winner falling to dust at this last hurdle; a frantic thought on which to cling, this short-straw-of-a-moment million. And so again I placed a glossy sole upon a Jolly Fisherman's sun-bathed stairway, in past imitation or practice for the future – I had the world at my feet after all...

Teeth penetrated the footwear in *Morph*-ish splatter. *Courage* cared for the spine.

*"You're going to fall flat on your face,"* echoed a warning, before a nervous laugh above...

20

*'... Yet from those flames No light, but rather darkness visible.'*

A scrambled descent, a thud. The dull, dull thud of another. There he thudded, here he glanced, there he scampered. Either our contemporary warriors were sparing me in recognition of valour, or the pesky parasites couldn't in fact see me, their shadowy bulks becoming more prominent... to an eventual new light-show from over the wall.

*Dr Marten* clarified all by a plod, rather than a thud. Jed had convened The Cavalry.

'Can you move, young man?' queried a voice behind a dazzle. 'Jed reckons you did a bit of a Lester Piggott.'

'Is he your friend?' I asked, but only part-regretted my second question, concerning myself for 'the lad who copped the bottle on his head?'

'Which one?'

'He had a parka on.'

'That narrows it down a bit.'

On that note I'd wallow no more, and so gripped something with which I'd never hope to be clobbered, allowing my officer and his colleague to each take an arm and guide me back with a foot-clamber. 'Grab hold o' that and give yourself a pull,' advised the latter, referring to the steel bar protruding from the wall by about six feet, radius of around...

Taking another peek, the three of us didn't so much speak for a shared groan. What might have been...

'So this is Lester Piggott, is it?' nodded the six-foot sergeant, to Jed's unambiguous delight; he was leaning against a black van in one more every-picture-tells-a-story. I'd never seen a policeman smoke before, not in real life.

I was ready to make light of matters, when one of the bald arrestees, pinned by three or four captors, launched into to what he would have done to me had things panned out his way, foaming at the mouth in a quasi-cockney accent.

"Got the wrong coat on, lad,' smiled our sergeant, and threw a Pat Jennings-type hand into Baldy's gullet.

He compelled me to hate *him,* too, did Baldy, and not solely for hating me, or the bloodshed, or the bottles. I heard a tune, eerie swishes, *House of the Rising Sun* originating from another scream-filled ride, floating about a pale tea-time sky...

* * * * *

War had been organised with backup plans to boot: if the Hell's Angels didn't turn out, the daffs, in bank holiday bloom, would prove a less painful contingency. So many cropped heads – I'd never seen a cropped head before! The white shirts, the braces; when in a chemistry class our teacher drew on the term 'homogeneity', I knew what it meant.

My kings, they'd be, homogeneous yet smartly removed. Not that I'd never wonder where they resided in wintertime, these kings, as the backs of my legs froze over the brittle seat of an outside toilet on an early black evening.

My itchy shorts itched; my *Man from U.N.C.L.E.* felt hat felt hot; I longed to get nearer, as two handfuls of bobbies bordered the gardens in wait for reinforcements. My dad's icy eyes didn't budge. There were no idling deckchairs at hand's reach...

* * * * *

For this here Baldy character, he resembled nothing of the sort. He wriggled no more.

April's head alternated between Sid Vicious and a Technicolor Twiggy: 'We did it! They let us do it – They let us...' Over the moon, she bragged of free bumper car rides. As I flew over a wall, her army flew over the moon.

I let Jed take off in running commentary of happenings on our side of the street, favouring a scan for Victoria... only for my eyes to touchdown on a familiar swagger, belonging to no other than our Windmill bouncer, or ex-Windmill bouncer; the one having lost his job to a loathing for Soul boys, and this here Soul boy in particular. The moment our eyes met – he wanted me at that door – the day's knocks confirmed tonight was not meant to be...

''Arms an' legs out in mid-air at the same time!' Jed cried

I wouldn't try throwing it all away again, not on the Rotherham brain-dead – he already had an arm in a sling, while the other had grown to compensate. It was as if a sword had spent its day thrusting at me via an alcohol glut and I'd only just noticed.

I wished them the best, hoping Victoria might think of me from time to time...

## 21

*'Speak, father, speak to your little boy, Or else I shall be lost."*

I'd revelled in all-nightness, crossed a country and revelled again. I'd flown rockets high, fallen walls *Milk Tray* deep, and why? All because...

Only the sea would understand.

Yet as shingle mailed tingles of an ensuing day's aches, as water ran amid my toes for getting too intimate, I pictured another temptation: tea bags on a silver platter. Duck-flocked walls, prominent, furry patterns to, lights out, seize in reverse; artex begging a finger about its continual crevice. Pillows to get lost in, frills and furbelows to tie all together – swirling carpet! And that bathroom suite: avocado lime-scale indicator, hip-height sink for getting carried away... toilet-roll holder in party-doll guise.

Bed and breakfast never felt so alluring, even a grabber with hardboard-partitioned rooms.

My welcome arrived in gaudy green, an 'Oceans Welcome'. I'd fuss neither over the missing apostrophe nor the four pounds fifty per night.

'Can I help?' rang a voice in a blue rinse, half-smoked cigarette between remaining teeth. She cut me off with a supercilious blade, nodded to the Vacancies sign in the window, above the stuffed dog's head on the sill. ''Needs turnin',' she said, ash dropping onto a bedroom slipper like not for the first time.

And so I winked at the hound and headed north, beating off further designations *en route*: Travellers Rest, Happy Haven. Cosy Comforts Inn, Floral Retreat – 'Liars!' I may have pronounced, faced with a whole host of venting-spleen classics.

In no time I worked out an outlined 'Uncle Tom's Cabin', or Uncle Tom's Cabin once was, my dad's cherished little club beside the sea. He was happier nowhere else, *Watneys* in a hand, my mum's knees in the other, as his offspring strove by non-authorized means to rid Rich Gypsy – a fortune-telling card-machine – of her bounteous sixpenny pieces. Those enticing Romany eyes…

And just over, there, East Gate caravan site, its ex-cinema opposite, the place I'd met young BB – *Shalako* – gone-tombola hall like there'd been a shortage.

And back across, an arcade in which Jenny took her pick among the throng of Skinhead wooers, seemingly all from Wolverhampton. Sixpence after sixpence, I'd slot into that jukebox, hand-written a- and b-sides; same records year after year. One-armed bandits weren't for me, nor was flicking ball bearings about a tinny face – a flat thing on the wall; its glass never broke despite the effort, but its balls would tiresomely swing before declining into that ever growing hole: loser… loser, loser… No, while ever *There's A Ghost In My House* was around to haunt me, I stood haunted, by the sound as with that black and steely rotating rectangle, *Tamla Motown,* evoking the miniature *Cadbury's* chocolate bars I'd hunt out of my mum's Christmas box of *Quality Street.* The Skinheads topped up the coins with a pat on the head, an odd 'Keep up the good work, little bruv.'

I didn't half find those accents strange.

Vickers Point was where I'd ended up, and another dreamless pool. Maybe I, too, had never been happier than around these parts. Old Uncle Tom's Cabin down the road… the place with the apostrophe…

## 22

*'When the wind of change blows, some people build walls while
others build windmills.'*

'Come on,' he tried again, 'it looks like it's goin' be a nice
day.' He told them he'd not tell them anymore, that he'd go
without them, adding: 'Come on, it's beautiful out there, I'll not
tell you anymore.' I heard the giggles, amid a Dean Martin
impersonation.

I banged my head but was saved by the children's efforts to
evade whatever punishment – cold water, I imagined – the
dedicated father was dishing out. Powerless to part with the
sunup caravan park scents I trapped down here, I decided to stay
put until our happy family, stocked shoulder-high in buckets and
spades, had headed on to the beach.

'Can I take my Shakin' Stevens tape?' begged the girl, when
mum mentioned the radio.

Dad made two stipulations: one, that they get a move on, and
two, that they 'have a break from the bloody thing now an'
again.'

Mum beckoned Jamie to eat his fried egg; dad prompted him to
have a go at the bacon, both asserting that Sarah had eaten hers.
He wouldn't get an ice cream otherwise. And so Sarah teased
while mum told Jamie not to listen. Pots and suds, was mum,
slotting washed plates into a drying rack on the sink – I saw
without seeing; just knew Sarah was about to cop the tea-towel
treatment. 'Come and dry a few o' these, Sarah, I'm runnin' out
o' space.' Dad stuck to his guns for nigh on thirty seconds,
zooming in to rescue Jamie's bottom-lip. The egg and bacon
rashers went to the dog.

'The Eagle has landed!' dad at last declared, the door swinging
open with a skull-splitting crack, his feet touching down on

heaven-scented grass, blue and white beach ball arriving a second on.

Sarah performed an on-the-spot jog before her feet made the field: 'Can I play my tape now?'

'Houston, I think we godda problem.'

She was riled by dad's old act, as per what she said once our northern *Major Tom* claimed he couldn't hear her, that the problem was technical: 'You're allus cuttin' out!'

Four pairs of feet for the flip-flopped march away, each tool vital for fortifying the coast against another Viking invasion; a chain gang of sorts, Shakin' Stevens to dispel the working blues.

'Are you comin'?' asked dad, about to lock the portal, the dog still lapping up the remnants of its full English.

When the four golden paws hit the green, the sun-lit pedigree tilted its head and tossed me a lifetime glance, eyes asking Jamie, head-height, why there was a man lying beneath the caravan. Off, they then marched, to earn that ice cream dessert.

I clutched something rusty, tugged myself from the chopped-stone mattress, chalk taking a liking to my once green coat. Hand for sunshield, I squinted toward the gravelled entrance, either side of which privet-fencing accomplished the stature of cacti, if those spaghetti westerns were anything to go by.

I took my first step, took another for second opinion: my doubts alone were assembled on solid footing – 'Wherrrre *doe*sn't it hurrrt?' our family doctor would have laughed, wide-eyes and madras, pressing something sensitive and I'd smile back. Nets twitched as in ten-to-two, creating a domino effect to our cacti high; someone openly drew their curtains. A young Clint Eastward beaten to a pulp, left to rot in Andalusia. That was me. Creaking my stubbly way across a cross-eyed Andalusia.

Since my remaining cigarette was in thirds, I lit up the furthest from the tip, and spat what I first judged to be tobacco bits, until the back of my hand illustrated a bloody, chipped-teeth mix. I'd made it here on foot but wouldn't make the return journey as easily.

Even my fifty-yard hooked-hobble to the bus stop/terminus proved a tall order. Children grabbed their mothers' hands, others scampered to their dads; a boy dropped a cornet jumping from *Goofy*'s rocking back.

At least the shops stayed open.

I asked the driver if he'd be leaving straight away.

'Two minutes,' he said. ''Swear on my Vickers Point.'

The local toilets stank like a place time had forgotten, where I wouldn't heave for keeping an eye out of the thick, grey-tinted window, should my Lincolnshire green open-top flee with everything else. Teeth smacked the mirror like semi-munched peanuts against a chicken-pocked forehead... *'You've got the wrong coat on, lad,'* guessed a voice. *'She wants your kit off,'* guessed another. *'She wants...'*

''Comin'?' I heard.

I checked in my coat's cavernous pockets before letting it fall, and pulled out a pair of record sleeves, their contents but fragmentations, like burned sand, occupying the creases. And I kicked... and it hurt. And I kicked, and again, and staggered back into the sunshine.

I held up the former records for the driver.

'Aye, they're nice,' he said. 'Didn't you have a coat earlier? Hold tight, we're off.'

Although, with patience, I reached the top deck, hoping a sea breeze might act medicinally, I had no time to sit. Opposite The Jolly Fisherman I thanked both the driver and an elderly lady for helping me off...

... where at once a whole barrel of quandaries rolled in. Like, what to say to Victoria about my absence? Or to the crowd, unfit as I was for speeches? Was I a bore? Was I? Worse, would be hearing about the exhilarating night they'd have spent. How Mogga had 'got down to any ol' crap', insisting Gene 'The Duke' Chandler, in case anyone had wondered, recorded the original, the sole singer he'd succeed in summoning when in his fast-becoming-a-permanent state. Or how Chris had 'got off with some posh bird from Newark-on-Trent.' How Paul had taken a slap post-one too many wisecracks *a propos* Boston bikes and loose women. How my best friend had somehow come away untouched, despite having addressed every two out of three males in the place as 'wanker'.

Those steps looked higher today, too. I first nipped next door...

We didn't know the name of the pub next door because it didn't have one, or didn't display one. It had all the qualities of The Jolly Fisherman without serving the indispensable: the *Courage*. Today I'd make use of its gents', perform the beauty essentials, tone down the war paint; rinse my mouth into the sink. My lead fillings joined the orgy.

If drying proved complex for the knife-edged toilet paper, looking omnipotent felt good again. I'd make it through my weekend if it killed me...

'It's Lester Piggot!' was right on time.

''Pint o' *Courage*, please,' I requested, with an inadvertent spit at Vicky's scenic colleague.

She said I'd forgotten my 'motorbike helmet' last night, ahead of asking whether I'd been a naughty boy, given Vicky hadn't turned in today. That one made life a little easier.

I'd have liked to defend her workmate's absence with a diagnosis of a week's recovery, but the words wouldn't leave my lips. And so I just winked.

April's rescuing call invited me to a chair: 'Christ, you look awful!'

''That your breakfast?' asked Chris, beside printed Sunday boobs.

Jed wasn't around.

''Still be in bed, no doubt,' April supposed, turning to tap ash into a heaving metal tray. ''Got off with that girl.' She made sure to turn back on 'Her that wanted your kit off but you weren't bothered.' As if to emphasise the last three or four words.

She left it there, leaving me to lose my breath. Feeling like I'd never regain it, I carted out my stuffed ribs by way of another *Strange Town* intro.

'Don't forget your helmet,' I heard, before the sun's glare.

I shambled across the road, blood-spit route, and in and around an endless arcade, to falter at wooden slats; to go no further. Cut off at the neck, was the place I'd shaken hands with Dick Emery. That old pier. And I recalled a newsreel, how, between last summer and this, a storm had swept in like a sea of change. The council's one flaw in its master plan. I'd only just noticed...

147

Ghosts crowded the artists' entrance, until the sea tapped a beam with a snort. I hit back with a sputter, with a stamp, flipped sparkly vinyl specks to The silver-grey Wash. I kept Jed's specks like he'd still need them.

At the same time, I couldn't understand what my problem was, why I was so hot...

... when here he was again, in the water's glint, a younger Jed, delivering oxblood wax remains to assist my labouring *Dr Marten's*. Another winter Sunday I'd never have survived without him, when *Wherever I Lay My Hat* said it all.

A flaw in our master plan? But it was the road we'd taken and for me to stop letting the side down. And as my breathing returned to a more normal rhythm, I made my way back over.

Spotting him in my chair was to know this gun-fighting finger wouldn't behave. He was drinking my drink.

April described how Alan Wicker had since been substituted for Lester Piggot, by how I kept wandering off.

Jed was more discreet.

I pushed him up for room. 'Sorry, I said, ''got some sliced tongue in my throat.' And asked whether he planned to always live off my leftovers. I pointed to my seat, to my beer, and then to the door on 'my bird.' I depicted how my night had consisted of losing four teeth, and that I'd requested a bonus from my tooth fairy.

Mogga laughed but didn't know why.

Jed smiled... and I could have killed him for it.

'No Nottingham Palais today, then?' I said – I was being rhetorical again – adding I'd never understand his contempt for 'Funkateers' – the Palais had a Funk room, which Jed despised the thought of; he saw it and them as a threat to real Soul. It was just that, well, right here, right now, his hatred didn't seem to make any sense to me. Surely they, the Funkateers, were the real Mods, I said, unlike us, the retro crowd. He didn't like it, either; I saw it in his eyes... just not enough. And so I handed back his record from my jacket's inside pocket, all three thousand bits, signed, I smiled, by Lester Piggot.

That was me burnt out. Jed never mentioned Victoria again.

Once we'd laid Mogga to rest in the back of the *Hillman,* April took off for one last breath-taker on the Twisters, acquiring

148

Chris' accompaniment by a dragged ear. The rest debated whether we'd get back in time for The Windmill. But as I'd had my rib-full of Rotherham for a weekend, I checked what money I had left and picked up a plant for my old mum, which I hoped would make up for wasting her hectic hands' time on the green fishtail, only for me to give it a good kicking.

Thinking about it, Jed never asked where the coat had gone, either.

It had turned into a nippy evening, with a sense of symbolism attached, like the lid had been blown from our weekends in Nirvana, like the gate had been crashed at the front of forevermore. Maybe there *was* something in the air. And just maybe I shouldn't have taken that last glance at the pier's head, out there, all alone...

Apart from my insistence we avoid Grantham, we didn't speak, Jed and me, on our way home. But then that could have been due to the weight of the daisy-thing's pot swinging about my neck – I thought it might bring me off. There were the usual grunts on Jed's part, the self-proclamations: abhorrence for anyone with a scooter barring himself – you didn't become a Mod, you were or you weren't. Individual style mattered...

I had all on with the flower.

Still, he did evoke something I'd have otherwise forgotten, something he'd slurred our evening previous, about 'Mod' and 'Ted' rhyming, both with three letters ending in 'd'.

Like 'Jed', it dawned on me. *One of those quick-fire thoughts my Nathalie might have shot. I saw that twinkle in her eyes. But I kept it all to myself...*

3

# 23

*'Thou know'st 'tis common – all that lives must die,*
*Passing through nature to eternity.'*

The fractured fortifications consented to another rushing ray, heralding the dark season's end, or the beginning – Easter! – of brighter things to come. Jed declared that when *the* time came, he'd go down with this ship...

I just couldn't understand why he'd want to partake in this weekend's national scooter run, not with the alternative of letting our hair down to Chaka Khan's *I'm Every Woman*, even if he'd made himself scarce on Sands nights last summer; *One Nation Under A Groove* and he was off. No, Scarborough had to be worth the ordeal.

He now enlightened me on his motive: someone was ready to purchase our very own, two-wheeled friend, in Scarborough. £250 sounded about right.

There was no stopping him. As I distributed belated hugs, he skipped his lucky-loafers over to the station like the train might come early, bounding to his black spot; to his, our, sinister little corner, a tunnel outdone, week after month after year. 'Not today!' he crowed, backed by a defiant westward echo. I kept my distance and thrust a victory V.

No sooner had our wiry assembly crammed the station than we learned the other four had agreed to stay on until tomorrow. But if the train pulled away with a wrench, it could have been worse: at least my best friend was on this side of the glass.

It was a wrench strengthened by the fact I'd partaken in the gear last night. The one pill: a 'black bomber' – on Jed's word, I'd be up and running until next weekend.

I sensed the other five had seen me off our Soul train – everyone had gone pill mad. And maybe this was my way of catching back up.

Jed told my dad he'd lost his job rather than me – I was *there* but he told him, not me; they were ogling Debbie Harry at the time. And again I didn't dare to ask where he was getting his money from – though I did think of asking my dad – since the least of Jed's problems were financial. Either it was right what they said about social security or his mum and dad were picking up one hell of a war pension. Why I should spend 40 odd hours a week in Purgatory while he played urbane *flaneur* with a bottomless mohair pocket, I couldn't work out, not when 'she' was meant to be ripping her claws into those kinds of pockets as well. But yes, my dad knew him better than I did...

And then there was Sands – it had only taken a week for our Rotherham troll to get the rest of his body broken, with another notice. Jed would simply take off. What I considered an aberration became a total regularity, to the first five or six bars of Funkadelic's *One Nation...* – and there were worse tunes than that one. Victoria had returned to Ilkeston, back to the shop, as per her ever playful colleague, the one I accidently spat at: Kerry Spalding from Wainfleet. And so I was spared embarrassment on that front.

She looked after me, Kerry. On cue, Jed's funky disappearing act, she'd literally jump on me. They both became that predictable. 'You are the *swee*test thing!' she'd whisper, peering up, as if moved by the sight of my manliness, once we'd settled in beneath the remaining land-end piece of the pier.

As she was living with a friend and didn't like troubling her, we never went back to her place. But she still made me feel good, weekend after weekend, and had no qualms about it being our little secret.

Alas, the relationship was doomed the moment she told me her name and place of birth. Come autumn, my dad fell into frenzies reading the back of her envelopes, each scented with some French fixation only she could pronounce. Due to those frenzies I couldn't bring myself to reply, preferring to believe the sex had been good to the point of wearing itself out. Besides, news of our affair would have gotten back to Jed sooner or later; it was amazing he'd never caught on.

'Where'd *you* get to last night?' I'd ask him.

'Oh, 'bit o' gear.'

I was meant to understand.

There'd been more oddness vis-à-vis his association with the law, too, summer and winter alike. Not so much lifts, but every-other-evening ride-bys: 'Now then, Jed?' Like clockwork: ''Been a good boy, Jed?' He no longer enjoyed their company, either, or wasn't as cocky, before a faraway look beyond all I could see...

Fits and starts was how I'd come to think of Jed; he was only ever with me in fits and starts. And nowhere were they better demonstrated than in The Grouse's concert room, where everyone barring the Yetis, Frank and Marlene had taken to wearing khaki badged up to the nines, a pint-puller and a couple of old commandos in the other side included, whatever the weather. When the fits started, my mate would need some stopping. And he'd have been expelled without Armageddon's bearish hugs, lifting him from the ground, squeezing the fit out of him.

Afghan put the calming lid on proceedings: 'Way d' go, yeah, like it, man!' He seemed to think they were performing some kind of mystical dance.

He'd open fire, Jed, the second we'd swung through the main doors: he was no fan of those Secret Affair entrances: 'Tie under a v-neck jumper, for Christ's sake!' Or entrances along to any of his re-named 'bandwagon-jumpin' bands', those claiming to have awaited this moment all their lives – as per a song title of *Time For Action*; those claiming to have been formerly misunderstood in their unparalleled worship of Smokey Robinson and The Miracles. Jed just wasn't buying it. He threatened to trash the jukebox, get his hand through the glass and smash up the records.

'And you'll be barred,' Marlene returned, wiping *Smith*'s from the bar-top with a *Magnet* printed towel.

'Then pull the plug – Quick!'

153

'You *are,* you're bloody loopy!'

She'd then terrorize the khaki lot for getting too rowdy, with that sexy index. Geddon's locks twitched about his face.

Last October was the worst, with the release of *Quadrophenia,* above the subtitle *A Way of Life.*

The film's sole positive, as per Jed's unpaid, unremitting running-commentary, a café scene set to the background of Marvin Gaye's *Baby Don't You Do It,* provoked his 'Now that's more like it!' But when the Police man made his pouted-lipped, grey speck in heaps of green appearance, he looked like he was ready to slash the seats: 'As if a pop star can act...!'

'*Oy!*' the usherette ushered again.

'Shuddup,' April prodded.

Nor did he welcome our protagonist's getting his wicked way with Leslie Ash up some Brighton back-alley: 'He could never do that after speed!' No, torches a go-go.

Mirrors a go-go, our Grouse lot were off to see their favourite film for the ninth and tenth time. While it blew Jed's mind, I found it a blessing, respite from Back To Parkas, The Direct Mertons and The Purple Zeros, or something like that.

Many – not our Grouse lot this time, though some were asking questions – were even squeezing their way through our Casino Club's main doors, if looking at a loss once inside. All going by the name of Jimmy, most would swagger into deep sleep; others needed a makeshift stomach pump before one o'clock.

Over the months, I'd experienced unprecedented panic-attacks, whenever anything was presented as 'an old Mod classic': would it be The Who and what should I do with it? It never happened, but the onetime dedicated scene was being put to the test...

The year had also been a trial in other respects. Like the day after Boxing Day and how we attacked the sales, snatching *Levi's* from the hands of shoppers, shoppers who'd never known Miss Bland and her bile-bringing films, shoppers who checked a clothing-item's size before buying it. Of course, we weren't talking any old Christmas sales: those Russians had finally gone and done it, in Afghanistan, on Boxing Day of all days – or that was when we got wind of it, in The Grouse, as if the day hadn't been dreadful enough for two of us. I borrowed money right, left and centre, supposing I'd never have to pay it back, while Jed claimed his jeans from the DHSS, or so he said. I even asked for an advance back at work.

Actually, I blamed Alcrap for the lot. Doomsday personified.

On he went during the Christmas run-up, judging 1980 to possess an apocalyptic ring. Four years at the most, 'so we should be grabbin' life by the balls.' I knew somebody's big brother was at fault but didn't get most of it. Wigan Pier's connection would be the bit to wake me. If we were going to go, then that would be the perfect way.

More depressing still, for Jed and me, was that we'd have indulged in the comfort shopping even without the Russian drama, after all we'd endured that afternoon: 'The Boxing Day Massacre' – like its predecessor could have been as important. Sheffield Wednesday 4: Sheffield United 0, the history books would read, as would the record books with a 49,000 attendance for the Third Division. Before the match, the then Mogga suggested that if they, the blue and white four, waved from yon hill, the biggest kop in England, filled to capacity of something like 25,000, then we two, back over on Leppings Lane, where their team kept knocking them in, could wave back. We never did make them out, no matter how hard Mogga and April claimed they'd tried. A goal each, and they'd re-enacted them ever since.

Wednesday Keith, or 'Guy', post-Boxing Day, was as bad. Him and his *Singin' The Blues* number; he even sounded like Guy Mitchell...

But, as with today and our rain-free, Sheffield-bound stroll through Manchester, it hadn't been total doom and gloom. Mogga, this time, supplied us with the anecdote of the year.

One Monday evening last June, Mick, now only seen in The Grouse with my dad, popped his head round the door and, with a frown, announced: 'The Duke's dead.'

News couldn't come worse for the disowned brother, who fell straight into mourning against the bar, April holding on. 'Drinks all round' were as soon pulled from Mogga's pocket for the rest of the evening. He also monopolised the jukebox, picking out anything remotely like Gene 'The Duke' Chandler. No-one complained and Armageddon made sure they didn't, appearing to have also been a fan – who'd have thought! The rest of us cottoned on only when Mogga stumbled from the gents' at a quarter to ten. 'John Wayne's copped it as well,' he said, right after which Geddon slotted another coin into the record machine and out zoomed The Trammps' *Zing Went The Strings Of My Heart*. Worth a replay, that one…

Poor Mogga. Or rather, poor 'Half Dead'. Sartorially, he still put princes to shame, though the dancing had become rabid, rhythm-lost, like his juddery being was at conflict with itself. Neck upward, it was as plain as the night what the 101 percenter was up for, but as if the downward part had gotten too cosy with the wreckage.

April, too, was looking more drawn of late, if still as scenic. The weight of love must have felt heavier than it ought. Still, Chris was always there, when things looked too heavy, kind word and a promise. Paul collected records like the bomb *had* been pledged for tomorrow. He'd never get a car at that rate.

There'd been just as many news-worthy events of an up-and-down nature in the house, the major down being that Ida, my grom's sister, the tippler, had died. Overwhelmed by news of John Lennon's death one early English, early December morning, she'd gotten so drunk throughout the day that she fell asleep standing by the coal fire. Up in flames, she went, without noticing, or not until it was too late, according to Uncle Jack's report, the inebriated husband. He'd sat and poured pale-ale over his lap, dousing his own trousers in disbelief.

My dad was as sensitive as ever: 'What a silly bleedin' thing to do!'

Connected – 'She wasn't happy at the funeral,' my mum noted – or coincidence, my grom hadn't been the same since, and was now living with us.

She'd stopped work but for the times 'they' were desperate, via a word from Uncle Jeff. ''Don't want work, these young uns,' griped my dad each time.

Whether no longer good for bashing silver plate against spindles the radius of 78s, eight hours a day, five days a week, up to her eyes in grime, she'd always be my reckless old Guardian Hell's Angel, with a thirst for tombola and a slap o' tripe.

She slept in Jenny's bed; the wardrobe was divided into three – I had recommended throwing Jenny's stuff out but was voted down. The bedtime stories made up for it, though, even if she hadn't added anything new to her ancient repertoire. They just seemed to sound bluer than they used to.

'Can you two stop laughin', I've got to get up for work in the mornin'!'

'So's he, get back in bed, miserable sod!'

It meant we had Uncle Jeff popping in those Tuesdays and Thursdays as a matter of routine. He'd get the ball rolling with 'She's at it again, another ten laid off at our place. Watch your back, Phill – An' *he* threatened to vote for her!'

'I'm not kiddin',' bit my dad, as if programmed, 'he comes round here in his bloody car' – outright luxury in my dad's world – 'he's got a phone' – and another – 'an' says *his* mates are bein' laid off – *You* bought him them, Phillip, payin' union money week after week!'

Brainy never knew where to turn when Uncle Jeff called by. But it was all in good spirit... well, except for when my mum joined in, learning the price of a pint of milk had soared to fifteen pence: 'The vindictive cow, she's nowt else!'

There were ideas my mum couldn't accept. She was like that. As with how she viewed the Nathalie situation, how she hoped I might yet make amends – I'd have to *see* Nathalie first. Maybe she was simply more honest about it, whilst I'd keep vigil at our little hilltop nest.

*Who knew what today might bring...*

The other important change was in our no-longer-so-little Sam. Or not change exactly, for people didn't change; they evolved, in accordance with one of my dad's morning lectures – those self-labelled 'comrades' were at present endeavouring to pass themselves off as "grafters", given a better paid position was up for grabs, despite redundancy proposals for thirty unfortunates.

157

But if that's what Sam had done, evolved, then he'd done it in a less sinister fashion, and overnight.

* * * * *

It was a familiar tune, ol' Jimmy Ruffin's *Baby, I've got it,* amid an early January, bluesy Tuesday. Sam finger-clicked in the kitchen.

''You singin'?' I asked.

'For your information,' he pointed, handgun-style, 'Jimmy done good.' Ahead of raising a foot and executing the sole spin. ''Found it upstairs, so I played it, and digged it.' Confusion checked my seizing him by the throat: I didn't own Jimmy Ruffin's *Baby I've Got It.* As when he also said: 'But keep cool, I'd never go near your big black box.' He found said tune 'hangin' out in one o' my mam's neat piles.' He 'just stepped in and Souled out...'

So Sam had evolved into a Detroit dude, unearthing gems among un-boxed *Tamla Motown.* Recalling what the black label with the silver rectangle did for me at his age, there was only one thing left to do. I placed a light hand around the back of his silky neck and lead him upward to spin some American imports.

'Have I got to go through all this again?' said my mum, to no-one in particular.

The lesson commenced, together with how to play records without the bit, just in case, to which *he* responded without a glitch.

It wasn't all one-way traffic, either. Sam introduced me to more bravura b-sides I never knew I owned, like, say, The Four Tops' *I've Got A Feeling,* b-side to *Bernadette* – 'Phill, my man, where you been!' We spoke jive-speak that evening onward, and I became so eager to recount Wigan tales that I'd let rip before he asked.

Jed also loved having Sam on board, and promised a Pennines pillion when he was old enough, in around seven years, going by our example. He stressed to me that our task would be to steer the lad clear of Northern Soul's amphetamine-fuelled side; dry wasn't the word...

*  *  *  *  *

The promise was prior to Jed's £250 offer this morning, leading us to the northeast. We now placed our Easter weekend feet on Sheffield Midland's platform 3.

I sensed by jolts the electric currents running through England's fourth biggest city, as went the claim, were doing so at a quicker rate than usual, even for a midday Saturday.

And then Jed remembered: 'It's the big un today!' His speedy black eyes chauffeured mine to the heavy booted law enforcers about to steam into a band of Wednesday provocateurs, whose team allegiance would otherwise have been hard to make out without knowing their faces. Here were the beginnings of a new underground style scene, first division apparel, club colours cast off for an expensive taste in sports attire with a golf slant. Our casual sorts of an invisible blue and white layer had given themselves away with a chant, despite the fact their equally modish United teasers had begun to scamper.

As unmoved as he would be on this United-Wednesday match-day, after Boxing Day, Jed stepped over a horse's pile like carrying an eye he'd not yet told me about, whilst I'd covered a dry Manchester on consecutive days only to be thwarted by a charger in Sin City. I jumped from our bus to old-time hushed relief.

We then headed our separate ways, both to get changed and Jed to pick up the scooter.

Stan's head was lost in the engine of his long-standing, ever precarious *Cortina*. My dad twiddled with roses-to-bud on the front garden, one among which he'd let me plant when I was five. 'What are you doin' here?' he said, happy to see me, all the more noting my right leg's bottom bit. Stifling his glee, he warned me to get the lot off, 'or she'll have a do-dar...'

In the interim, we rode a high-pitched-to-window-breaking scream from next door. It had nothing to do with my semi-streak, more the antics of some semi-clad semi-whale; one of Dickey's wrestling sensations. Sprawled and canvas-slapping, he'd be, pleading for mercy, while she, our voracious old bat, Mrs Bashforth, soaked up every last drop for real, and had done so as long as I could remember.

159

My dad guffawed to another secateurs-snip, and then nodded: 'Go and get Sam out for some fresh air. He won't even play cricket with me anymore.'

I called up on a whim, that his dad had got no-one to play with, provoking a snort from Stan's car.

'I bet that's him, not his engine,' my dad snorted back. He told me off for laughing, that it was my fault Sam thought *Tiz Waz* was for kids, and that he wouldn't leave the bedroom. 'Since he's become one o' your lot, that's all he does, play bloody records...'

'We don't "become", Dad, we just are.' I helped out by lobbing a couple of small stones up to the window, achieving the rumble of an excited descent. But by the time I clarified *Tiz Waz* was for grown-ups, Sam was already taken by my standing outside with no trousers on. He leaped over the threshold. My mum was more discreetly shocked.

It was as if he'd needed to consult a plant, when my dad asked what was wrong with my eyes, in response to my amphetamine dilated pupils: '"Seen a ghost?"

I said I'd fallen asleep on the train. They stung from the week's fume-intake.

My mum grabbed the *Levi's* by a loop and an unwitting rescue, took them round the back for fumigation, holding up a number 8 without turning her head: 'What do I do with these?'

'Bin 'em.' Via a nod to my grom from the bottom of the stairs, I flew up. Sam tagged on like a nervous bodyguard.

He preferred to croon his current favourites' titles, rather than list them, until they played a secondary importance. By the time I'd made love to my reflection, the concentration in his eyes focussed elsewhere. 'What's wrong with my grom?' he asked. He was sitting on her bed, and turned away again. 'She keeps lookin' at me funny.'

I took the shortest trip for a cold water face-splash, returning with the notion she'd no idea how to treat him since he'd 'traded in *Captain America* for *'The Sound of Young America'.'*

He liked the sound of that.

He made a dive to the floor and, with the fingertips of a single hand, pulled at the corner of a jealously protective cover belonging to Dee Dee Sharp's *What Kind Of Lady*, laying the disc onto the black bit-free, 45 rpm rotating deck, straight as a dye.

As Dee Dee faded away, a happy-go-lucky purr indicated Jed was sitting before my dad's cherished garden. And for the first time, since five to eight this morning, I realised I was going to miss that old blue friend of ours.

*On all accounts, it was turning into an important weekend. End of an era, I supposed...*

Sam sprung to the window and I peered over his shoulder, viewed the composed head-sneak from a starry-night helmet. I'd never tired of this show, and if I ordered Sam to put the records away, I'd trip over his springy ankles on the stairs' bottom step.

My grom was toothless again, tripe-free, eyes on a winning black horse she'd not backed.

'She is, Jed, she's a belter,' my dad enthused, stepping in. 'Sheena Easton, she's called...'

Jed greeted my grom by drawing a packet of Lincolnshire's finest links from the breast pocket of a newly acquired *café au lait* leather box-jacket.

'Oh, thanks, Jed, you *are* good to me!'

'Your jacket's where it's at,' deemed our young American, as I hung by the door.

Jed patted Sam's head and strutted off to a Maureen O' Sullivan-type yodel, Bashforth still adrift in a *World of Sport*.

When my dad grabbed my wrist, I expected the worst. He said to go back in and say goodbye to my grom, 'properly.' I did as told. I put an arm around her shoulder, placed a kiss on her cheek, and squeezed. 'He says he'll see you later,' my dad repeated.

'I heard him the first time,' my grom retorted. 'Silly sod!'

Sam reciprocated the laugh; my mum smiled and returned to the kitchen. My dad smiled, too, one of those father-to-son smiles, telling me something just wasn't right.

'Come out and play,' whispered the midnight-blue, for the last time...

## 24

*'... The fewer men, the greater share of...'*

We didn't know the words to *Scarborough Fair*; we based our raucous attempt solely on the context. Then again, considering we didn't know this neck of the woods, my easy-rider couldn't have been steadier in acknowledgement of the place signs every odd mile; unlike me, he didn't appear lost after Pontefract.

'Selby?'

Steady acknowledgement.

'Crockey Hill?'

Steady acknowledgement.

'Claxton? Flaxton? Huttons Arnbo?'

Steady acknowledgements, as sapphire and emerald intertwined at head-level on this God-sent summery day. When I pointed up to another signpost, told him Kirby Misperton sounded like she ought to be duetting with Bobby Womack, he said we'd wandered too far north, that we'd turn right at Pickering, and: 'Look here!' Testing me beneath a sky I ached to fall a foot up and into.

Black dots in the narrow road's distance.

Given our machine wasn't designed for carefree ton-ups, and that the dots never concealed themselves behind our divinely rolled hillocks, we agreed they were heading in our direction, away from Scarborough, leaving early at that.

Jed guessed they'd been kicked out by his style police, a branch of the law I was sure he'd come to believe was a real one. The line proved just enough to get the barrels rolling for a hyperactive head-on meeting from a dip into the wrong side of the road. I wondered whether we were doing the right thing; the Vespa GS laughed with us on days like these, rebounding beams, beams merging into waves of deep sky at mounts...

And then I tripped from my cloud, over a chortle that had helped keep Jed a Grouse regular; or rather over its usurper: a laugh at best atypical. Looking to the fore, I fathomed why. I let him know: 'We're gonna die!'

He kept up the laugh...

'I want to go to Skegness.'

On, he went...

'My grom's not well...'

The earlier black dots were everything but black dots by the time he collected himself, redressed his posture, as in sudden recall of who we were and what that should denote. 'Look up,' he instructed. 'For Henry an' our Steve.' If each of them would have eaten Armageddon for breakfast, and maybe did that kind of thing unable to sleep, my once celestial setting now comprised a scene more fit for white knights and black princes, a scene leading right up Jed's Shakespearean street.

He stiffened the sinews. The devils appeared to come up out of the ground.

At spitting space, I doubted my heraldic leader had closed his eyes to pray, going by our straight-lined advance. I calculated by which instrument, axe, mace, monkey wrench, this passing array of arms, I'd rather be slain. And although we'd reach the end of the line assault-free, it would come via a never-ending journey.

I returned greetings with a benign smile, entreated Jed do likewise. And implored their forsaking shouldn't be some great tease – ironically, I got a lot of this flowery expression from Jed's favourite film, even if I wasn't thinking in it right now, clinging on to his behind...

Jed confirmed the Hell's Angels were, indeed, turning round, stapling his eyes to our one wing-mirror, prior to donating me another split-second profile: *'Good God, why should they mock poor fellows thus?'* One more line seized from our senior school viewing, normally utilised post-a furtive glance some cat-walker's way, a line alarming me as much as our ordeal. I was taken even further by his drop and delicate shake of head, eyes to the road, not so much fearless as reflective, like he'd at last understood his quotation's significance. No more, no less...

It prevented me from puking over his neck, awarded me the smidgen of pluck to take that dreaded peek, to recognise they

163

were merely rolling back onto their Scottish highroad. The mighty rumble faded…

We showed 'em! And I'd make sure it went down in the annals.

Jed stayed silent a while longer… until: 'Decent blokes. Respect.'

I asked if he'd noticed any women. And asked myself whether I'd ever known Jed at all.

'No. They meant business.' The beards should have given it away, he said, with a rev.

Falsgrave, our signpost hailed, with a wince. If Jed copped one too, he didn't say, though I caught his disapproval at the approach of our season's first police roadblock. Where I presently felt a need to embrace the Human race, he wanted to take it all on, it seemed.

Our officer looked as eager, clapped: 'Right, search-time!' He wasn't expecting my brother in arms' suggestion that he wouldn't have been so keen before a chapter of Glasgow Angels, according to the ice pick gaze. He spoke with effort: 'Do *you* want sending back as well?'

I tapped Jed's coffee-coloured shoulder, trusting he might be in there somewhere; I wouldn't have minded, but it wasn't as if we were dealing with some greasy sort on the mouthy streets of our early teens. This was the police.

When he *did* unearth the old grin, our young hopeful retreated like from a stab to an unseen bag of wind. With a cough, eyes for guidance, he ordered us on our way. The yell came from afar: 'And behave!'

I clutched Jed's hips, in a signal he should take heed. We'd not reached Scarborough yet.

Oh, but we had now…

## 25

*'Darkness had set in; it was a low neighbourhood; no help was near; resistance was useless.'*

Lighting up a big fat thing, he said he first wanted to bring me round North Bay. For here, at the zenith of our sheer drop, sailed a Viking breeze I hoped might steal me away, a salt-zing gush via a breathtaking relic on yon hill, or purpose-built snout for the seaside town folk's daily quota. The sea's meeting with the sky must have been Heaven's secret, while Jed hinted he was revelling in a secret of his own: the miraculous air's meeting with his funniest smoke to date? He'd have sat here forever. I knew *I* would have...

But some force preferred otherwise. That we get business over with.

And so back onto a route already taken, for a final dismount from chrome and leather, into the glass-laden car park of The Ship Aground, an outlandish location, given our purpose, at the inland end of the town. The scooter stood alone. I would never have predicted it.

The pub's door, gnawed at, by the looks, boasted carved allegiance to *'The Whites'* and *'LUFC'*; should you *'come in red your fukin dead'*, signed the *'Gelgard end boot boyz'*. I wished I'd waited on North Bay.

Darts were thrown, snooker was shot, ale plied and spilled with ash, as some flashing game pinned to the wall pleaded for mercy. That stencilled skin...

When I asked what we were doing here, Jed offered a steady acknowledgement.

'Jed!' yelled yon shorn head, inviting us to a couple of crippled stools.

''Can't stop long, 'sellin' the scooter.' Jed introduced me to Wiffa...

... who introduced me to his bald other half, and then to the dog beneath the table, before establishing *he* was the one to wear the trousers, by the way he told her, the bald other half, to get the drinks – everything he said was a growl. Like when he nodded to the door: 'If any o' them bastards' – the scooter crowd – 'come up here, they're finished!'

He talked between swigs and spits about how the pigs kept poking their heads in to keep an eye on them.

I just wished for a change of record – some rowdy new-wave thing about capitulation, and how he, the 'singer', deemed it out of the question.

For the Glasgow lot, you'd have thought Wiffa had sent them back himself.

'We met 'em a while back,' said Jed, like he met with such calamities daily.

His friend then got to his feet, leaned over the table, and thrust his swastika-labelled brow to the ridge of my nose. ''Shit yourself?' he asked. Barrel-breath, he returned to his chair with a dagger-to-dagger, keyboard grin.

I pressed on a foot, all but dropped from my seat, and recalled Oliver Reed, in *Oliver – Bill Sikes*! How I'd buried my face in Jenny's lap until it was safe to come back up. My artful mate had introduced me to his modern day counterpart. Pints served, I quaffed at the double.

At half-four the place veered from sporadic outburst to swear in unison, forcing beer down my white *Lonsdale* shirt. But since the Skinhead licensee had just relayed Leeds' 2:0 defeat at the hands of Derby County, I thought I'd let it go.

'What bout Sheff United?' asked someone I once knew.

'1:1.' Going by the same wireless.

Wiffa wanted to buy us another, until Jed explained we needed to be at The Horse and Groom for opening time.

And so, as I sat and mused on how the landlord had come by an all-day licence – it was hardly a 'lock in' – Wiffa slipped a hand into a *sta-prest* pocket, tugged at a small packet, and passed it over the top of the table. Jed placed the packet into the inner pocket of his jacket, like he would a pair of sunglasses, pulled out a five pound note, and let it fall onto the ash and ale-sodden table.

Pockets, packets, jackets. A *Fagin*-like underworld worsened to an indifferent overworld, as it were.

Leaving, I closed my eyes before patting Wiffa's shoulder, should he or *Bull's-eye* take a playful snap at my fingers.

''Bit o' gear,' Jed coughed.

'I noticed.'

## 26

*'For once she was a true love of mine.'*


Sulking was tricky. Sea surveying via the colossal arches of a puffy-cloud-connecting bridge. Invading white horses in magical mass – an ocean's welcome. To our left, below trees of already-green, stood a sun-speckled café, at the foot of a precipitous Parisian walkway, or a Parisian walkway of my mind, name served on tricolour over a *terrasse* of ornate tables and chairs. Our nosey relic's south side surely wondered what we were waiting for, while a Paul Weller spray-alike reflecting moody felt-lettered *Lonsdale,* a messenger sent, appeared to pose the very question, above the Weller-prompted title of *'When You're Young',* in pea-rattling pink…

I should concentrate on the lighthouse, said Jed, over at the promenade's far end, ahead of reminding me I had a beer blot down my top.

Now for the old roundabout trick, as a run-up; a preview of the competition. And, raising my head, I beheld an interim world of seagull-assisted whirling trees, and higher, a mammoth bridge-like propeller preparing for some gigantic flight.

Jed reckoned the tower's clock in Skegness had never told the correct time as far back as he could remember...

For swansong, we rode into a valley of colour. A kaleidoscopic esplanade, without the globe's longest scooter parkway. Energetic arcades amid rainbow-dappled smugglers' alleyways; braved bikinis amid duly arrived white stallions – even the snail-esque chairlifts looked rich and ready! But this myriad of chromed gleam, this array of shapely-figured, doted-on Italian genius.

I'd never focus head-on with such a coastline for my oyster.

Transcending the cobbled paving and we were back round North Bay, pinpointing our spot of first arrival. We witnessed the jovial North Sea at almost sea-level, how she endeavoured to saturate anyone who dared to come close enough long enough, billowing like an extra-large Monroe thrill.

Jed got us through, and soaked up the cheers.

At the top of the cliff, I stayed put, proffered the old Vespa a last spank, and passed Jed the helmet. I said to go no less than a fiver for it.

'What did you mean about your grom not being well?' he asked, prior to some comment on my limp hair.

I nodded him away. I wouldn't dwell on it.

Nor would I dwell on the fact this wasn't his first visit. Nor on the midweek Russian bombs, the bemoaning a nation's Ripper, satanic mills. More, I'd marvel at this country's youth. But then, maybe the midweek tedium had a lot to say in the matter...

*'So scared of getting old,'* read a similar seascape, above some silhouetted teenager, reciting my own early evening dream. On a wing, he flew.

*'Can't Get You Out Of My Sight',* declared the next, the turning of a page: a Chuck Jackson and Maxine Browne title, the old magic *Wand* treatment; hand held disc; real professionals, those spray-painters!

I proffered a black-fisted salute, which was returned with a knowing smile, and I liked the feeling. I considered a breast-pocket *Benson,* yet wouldn't spoil the air...

*... when, out of my dizzy orb, I heard a voice, a beautiful voice, however lethal the incision.*

I spit my heart in bits, clung to the railing to avoid that one-in-one drop.

'We're going to have to take a walk over one of these days.'

I prepared to squat but dreaded the attention to such a half-measure. And so I sat beneath the cliff-rail's bottom bar, and onto it placed my elbows, rested my chin in v-fixed knuckles, tucked in my head, vertigo for pretext, and peeped out to sea, to be unnoticed at all costs... yet couldn't work out why...

The seagulls took a fancy to my legs, my mohair covered... Were they laughing at me?

'Look at these birds,' laughed Denise, pointed hand above my head, 'they're mad!'

I swung a loafer like I did it for a living.

'They're wapped,' said Nathalie, corrective tone, '… wapped.'

Back on my feet, I caught them on either arm of a tall man, who'd never uttered a word; I'd always imagined this kind of thing only happened in magazines Jed borrowed from Steve! And then sprung the spring of hope: her brother – 'Dave!'

I needed to say something – *sing* something! And harked back to a fight with my dad for his hooting at my friend Rod – You were never a *Blue Peter* badge, Nathalie! But it all sounded daft up until the last three words to leave my lips…

They crossed the road, made to what resembled the single non-hotel in the vicinity. Beyond the *Vespas*, they pushed open the gate. I'd call her back once all three of them were down the path.

If only.

The sick joke on wheels – a brown thing; I barely recognised *Fords* – seemingly crash-landed from a motorway in the sky, forcing itself between us, screeching its stoppers onto the pavement.

She glanced over to my No-man's Land.

I turned away, and yet continued to stare, unable to imagine my face's contortion. She was beautiful.

Jed ordered me in: 'It's Wigan time!'

But I didn't want to go to Wigan…

## 27

*'It was on the moral side, and in my own person, that I learned
to recognise the thorough and primitive duality of man...'*

I'd conquered the G-force by the time Jed, maintaining his
one-man crusade for a Sam's drug-free England, made a one-
handed lunge at the radio. He'd got it in for Dexy's Midnight
Runners: ''Probably never seen *Dexedrine*, never mind Gino
Washington...' He half-hit on some local station, and predicted
the other four wouldn't half get a shock.

'They're wapped.'

'They will be,' he said, 'when they see us.' He asked if I'd
seen a ghost in the same breath.

'Do you remember that Naaa... Victoria number?'

'W...? 'Can't remember.'

It was like I'd stabbed him in the thigh. The car veered. 'You
went with her mate, ''Four Times''... Raquel, was it?'

'Phew... *you're* goin' back a bit!'

There was nothing new anymore about Jed acting oddly, and
although he added that the girl in question was crazy for me –
'Or *was,* back *then'* – my attempt at getting him to turn round
would go no further than letting him know I'd just seen her in
Scarborough. I'd be better working on how it was we were off to
Wigan, all of a sudden, and where this car came from – I was
sick of his frivolity! I lost my patience when he asked if I wanted
a *Blue Peter* badge – he'd never done that before, it was always a
*Crackerjack* pencil!

His peace offering came in guise of a pre-rolled fat thing. ''Be
no good in that department anyhow,' he said, glimpsing
downward, knowledgeable in amphetamine effects. 'Till about
Tuesday. Smoke that and let me find a proper station.'

Once he'd done fiddling with his silver knob and filling me in
on the scooter buyer, 'some Loiner' – meaning from Leeds –

who'd paid up and lent us his car, he'd trap me in the old cackling snare: it all seemed to make sense now, and was entertaining with it. I laughed at the windscreen, at my attempt to revive my loins, at my tugging at Jed's breast pocket for more funny cigarettes. I also learned that Jed had been to Scarborough before, 'for some gear', and that he knew all the words to The Jam's *When You're Young,* like he'd written them; two and half minutes during which the Yorkshire Moors detached themselves from our wheels. My giggles united with the hiccups, which made me laugh on their own…

I needed to get back to the house before going any further, to get the mohair home, restore the binned bowlers; pick up more talc, that kind of thing. There was something else, too, but I couldn't think what it was. Jed didn't mind, it meant we wouldn't get lost that way. And Leeds could always result in a bit of a beating for our trouble.

By the shelter, my chauffeur looked like he'd had a change of heart. He eyed the mirror with a whisper, as if those in the car behind might hear: 'They've been there ages.'

As soon, a police *Ford* pulled out of Nathalie's road and blocked our route. Its busy-bodied bobbies laid siege to our brown thing.

'What's goin' on?'

Jed locked his door and bent over to mine: 'Promise me you won't tell your dad.'

'What's happening?'

'Promise me.'

'Open the door, Jed, or I'll put this baton through your window.'

'Jed…?'

He took my shoulder: 'Promise me!'

*''Pro*mise! I promise… 'promise.'

He responded to the policeman: 'I'll open this door when you promise me you'll let him go. He didn't know I'd nicked it – Promise me!'

The baton menace bent further to look me in the eye: 'Get out, son, and on your way.'

Jed nodded, indicating I should do as ordered. Once I was out of the car, he made to open his door, when, in *Mr. Hyde*-return, he wound the window back, threw the machine into reverse, backed up, and, with a feral beam, rammed it into to the flashing-topped car in front. It went with a hell of a bang.

The baton entered via an assortment of excited epithets. Door open, Jed was ripped from the vehicle: 'Watch my jacket!'

There'd been no last-second attempt to escape. He'd wanted to hit them hard for a while.

I sat behind the shelter, trying to work out when it was he'd learned to drive, until the door-slams, a revved engine, the tyre-skids, jolted me back. And along chased the anger. Crook. Car thief. Drug addict, liar. And the hurt: 'Liar!' The bastard...

Roadside, I greeted twitching nets with defiant poise. I knew my place, I'd lived it all here. The early morning yearnings, early evening kicks; later evening riots, wood bound lusts. The eternal triangle, me, myself and I...

I gave the shelter a right-handed chop.

The shelter retaliated with its latest literary submission: *'If its black send it back! NF.'*

But I wouldn't go down easily; I'd summon an army: a mirage of wishful thought. Curtis. Junior. Smokey, Bobby W – Jackie W! Millie J, Marvin, Tammi... For if I couldn't be where I wanted to be, wherever that was, then I wanted *them* to be here, to rescue me from this desolate English shelter.

They just wouldn't stay long enough.

At the flash of an ambulance exiting my own street, I believed it time to get a grip. Saturday night or not, there might have been people in a worse state than me. After all, what would my best friend have given at present for a pint just yonder?

He was quick echoing his blessing, stealing away from a picturesque coastline, courtesy of The Jam: something about what youth tends to do whenever the going gets tough.

My mouth never felt so dry...

## 28

*'Men of few words are the best men.'*

Marlene wasn't surprised by my request of six pints, more by my being here in the first place, though conceded to a lie I struggled with. Rushed off her feet, she looked toward the concert room: 'Madness.'

'As in *One Step Beyond*?'

'Hey, not far off, when you can hear 'em. Two-tone group. The Specialities. And who are these other five for?'

'My double in the other side.'

Two-tone regimented swagger held centre-stage. Unruly running-around held everywhere else. Unconnected, two separate worlds.

Madness.

'Now then, Phill-pot!' Mick acknowledged from his former-favoured end piece of the bar. Despite his catching me ship aground once more, I was glad to see him, if only that he was guarding my drinks. He didn't say anything else, just eyed the filled pots. In truth, I felt nervous around Mick at the best of times. Not because of his witty one-liners, more by what he wouldn't say, like his mere presence did all the talking…

''Thirsty work watchin' your mate get arrested,' I bit, without any verbal provocation, during which two grown men attempted to strangle each other at four paces over three tables.

He brought down my sails with a nudge to the shoulder: 'Enjoy 'em, then, kid, you've earned 'em.'

It was turning out to be a fraught day. 'Cheers.'

'Where's your dad?'

'Dunno…'

'He's not next door.'

'He'll be in.'

'It's a quarter past ten.'

I picked up two of the pints: ''Want one o' these?'

He didn't answer this time because the noise had hit a new level of nullity, after one of the Wednesday scrappers got himself caught beneath a gangly guitarist's stomping feet. Frank tossed him and the United scrapper that put him there through the door before things got out of hand. Our giant was on his own this evening. It was The Wapentake for our Yetis.

'Where's this lot from?' I asked on his return to bar-duty.

'The Snooty Fox.' He deemed them bad enough without having to play each other. ''Only glad they drew.'

Mick smiled like the big brother I'd never had, when I said there were worse places.

Frank's reaction was an absorbed gaze. Pulling and wiping again, he said: ''See your dad's not in. He could knock 'em down, as I remember.' And before being summoned back to the other room, he eyed my drinks: 'I'm not talkin' about his ale, either.'

I asked Mick whether his suit was new, odds on my side this time: no-one worked through Saturday night, there must have been a law against it.

''Gettin' our marchin' papers,' he grinned, stoically. 'That's it. Finito. So we're doin' it all now as overtime. Looking at his watch, he placed his empty glass down and told me to give my dad his best: 'Tell him I've missed him.' Almost out, he popped his head back, helped on by a tiptoe. 'Keep the faith, Soul brother!' he shouted.

That one meant everything.

'Corrr! Ye no' 'opin' te get scattered on all that drink, now, are ye?' enquired a warm-bedded voice out of a stormy port, accent Glaswegian, if Tommy Docherty was anything to go by.

I swivelled to meet its donor, told her she'd just caught me with my mohairs down.

'Oh, aye? Ah missed that one, can ah do it again?'

'Only if you let me walk you home.'

'Well, if ye play ye cards right, ah might just let ye…'

'Woah, woah!' Frank came a choking. 'What the bloody hell's goin' on in here!?'

'Are they singin' what I think they're singin'?' Marlene came running after.

'It's Prince Buster,' I told them – I'd once borrowed a couple of his reggae classics from Steve; catching a few of their dirty lines from the opposite bedroom, my mum hit them back like golf balls from a nine iron.

'Sup up,' my lowland-lust-affaire now ordered, burying her nose into my ear and moving on to biting mode.

When she yanked me through the main road end, I met with Frail ol' Jim's frail old drinking hand. ''Not dancin', young man?' he asked.

I was off for a bit of pair work, I winked.

My own drinking hand was on the door's handle when Marlene beckoned me back. She warned me to be careful, that 'she' was 'one o' them Mods' girlfriends.'

Those wild horses wouldn't have stopped me getting through the doors a third time, with a Celtic bombshell I'd never before noticed.

Making right as opposed to my usual left, I could have sworn I heard my big brother call through: *"'Nothin' false about this place."*

## 29

*'... O most lame and impotent conclusion!'*

'Ah'm surprised ye want anythin' to do wi' me at all,' ribbed my wee young lassie. 'You six, ye think y''re the cock o' the walk.' She pinched a cheek: 'Superior an' all that.'

'If you lot had what was needed, we might have a bit less.'

'Ah mean, ah bet ye don't even know about Chris, do ye? Ah've bin seein' him for a year now, an' ah bet the rest o' yiz don't even know...'

'Chris?' I knew he was a dark horse but not trotting from camp to camp.

'There ye go!' she said, as if knocking one in at Ibrox Park. 'It's kind of a love-hate relationship...'

It sounded too false for my liking. ''Not in Scarborough today, then?'

'Och.'

Whatever that meant, I proffered a nod. 'What's your name?'

'Call me 'J'' She wore it on the left breast of the same Blackburn Rovers-like rugby shirt Nathalie sported that long ago Friday evening.

'Did your mam sew it on?'

*'I* did it, Mr. Gallus! Though ah s'pose ah should be glad ye didnea ask if mae mammy could sew, ah might e' bin a wee bit feart at that.' My eyes must have requested subtitles, and so she drew a line down this same cheek, with: 'Can yae mammy *sew,* sunshine?' And hooted at something I believed I was meant to hoot at too...

I got there: 'Ahhhh, Glaswegians... 'bunch o' bike-riding nancy boys.'

'W...? Y' *are,* ye!

I observed how her *Levi's* sat on yachting slippers – 'boaters', which would be all the rage this summer – and yearned to eat her bare, brown feet, that Glaswegian ring scurrying about my mind, long-distance and tormenting. 'Take your top off.'

'Here? Now?'

I pressed her into the side-doorway of the pictures-gone-bingo hall, and, with just about manageable hands, unleashed her brown hair, pushing it further back. We went at each other like there'd be a prize for first fly open; I drowned in her lips, as we sank and sank... and just slowed down and stopped.

'Is it somethin' ah said? This's never happened to me before, ah can tell ye!'

'It's not you.'

'D' ye not really like girls, then? Ar' yiz really all queer after all?'

'*No* – I mean, of course I do! It's just...' My head span: *"He could never do that after speed!"* The speed king himself, railing at the implausibility of a young man, up on the big screen, achieving what this young man was failing miserably to achieve right now. He should know; he lived on the stuff – 'Four times, my...!'

'Is it the drink, d' ye think?'

'No, it's my pill... *"Strange, how he that abides by such a rule happens to be so first-night-shy..."*'

'You're losin' it, so ye are!'

As she pulled up her fly, I probed into her wary eyes, and caught her part-time lover whispering sweet-somethings into April's ear, Half Dead grappling with semi-oblivion. I brought back my beer down the wall.

'Look, ah... ah 'ave te go.'

'I'm sorry... come back...'

But I was talking to someone else, and my pretty young Scot knew it. 'Ah 'ave te go!'

She didn't hang around.

And so I leaned my head against a huge sycamore trunk, whose notches recalled how many times I'd fallen from its branches and broken my arm...

# 30

*'... and may fleets of angels... '*

*Four times... Four times... Four... I was stymied by a frozen-handed slap on the back of my neck. Why did she always do that?*

*'Well, I've' said goodnight four times,' she estimated...*

To wake was with painful consequences. Aches rushed my head. As did vivid recollections of the previous day.

Oh well, she got a smile at the worst of times. Goodnight...

It was out of this brisk light of an April morning that everything looked clearer, while the other four, I imagined, made their bulgy-eyed way out of a joint known to the few as The Casino Club, while he with the soulful eyes fought it out with Mr. Stir Crazy.

I envisaged my next Grouse visit, the stares of ridicule, word pandemic before mid-evening... but was caught mid-thought by church bells tolling a different tune. And then it dawned on me, why I'd been anxious to get back home yesterday. Something wasn't right yesterday but I'd been unable to put my finger on it, to allow my busy-bombed person the moment.

I slid down the banking, lost a loafer and my balance. Up the back yard there was an open door. 'Where is everybody?'

My mum was dusting. 'Dear me, have you seen yourself?'

'Where is everybody?'

'Listen, love, your grom's had to go into hospital for a while.'

'What for?' I flew upstairs...

*'Don't...* wake Sam, he's upset enough!'

He was on his grom's bed.

'She's comin' back.'

'But you said she was alright yesterday.'

'She's comin' back, now get up, we'll go an' see her.'

'Well get some *break...*fast!' my mum tried.

I stepped back into the yard. 'Which one's she in?'

'The Infirmary... 'Geriatric Unit.'

Sam shattered the shelter's Sunday silence: 'Phill' – I recoiled, knocked away an invisible wasp – 'if anythin' happens to my grom, it's sure gonna be a big thing!'

I looked down hard. 'Sometimes, there are things in life we can't allus control, things even more important than black America' – yesterday taught me that. 'And so, for the time being, it's better to stick with a Sheffield accent.'

He appeared more anxious. I patted his head, held him close.

'One an' a half to The Infirmary,' I was at last able to request, to a bus-driver-cum-bus-conductor, all-in one.

'Thirty an' a fifteen.'

Some sophisticated machine sprouted an all-in-one ticket.

I fumbled for more money: 'Jesus!'

'No good shooting' me, kid. I'm only the messenger.'

'Her, is it?'

'Oh, aye...'

I cut him off: 'Well, we were warned.' Like I knew what I was talking about.

'We were, that.' As we made to our downstairs spoilt-for-choice spots, he called along: 'We never had it so good, kid.'

Maintaining direction from that punch line-to-the-heart ought to have earned me a fraternal care prize. But then it *was* Sunday, a day when more time for reflection was permitted to our conductor-less drivers. And as he took new toy and all by the old market like the hound by The Dog and Duck, I studied in my mind's eye how our more generous lady would stare into space, or a place reserved for an extra special someone; how she mixed matters past and present, threatened the fainthearted with toothless pieces. And I squeezed Sam's shoulders...

Uncle Jeff was also staring into space, by the main entrance, enduring fixture smouldering between toffee-coloured fingers. 'Now then, Phill, 'not dancin'? She's down there, 3a.' Noticing Sam, he altered his bearing: 'No under-sixteens on Sundays, so you can stay here an' have a fag with your Uncle Jeff.'

I played along.

'Oh, and, don't forget she's old.'

A skating rink, was Ward 3a, where I met the reason for his apprehension: the eyes of a hare; a scrawny unfortunate lying next to my dad. No, I wasn't supposed to be here. My grom had left already.

'He's comin' tonight,' she warned my dead-beat dad, or the once young and tireless son, as I made out, 'so be here – An' watch them windows with that bloody football!'

I didn't catch the younger son's reply, it wasn't my business. All I understood was that there'd be no 'Shut up, you ol' coot!' on his part. Nor a 'Are you goin' senile?' on mine. And so I did what his eyes repeated: I left, partly consoling myself in the knowledge my guardian Hell's Angel had said goodbye this morning, as I slept upon a hill. I wanted to fly...

'He can sing as well!' waxed some doe-eyed model beneath a twin-pointed hat, as Sam flopped into a competition-winning back-fall.

'When are you takin' him?' his uncle asked me, flicking a stealthy brown thumb over to those same brown eyes, under that hat. 'Can you learn me a bit?'

But I'd learned enough for a weekend, and needed my spare time to take it in. Uncle Jeff looked like he'd noticed.

''Be seein' you again, sweetheart,' our nurse promised the tear-stained young strutter.

Sam's love for Northern Soul was unconditional. Uncle Jeff was all ears.

I'd not spoken on the way home, and didn't speak closing the car door, but marched up the path, bypassed my mother and the stairs, dropped whatever wherever, drew back the sheets, sunk my head into my pillow... and hoped Sam hadn't followed.

The front door knocker invited me to an out-of sync world before the clock tolled four, the middle of the night. The bank holiday relief died to two or three anxious groans from the worn stairs, to the door's belching that keyhole rattle, and to Uncle Jeff's sapped voice. ''Got a call, she's gone, brother.'

''Hear that, Phillip?' my dad whispered, around my door-ajar.

'He turned up then, did he?'

# 31

*'Give sorrow words. The grief that does not speak*
*Whispers the o'er-fraught heart and bids it break.'*

'Is Jed comin'?' asked my dad, shattering the bottomless bank holiday hush.

Well, a hush without my mum's odd murmur: 'Jenny's takin' her time'; the odd sob on Sam's part, face in her lap as she cracked the odd nit between well-rehearsed fingernails; and my Uncle Jeff's nipping by for a quick-if-quiet 'cup o' tea an' a fag'. The lot of us nodding off in spurts, a silence sacramental only my grom could leave behind.

For the sake of nitpicking, as it were, I wondered if my mum might leave Sam's head alone.

My dad raised a warning hand, eyes menacing the ceiling. He brought it back so hard I assumed he'd split the chair's arm in half: 'Imagine what she went through, seein' us comin' down in the air like that, and all that... bastard pilot could do...!'

''Don't know if he's comin' tonight,' I replied, to the Jed question.

'He needs to know!'

His concern was just. I told him I'd head on up and do the deed.

''Pity you can't take him,' he said, nodding toward his youngest.

It felt more like the end of summer, making through the downpour, than its beginning, the rain cleansing the sick-stained loafers, a wound I'd preferred not to erase, for some reason. If I again acted out the dropped fiver routine, it was only to prolong reaching The Grouse, the price to pay for putting all these eggs into this same basket.

I went to the back door, where *Vespas, Lambrettas, Suzuki, Honda,* and now three *Triumph-Bonnevilles* intermingled, each with an endeavour to outdo the other. It might have painted a nice picture...

A young Jackie Wilson's *Soul Galore!* rang from the concert room like an old boast, maybe just in time, alerting me to a pair of guarantees on which I would have wagered my life: a, the others were inside; and b, that, come the ups-and-downs, I'd be forever helpless to this indefinable pull.

I lit a cigarette.

'Look what the cat brought in!' April shot in her random-fire manner.

Jed resumed an anecdote about a couple of young fops who'd travelled to the seaside and met with cross-boarded Hell's Angels. I didn't hinder his form, his tickling of a Glaswegian's innards out there in the middle.

Marlene passed my pint: 'There you go, love.'

'Why didn't you come to The Windmill yesterday?' April looked anxious to know.

I didn't answer, for recognising an old antagonist with a new guise, sitting a convenient spit away, going by the khaki like he was expecting an imminent ice age. I thrust my pint to my lips.

''Thought we'd give Nigel one more chance,' Marlene reasoned. 'He came and asked, you see, and...'

'An' *he* just shouts,' Jed hollered: '''My grom's not well''!'

'How is your grom?' asked Marlene, in an attempt to keep the guffaws to a minimum.

I renounced the tried smiles.

'So why didn't you come to The Windmill yesterday?'

April again snuggled into Chris' side... or definitely maybe, one hand twiddling with Half-Dead's mohair shoulder, Jed still looking to the middle ground. I placed my empty glass onto a green towel and requested another, before parting with 'She died in the night.'

When Marlene took my hand, I took it back in exchange for some glib comment about old age. But the nonchalance wouldn't last. Our storyteller's eyes burned hot.

Whatever course of action I settled on, the jukebox beat me to it with a timely named tribe of Bad Manners. Our scooter lot wasted no time for a post-seaside hop, according to the part-cracked mirror behind the bar.

183

'Sit down!' Marlene ordered, re-gripping my hand.

'Why didn't you tell me?' Jed prodded, sounding wary and challenging at the same time.

'Do you want to pull me that pint?'

'Why didn't you tell me?'

'Jed,' April nudged, 'Phill...'

'Sit down!'

'You didn't come round, Jed.'

I turned to face him, for a fight, perhaps, when all I wanted, needed, was to apologise, for anything I could think of, and to rest these heavy eyes on one of those light-leather shoulders, as if a time, a place, existed...

Geddon got up on the third 'Sit down!'

'What's up?' Frank called through... too late.

Jed pulled away, selected the nearest chair to hand and, to everyone else's astonishment, rammed it through the jukebox's dome.

The last looming stare impressed me most, prior to his casual saunter out of the main doors.

Geddon was standing as if preset, scraggly chin on all-in carpet.

'Wow!' whirred Afghan, sooner or later.

I loosened myself from Marlene's gob-smacked grip, panted through the drizzly dark.

''Could be anywhere,' huffed his indifferent old mum, 'you know our Jed.' I should have known this to be the last place.

'What d' you mean, ''he's took off!''?' my dad insisted. 'Get lookin', scoot!'

I did them all: the bowling alley, The Wood, everywhere, anywhere, to find myself back in the Grouse, to a villain's welcome. A saloon brawl. It took three goes to get my head round the door, where I caught Frank knocking a couple of the khaki-clad to-and-fro, like on some arcade game. Geddon dropped Nigel from out of the sky for old time's sake. With a run-up, April kicked into his ribs.

The sausage supplier in *café au lait* had gotten what he wanted in the end.

I looked up, beyond the airborne glass, and wondered if she knew.

Marlene brought me back, via a pointed finger, other hand taken up with a beer towel whipping: 'You can tell him he's barred!'

4

## 32

*'Out of the day and night,*
*A joy has taken flight.'*

*'Would you marry me?'* – it was her fault: Lady Diana Spencer; even when you closed your eyes she was the first thing to pop up. We men were envious of that Charlie fellow…

*But surely my very own princess was being rhetorical?*

*'Well just ask… We could even get our Elvis to sing He Who Picks A Rose.'*

*'This'll do for me,'* I said, to a Bobby Thurston backing of *Just Ask Me.*

*'Well?'*

*And so I readjusted my posture: 'Ouch! Asked: 'Will you carry me?'*

*'You mean 'marry' me?'*

*'It's my feet.'*

*'But we'll have the world at our feet.'*

*'I already did… now they just…'*

'… Why didn't you take some gear?' enquired a voice with which I'd had the misfortune to be acquainted for too long. And besides, my choice of gear-abstention should be as respected as the next man's partaking; I was capable of holding my own at six o'clock on a Lancashire morning, thank you very much! I'd been doing it for years, for reasons he, Wiffa, would never understand. He brought his tattooed cranium closer: 'You were asleep. Dickhead!'

I couldn't believe to what point I hated him. But he scared me. 'Maybe.'

He tore Don Downing's *Lonely Days, Lonely Nights* from my defensive fingers: 'What's this?'

187

I feared he might fling it across the wood: 'Oh, Don... 'Only two quid.'

''Never heard of it.'

Jed drew him away with another apologetic smile.

One more outcome of present day outings to an all-night Wigan. A sign of the times, as with these bloody feet.

Yesterday proved a case in point.

\* \* \* \* \*

Friday, our first day of May, '81.

Half past four, the horn didn't so much blow as cough, as if continually disheartened by the increasing number of redundancy notices doled out, like it'd developed terminal rheumatism – the firm's manager was blowing it! If Friday buzz had been dismissed with severance pay, then Friday horn no longer wanted to know. Even Uncle Jeff had copped it – there was rarely anyone to clock-off *with*...

Guy had gone and I missed him, despite the Boxing Day Massacre having granted his beloved Owls the lift they'd been waiting for and taken the edge off our already blunting Blades, heralding an imminent plunge to the murky depths of the Fourth Division, the first time in our history. I still missed him, missed all the old characters. McGoohan hadn't gone anywhere, of course... Mister Conversation.

The weird thing about the whole sorry business was that my own post never looked to be under threat, and I thought of writing to ask why. I surmised my two-pounds a week rise was conspiratorial; 'Roll on your 21st, eh?' teased the remaining few. The consolatory straw I clung to was that if ever I *were* to kill Alcrap, well, there'd be no-one around to tell tales, just the sickly-sweet backing of 'So, have you got the year yet?'

Yes, things had plunged further on that front, too. A barometer of the age, Alcrap called it 'Our Choon'. It made its presence felt at eleven, post-the aforementioned Crime at Ten.

'See you Monday,' he reminded.

*En bus* and *en route* for home, I whistled between my teeth as the light evening rang bells of riotous summers from a not too distant past. We'd renounced our love affair with the east-coast, it having fizzled out toward the end of the last once miraculous season, along with a lot of other things.

Maybe this was what they meant by not being a teenager anymore.

Again the problem was narcotic. Many of the good guys were no longer attending our hallowed hall, while those enduring were turning bad, losing their way on the favoured route of 'crankin'' – injecting – to the extent of dropping dead one per week, hence why Wiffa never stood out for the Ned he was. It was a shame, really, given last year's tourists had realised all-night dancing required devotion, decided four wheels were better than two, and ridden back over to their normal lives via that sunless vista, as we'd wished...

As the white-walled, green-shuttered façade of our venerated Mojo came and went, I leaned my head against my top deck window and conjectured on whether that club's demise had been for similar reasons, when its drugs became more important than its Soul.

Then again, if *I'd* fallen from the habit of saluting the place of an ever enervated evening, my dad wasn't going to let me just walk away; he'd still have me raising a hand of a Monday to Friday morning. There was nothing new on that front...

... well, apart from the fireplace. Rather than gaze beyond shy blue flames, he now went for staring straight *at* the three white and orange chocolate-bar plates of the gas fire – no getting past those. The one he'd installed with a spot of 'help' from the Yorkshire *Rambo*-to-be, who'd confirmed himself as useless – if *he* was a fitter, *I* was a dentist... *and* he was drunk! Point being, my dad had evolved from being useless at DIY to being useless at a greater rate, attempting anything to prove us wrong, or searching for a change of trade by leaving out the college bit. What with my future brother-in-law's endeavours to impress *him,* the district often found itself in danger – *'Christ,'* blew the old soldier, pulling the three inch nail back out of the wall, 'I missed that gas-pipe by a thou!'

''Bit o' gas never hurt anybody,' scoffed the drunken young gunner.

On many occasion, my dad could have said goodnight to his precious gable-end even without the lightning. 'Pete,' my mum trod warily again, 'it's not only our lights you've put out but the whole street's.'

He'd hinted at knocking the old storm cupboard into the ground, now that 'we've got a bleedin' cowboy in The White House!' Onward and upward, lump hammer and pipedream at hand, that he might stumble over that well hidden gateway to self-employment, as far away from his rat race as possible.

Like me, it didn't look as if he'd otherwise be offered the opportunity. Though in his case it made sense – *he* was a ''sound an' contentious worker'', when reminded by one of his newer, pinstripe-suited inspectors, the one possessing the ''all-rectifying tool''. My dad now called the ex-comrade 'Inspector Comrade'.

While it provided more material for my eternal lectures, my mum spent all her time chasing round after him.

And the evenings were something else.

If King Arthur was still getting thumped back and forth – 'She'll get in again, I tell you!' – my dad had modified his tactics with the adverts: he now chuckled at them. And once those *Cadbury's Smash* robots got going, it was like he hoped we might outdo them. Or the bald man losing his wig and so lighting up a *Hamlet* – 'Watch this, Sam!'

'I've seen it.'

'Watch it again, Sam,' I advised.

Or *Cinzano* Rossiter putting Madame Collins on her back – she fell for it every time, as did my dad. But the *Shake 'n' Vac* was the thing. Now *there* was an advert on which the old Peter Rowlings would have vented his spleen – ''Size o' that house,' I'd pre-hear, ''take half a bleedin' week to clean it!' All we now got for our pains was a gormless grin of his own.

'Do you fancy her?' Sam asked him, one time. His old dad was already lost in a world of spotless carpets. And I couldn't understand why my mum never exploited it.

We missed the grumbles, they meant he was happy. Or happi*er,* even Sam knew that. And maybe my dad knew it, too. For old time's sake, then, he'd administer the odd one, deeming there was more Arab in our Brainy than the *Fry's Turkish Delight* man – 'Don't try tellin' me he's handsome, Joan!' The trouble was the ensuing gloomy silence, each of us hearing one of my grom's exasperated lines, none of us daring to take her place. ''Could always knock the kitchen through to the toilet and put on an inside door,' he finally thought aloud, breaking the collective contemplation.

'Leave it!' pleaded my mum. 'They're being modernized in five years.'

Of course, all this talk of more space badly disguised a need to fill a missing one. Even *I* was relieved to hear the season's first carol singer last October.

And then there was Jed, and the effect my grom had had on him. His unconventional exit brought about World War III. We got them all: the Attercliffe Teds, Hillsborough Hairies, Manor Mods, Wednesday Whackers from down The Snooty Fox, he none-the-wiser.

We now only met up at the weekends, in Manchester Piccadilly, Victoria, or Wigan Wallgate. Or in the Casino Club, where I was at present nursing my urine-bloody-wet feet. Inside this dump.

It was as if he'd been pushed to breaking point that bank holiday evening, and would go out in style. I knew why he'd left town, I just wished I could have done something earlier. My dad understood, too. Once he'd received news of my failure to find him, as with Nathalie, he never mentioned Jed's name again. Nor did my mum for that matter. Nor Sam – though I *felt* his withdrawal symptoms, which manifested themselves in hinting-for-news type questions. 'Is this yours or...?' he'd ask, placing The Vibrating Vibrations' *Surprise Party* on the old deck.

'Mine!'

But then it wasn't like I had news to offer. And if the other three and 'Just About' – ex-Half Dead, self-titled this time before the rest of us got there – knew anything, well, they hadn't bothered telling me, simply fallen into hushed hysteria each time the jukebox with the new dome disgorged more Bad Manners –

Geddon jumped like clockwork at that one, I was surprised it hadn't been taken off.

'*I* don't know,' the mother informed. 'He might've said somethin' about Ilkley.'

''*Il*kley?'''

''*Il*kley?''' echoed the three and a bit, tumbling into the same state of incivility with a similarly bad mannered Yorkshire folk song. My spurts of hatred were evolving into something less spurt-like.

I wouldn't ask Jed at the weekends, but witness how more decayed, aged, dishevelled he looked, how he no longer paid attention to items worn, the same items, week after week. I'd never have believed our once fresh-faced peacock, who'd left teachers rubbing their brows – ''Somethin' not right about that uniform' – outsmarted the headmaster – 'Young man, Wildon, is it? Err... well done...' – and blown me away each time he'd slid his torso around our front-room door, was capable of such ruin.

And yet, despite such indifference, the hair remained immaculate, while Geoff – who'd at last spruced up the glass coffee table with a handful of *Commando* comics – had had no say in the affair. During my Friday visits to the chair, he'd quiz me on his whereabouts...

... as with yesterday, after I'd dragged my unresponsive legs down the smoky-topped stairs of my bus.

''Might be Ilkley,' I said, eyeing his latest bombshell's reflection.

'Could you turn that noise down, Angela, please?' he asked, as if not for the first time. 'Before I throw the fucker through the window,' he whispered in my ear.

I'd never heard Geoff swear before.

He placed the tips of his proficient fingers on my temples and veered my head further, so I take a peek at the creature down the shop whose hair our newest Angela appeared to pamper with all the love in the world. One side short, the other was an in-curled ski-slope, which lay on a pierced left nipple, as I was able to note once Angela had removed his plastic poncho – without forgetting another of Geoff's swift head-veers.

'She's been pissin' around with that ponce for three quarts of an hour!'

'Isn't it great they're from Sheffield, tho'!' she enthused – the band gnawing its way out of the radio – with an extra comb-like motion down the obvious side.

'So's Tony Capstick, what's she want, a *Crackerjack* pencil!'

The New Romantics were taking over the City's nightclub scene, and Geoff's greying, *Jason King*-like moustache was on the blink.

Not that my number 8s pickup technique proved more effective, over at the shoe shop with the 28 lanes. The manager didn't so much man the helm as breathe down this itchy neck, along with a couple of burly understudies. If I made it away, unlucky 7s at hand, my dodge wasn't so artless; I left the blazer and lunch bag behind. Nay, I considered stopping, getting caught, to return the things, recognising I'd transcended my revenge-quota.

I'd given up bragging my wins to the family for Sam's sake.

Craving info about Jed was only natural for my young brother, but I couldn't sit by and watch history repeat itself. And all the signs it might were there. Just the other evening he brought a schoolmate home and my heart skipped a beat when I caught them at it – though the idea of two Soul buddies, Sam and Dave, did tickle me. I'd seen the effect Steve had had on Jed, and Mick on Macca. While Sam had had two brothers to gape up at. I couldn't yet tell which he took after most, though hoped the bit-less vinyl wizardry denoted something.

All this following the false friend he'd tendered me not too many months back.

\* \* \* \* \*

Usual entrenchment, profuse *Relish* helpings, my great war of attrition...

'My dad's bird's on, Phill.'

Trounced once more, I set the pie aside.

''Bit parasitic, if you ask me,' he said.

That was the sign I'd been waiting for. Sam had acquired an interest in words. And I'd ensure he continued on that path, make sure he made more of it than I'd ever managed.

From that evening I'd have him nudge up beside me with an endless supply of semantic-related questions. Except the evening I was able to put two and two together went like this:

'Phill, what's a 'blackleg'?'

'Well, it's kinda…'

'What's 'accosted' mean?'

'Well, it's…'

'What's 'tantamount'?'

'Well…'

''Sadistic'?'

'He won't learn you owt,' my mum warned again.

'What's 'flounderin'?'

'Give me a sentence. What have they got you reading?'

'Eh? Oh, nothin'.' He ferret-fought his way out, off and up to spin tunes, I presumed, but returned around five minutes later, looking to the steam-sodden ceiling. ''Remember it now: *Joe dumped the flounderin' Don on the floor…', an' eerrr… 'got to his feet, hand comin' from inside his shirt with the deadly 'tool' ready for his vicious work.''*

'Weakening,' I offered, only for him to fly off again, leaving me to relive a school reading episode of my own.

*''Finished already, Rowlings?'*

*''Only just started, Miss.'*

*Joe Hawkins,* my ex-shorn-headed literary hero, had kicked *Peter Parker* in the head, and I needed to step in before he reached the *Abercrombie* stage.

I not only concealed the literature that evening but also vowed to myself that I'd never touch pills again, either, save for a headache. It wasn't a hardship with my frontline view of the effects week after week.

And what with Mick now nipping by the house as a matter of routine, to see my dad, well, he, my dad, obviously knew more than he let on. I was always out by then.

They'd get together with Uncle Pete, or 'ol' Tomo', as Mick called him, a little later in The Grouse.

* * * * *

It was on a Sunday, following Sam's unplanned literary revelation, by coincidence, that my dad, bending double over his roses, drew me to a halt for the pills question, with a light grip to my wrist. He gripped his waist with his other hand: ''Must be gettin' on.'

'Well, you *are* forty three.'

'You wouldn't take drugs,' he said in a flash, smile more embarrassed than sinister, more like a pat-on-the-back than a put-on-the-spot. He held up a defending hand. 'I know, I know, your mam's been a bit worried. I told her she was bein' stupid, but she made me ask.'

In the sure-fire knowledge he'd never feel obliged to ask again, I tutted.

* * * * *

Getting changed yesterday evening still ran by its regular configuration. I brawled with a tricky fitting *Perry*. I demanded playlist after playlist, ready to be particular about the order of my requests, as Sam span the tunes and scrutinized the garb with the same precision and dream. He held up the disc's reflection: 'Jackie Beavers, *I Need My baby*?'

'Not yet.'

'*I'll Always Need You*, Dean Courtney?'

'Nope.'

'*I'll Always Love You*, Sam Moultrie?'

'No.'

'*Little Darlin' I Need You*, Marvin Gaye?'

'No – What's wrong with this shirt?'

'Nothin'... as I can see – *Cryin' Over You*, Duke Brown?'

'No.'

'*I Always Love You*, The Detroit Spinners? *My heart Cries for*...?'

'No – What is *wrong* with this shirt!'

'Nothin'... just don't have a cow.'

He was right. There was nothing wrong with it at all. Save that, had there been a bonnet attached, I'd have found a bee in it...

*'It'll Never Be Over For Me...?'*

I was out in an instant.

I rammed home the buried size 7 substitutes and, with an empty bag, left the house – realising I'd been taking the having-the-world-at-my-feet thing too literally, I'd since gotten used to bringing my loafers along, just in case. But I wasn't going back.

The shoes gripped tight as I knocked open the main road's swinging doors to Jim's nod and Springsteen's *Born To Run,* where an experienced looking landlady of around fifty asked my choice of drink.

Marlene and Frank had quit the establishment six weeks ago, never recovering from Jed's one-man Easter rising a year gone, or its repercussions – 'Even *he*'s not John Wayne!' Marlene insisted, tilting her head toward her knuckle-torn husband. They never pressed charges, and my dad and me lent a hand whenever able, preferring the Ted incursions, in belated response to the Cleethorpes chronicle.

The new management had also brought a reputation with it. Evenings were no longer violent and there'd been speculation as to what would become of the place. The idea was to refurbish it in its entirety, while ridding it of its existing patrons. Every pub in the area was doing the same.

The Yetis had taken their leave before being asked. It was odd entering the place without a whistle and a taunt, their *Alright Now*, oblivious as they must have been to their effects. I only hoped they rode into a sunset resplendent, that pastures new were the greatest of improvements – 'Far out, Geddon!' I heard someone eulogize, rolling a funny cigarette...

Our new landlady passed me a pint of Bitter with my card marked, to the backing of The Joe Dolce Music Theatre's *Shuddup You face.* Unconvinced with the Polka Dot, I prodded it back into the bag, punishment for what was beginning to feel like dithering – she made me nervous. Jed's guffaw in the other side, for the first time in a year, made me more so...

I headed to the jukebox and, to the opening bars of Roxy Music's *Jealous Guy,* caught his friend's reflection through the dome, grinning its dull grin. To boot, I discerned the landlord's manner – nowhere as big as Frank, short even, but looked liked he'd served time for Hull Kingston Rovers – holding on to a beer tap, keeping an eye on our lot, waiting for an excuse.

They were quiet, and had been quieter without Jed and his friend.

Whatever comment Wiffa slung my way, swastika reflecting true before my eventual turn, the landlord didn't so much swoop as give the briefest, direct order, like an old habit: n`o 'Sup up', just 'Out!'

If I suffered the public humiliation, it was nothing beside my satisfaction seeing the rest of them barred... I'd no idea what I'd tell my dad.

Wiffa knocked Jim's well-wishing hand away, and when I looked down, offered a contrite wink, the latter's sorry eyes confirmed what I'd known for some time: this Soul train's days were numbered, overworked and under-maintained.

The same Wiffa screamed like a baby through Sheffield's centre until we'd pointed out the spot The Yorkshire Ripper – of similar kind to our national leader, but with more discretion, thought many – had at last been arrested. He'd also point to a couple of his own landmarks: pubs his Gelgard gang had sacked seasons previous, some Saturday when Leeds had found themselves matchless.

The same Wiffa had the same effect in the station as he'd had in The Grouse, not for the inside-out swastika but for the prices he charged for the gear. He was neither reasonable nor low-key with it. Last Resort had just begun a five year stretch in Wakefield Prison, for possessing a "settee with enough inside it to start up his own chemist".

The same Wiffa went on to upset a group of City supporters at the opposite side of our wet Mancunian street. Where they were going to or coming from on a Friday, we didn't know or care to. I was bare-footing it by then, for the loafers boob. Just About copped a head-butt to the nose from the one traversing adherent, some young apprentice, by the looks, whereas I copped a bottle at my feet. I hopped, skipped and jumped for better times gone.

Jed's friend ran on in front. Jed chuckled alongside. And it all managed to look like it wasn't the first time.

The same Wiffa employed the same swindling tactics up to Bolton, a town whose station hadn't so much become a late

Friday evening battleground, with what remained of the Bolton posse fighting it out before we got there, but the start of one long battle-ride, the unfailing weekend scenario. If the khaki crews had ridden out sunless, their legacy was the huge number of disgruntled pan-Lancashire Yetis, who, having gotten so used to the taunting during evenings out in said town, no longer appeared able to do without it. Everyone off the train, on the train, change of carriage, off again. Brogues and boots at odds at this something-to-midnight culture clash.

Wiffa was a culture on his own...

I stayed in my seat last night, curled up in a ball. I held out my shoeless, bloody stubs for a sympathy vote, out of action until further notice. Eyes closed, I dreamed of other places – here, another time, Black Beam leading the way. No-one knew what had happened to him. Funny, my grom went, and he followed. But I lived to tell the tale.

And so on to the next assured running fracas, the central streets of Wigan, where it dawned on me that never once, from as far back as South Yorkshire, had I heard mention of a single sound, a tune, its title, artist, label – those flat round things Sam spun on the *Dansette*. Only rabbit ramblings between flying feet, of the increasing quantities of gear injected, of who'd 'o-deed' in the last week, never to be seen again, invisible hats removed for the short-lived moment it took.

Wallgate upon us, our wide-eyed freaks chewed in vicious anticipation of the violence still to come. I continued to nurse my feet, trusting, if I sat long enough, that the driver might take me back with him.

That stairway looked uncompromising.

My door was pushed open with a pant. ''Comin' o' what?' Jed wanted to know, but I just couldn't begin what I'd wanted to say, and he looked like he knew. I put an arm around his shoulder; he placed his around my waist, and on we limped in incoherence, stopping at the clatter of Hell breaking loose above our stairway to...

... an un-policed away game?

Five hundred to a thousand yards of gory glory, direct and directionless. Tanked up and armed, they'd waited, kicked out and eager to kick in, plastered eyes hatred-full for we, the wiry

198

invaders. To shirk, kick back and cuff was our sole route; heart at full pelt, bleeding feet or no… or was it the other way round? Sympathy would claim non-existence. My badged-up bag proclaimed something else.

Jed seized my collar a mere bend from a former cloud nine: ''Want a piggy-back?'

As it was too late, he pushed me into a shop doorway, a finger to my lips. And when our two boozers made their blind approach, he stepped out an unpolished shoe, legging them as a whole, a spiky skull cracking enough to vibrate the shop's window. Then would he make the kick: 'Bastard!' The repeated: 'Bastard!' Like from the depths of another dormant rage.

The queerest thing about this one-sided business was the mention of Sam's name. Or was I mistaken?

Reinforcements appeared at either end. I slipped away with a limp, to meet more turmoil.

Casino Club, the sky reflected, in red on white, like a short-term lump for reasons old, according to the window of a car caught in the mêlée. 'Come on,' goaded *Herman Munster,* blocking the vehicle's route, black drape meeting black boots below the knees.

Bovine had a different idea: 'Right, let's give these bastards a lesson!'

The queue, utilising the car as a pontoon, had awaited the order from the top. For *Mr. Munster,* I couldn't work out if I was impressed or not. It was one thing having your head rammed into the hub of a moving front wheel, but surely something else to come up for more.

He was onto a loser with the arrival of the Glaswegian charabanc. The tartan army; the odd black fist-patched kilt. They were always off and in before the driver put the brakes on.

A Wigan Friday, Saturdays alike. And all I desired was a spot to get my head down.

I made for a rocky chair and an eight hour sit on a flank, where I'd behold relics of performances passed on, a crowd looking like it only half remembered why it had turned up, the secret lying in the other half. Could a private hemisphere's spirit have seeped through the cracks one despondent morning and forgotten to return? Minds blown to pieces, hearts cheated, cheated and at risk; these losers, ever quitting, losers all. A synchronised shambles, claps singular and ungainly, where a girl with no name had carried herself like a nocturnal nymph on ice.

And I, the involuntary spectator, rank outsider caught inside, no longer wanted dealings with it. I'd look beyond the fractured walls... well, barring a few minutes' trip to what was known as the 'gents', a spot, as a rule, I'd risk a burst bladder to avoid.

'Pool o' piss!' yon relic exclaimed, hovering above bucket-sized brogues, baggy trousers rolled to knees – I could've done with that piggyback now. I disregarded the penny and went for the pound...

* * * * *

But this after-sting! Back here in my chair, where I'd remain until eight on the dot, to the odd heart-racer of an opening spin...
... and the uncontrollable drifts-away, to a finer elsewhere:

*'Would you marry me?' she asked, like she needed to...*

## 33

*'We are time's subjects, and time bids be gone.'*

*'Georgie Best, wunderbar... Wears purple knickers an' a see-through bra...'*

Lyrics adapted from some... big showy thing. As kids, we sang the same, Jed and me, except we'd employ a current Wednesday hero, to entice street roaming Skinheads and Boot boys displaying full colours, while we were far enough away from them. We'd then run hell for leather, like my cousin and me from old Batty.

For Wiffa, poking at some broad, sweaty back whose head was lost inside a fresh Manchester United shirt, it was the same old song. I prayed the Mancunian, head and arms through holes, wouldn't take it too well and shatter his jaw.

Alas. He looked unimpressed, heading on down the corridor to our blinding bright, one minute past eight.

It all left me wondering whether Wiffa, like Jed, had hidden behind the sofa from *Dr Who*'s foes *The Ice Warriors* – I teased Jed for years. And just when he'd swapped sucking his thumb for a shorn head and back-to-front tattoo.

An early May's sun ran through as a ruthless taunt.

The one amphetamine fuel-injected word to have whizzed from bandit to bandit this dismal night was the one no-one wanted anyone else to hear, if collective paranoia was unable to keep quiet about it – some wreck had had the gall to wake me: 'But that's just between me and thee...' There was gear to be had in them there hills, 'stashed before the poor bastard got arrested', to which our insatiable outlaws adhered without the slightest hint of hesitation but with the utmost enthusiasm. There'd be 'enough to go round for another six weekends,' so they reckoned. Tonight, they'd be hitting the roof.

I used my feet as an excuse to wait in some café, said I'd catch them up hunt over. I'd done one of those before, traipsed about Wigan in half a foot of snow, feet cobalt on shoe dye and frost. The gear was never found.

And so off they fused into the glare. Chris, who never brought up my encounter with J, placed an arm about April's leather-clad waist. Paul, hands in pockets, hoped to grind his *Wrigley's* into oblivion. Jed giggled at something Wiffa spat, whose bald head faded like a *Heinz* bean in sauce.

I hung back on the stairs, when Just About pulled his beaten body away and cast over a stage-struck grin of old, like in belated recognition of better bowling shoes honoured, thumbs up for erstwhile measure... before turning to fizzle out with the rest.

Neil McIntyre. Macca. Mogga, Half Dead, Just About... We called him Duke, too, after his black American hero – he'd croon his tunes all day long, especially *Nothing Can Stop Me*, clicking a finger along the school's top corridor. He knew his own mind alright, what was left of it. It was written for him, that one...

And then I remembered. I'd not collected my bag from the upstairs cloakroom; Jed had only thrown my jacket.

I got there in time, to the attendant's grievance. Following a petty gripe about me not having a ticket, he hurled me the bag.

It was weird hobbling about this empty space in the half light of day, ghosts gracing ancient maple to the echo of a far-off dulcet horn; someone beckoned me over, coke in either hand. And it was here – I'd never thought of it like this until now – I recalled Nathalie relating her Wigan adventure. She must have leaned over this part of the balcony, the semi-circle's apex – everyone leant over this part of the balcony on first attendance, we did nothing else. I saw Dave, too, thanks to an encounter of which he'd been unaware...

'What are you doin'?' asked a buxom young lady in bottle-green, from nowhere, mop and bucket in hand. 'Hopin' to get locked in till tonight?'

I didn't know what I was doing.

'Dear me! Have you been sittin' on too many cold floors?'

'No, it's my feet.'

''Bit too much?'

''Suppose so.'

202

'Then get home an' have tonight off. 'Don't know how you do it every week as it is. Well, I do, but it's illegal.'

It wasn't only what this bottle-green uniformed lady said, but how she said it. I asked whether she spoke French.

'I do, aye!' Putting the mop back to work, she stopped again and bawled down to an older looking colleague in front of the stage: 'Here, Mavis, *avez-vous une cuppa?*'

''Just had one. And so have *you...* lazy mare!'

I chuckled down the corridor, with the sole requisite of genuine humour, unscathed by the synthetic. I didn't belong here anymore, and so wouldn't come here anymore. But then I'd said the same last week...

On Station Road, I thought I'd wrap up my neck against an early May morning nip. Except the Polka Dot wasn't in the bag. Filched from the place Jed had paid to keep it safe.

No, I didn't belong here anymore. 'Thievin' bastard!'

And no, the unsuspecting morning shopper over the road didn't need to hear that. I'd word it better telling Sam...

## 34

*'Come what come may, time and the hour run through the*
*roughest day.'*

'… stop. It's your stop.'

'Where…?'

'At the terminus,' informed a silver, scraggly beard. As his
eyes came into focus, the bus driver wanted to know if I ever
hoped to get off.

'Yeah, this'll do.' I only lived over the hill.

He apologised that, me being upstairs, head down on the
backseat, he'd taken me to Abbeydale and back twice, as he
could remember.

'What time is it?'

He didn't look at his watch: 'Half two.' Said he wanted to get
to Bramall Lane, 'to see them idiots get relegated.' He'd 'nearly
finished, so it'll be 'out o' service' back to town – Between me
an' you, that is.' And then he frowned: 'Walsall today.'

Prising off the sticky 7s, I asked him if he relished the idea of
Fourth Division football.

He aided my pain with ''Not football in the Fourth, is it?' And
besides, he said, it hadn't been football down there for a long
time, so we wouldn't find it too different. He called me a silly
sod for pulling the extra fare out of my pocket. And so I showed
him my feet. 'Jesus, lad!' he blew. 'Stag-night? All-night job?
What time's the weddin'?'

But I didn't want to talk about weddings. I told him to get off
and not miss that kick-off.

'Some luck.' As he helped me down the stairs, I wondered
how, and why, I'd gotten up them. He deemed I'd do better to
put my shoes back on, before marching off.

I couldn't see myself marching anywhere again. 'Have a cheer
for me!'

Un-sticking toes of a coagulate red, I sat on the little grass-island terminus, around which a driver would swing the vehicle, take a ten-minute smoke-stop, ride back into town and beyond, and come back and do it again. I recalled how Just About, only weeks previous, had added a fresh stunt to the death-defying repertoire, with his sharpest performance to date. Standing too early as the bus made said swing, he crashed through the top deck window and landed on this very spot – the slope's fault. For me, the feat was how he got back to his feet and checked for mohair damage, of which there was none...

I rammed home the 7s for the umpteenth time, limped onward by the Pictures-gone-Bingo Hall, snail-paced the perimeter of St Michael's Church. The bells told me I must have dozed off again: it was already three o'clock. They didn't leave it there, either, like young lovers, the one chasing the other around the belfry... And when such a young couple stepped into a sea of blue and white confetti, I recognised the groom, his head towering above: Dave, from my indelible snapshot. Divorced *and* re-married.

I leaned against one of the churchyard's wrought iron entrance gates for a longer peek.

On the bells tolled.

Denise was next, bridesmaid, by the looks.

And now I twigged. Today made part of something greater. I'd been forced to abandon that Lancashire hovel for this.

I kissed the watery-eyed, elderly lady to my left, made her cry all the more, and thought about getting nearer, but feared ruining the album. Instead, as the admiring crowd snuggled in, as my vertigo ascended another gear, I crouched, squatted, allowed my inner dither to do what it would. And I hoped and I dreamed, and pulled myself back up...

... to lose every last hope, to kill every last dream. To clutch a glimpse everlasting. To behold a most beautiful bride, when whatever-his-name opened the love mobile's door and drew my Nathalie from the showered kisses and petals eternal...

Were those bells laughing at me?

'Isn't she beautiful, her, though!' the old lady nudged.

I turned my head away, met my dad's exasperation from afar, and so turned it back. I placed the bag between my knees, and finally accepted the held-out hanky like I'd known the woman all my life: 'Cheers.'

She poked the exhausted cloth into an elderly shopping bag, rested a hand on my shoulder, and said: ''Got the world at your feet, if you only knew.'

'I *do* know!' I choked, spat or something. 'You should *see* my feet!'

She glanced downward, and shook her head. It was a subtle gesture, a gesture granting me the resolve to drop my bag right here and kick the 7s from my heels for the last time... She looked worried I was going to go The Full Monty.

I hobbled past the bus shelter with more purpose, trusted the bride might catch sight of the cast-offs, and so catch on to my making part of the happiest day of her life...

## 35

*'Excessive sorrow laughs....'*

I'd say the least possible about everything. I couldn't face another sermon, not today. He'd be right and...

Sneaking by the old *Cortina* would have been simpler than by the blinding patina of Stan's new vehicle, the one with the "crisp hatchback stylin' and plastic bumpers", as per my dad's report. Not that Stan went anywhere in it, reckoned the same. Where once he spent every free minute with his head inside the banger's engine, he now spent it beside the dazzler's bonnet, "washing, polishing and staring gormless."

'Hey, it's The Milky Bar Kid!' he laughed, rubbing away to Hall & Oats' *She's Gone*. He gawked down as I got closer: ''No wonder you're walking funny.' And then back to the machine: 'What do you think?'

''Prefer Tavares' version.' He thought I was talking about a better car, until I nodded to the radio, via a reflection looking like it had already seen better days.

''My new tape,' he said. ''Couldn't listen to the radio anymore, 'sounds like United have gone down in style.' He narrowed his eyes: 'You're lookin' positively rough.'

As custom dictated, I was at the ready with 'Positive being the operative word.' But the conviction proved a thorny grasp.

And the old tease looked like he'd noticed.

He ceased polishing and took my elbow, eyes calling an unexpected truce. 'You alright, love?' he said. He'd never called me that before, it was a Sheffield thing; we'd melt at those. Bidding my new-found friend a great Saturday night, I almost moved on, when he stopped me again, to ask who the 'smart bloke' was he'd seen coming to our house. I thought he meant Jed, but then Stan, like the district, knew or had heard of him. It clicked on his stating the bloke in question stood with my dad in The Grouse. Not Pete, but Mick.

'My big brother.'

Once his eyes had done rolling, he said Mick was at ours as we spoke, except he didn't look happy, by the way he'd passed by. 'One minute, your dad was doing' his Eddie Warring bit' – Hull and Widnes were fighting it out in the final today; he gave Bashforth a run for her money on those occasions – 'but then it did seem to go quiet.'

Stan was either being nosy or worrying over nothing. I was contented just knowing Mick was around, and that I'd made it through my longest ever three minutes still standing, to Hall and Oats perfectly-timed masterpiece.

There *was* life after all this. And perhaps other pubs, too. I'd look for Marlene's, see if the Yetis had gone there. We'd fight our way out of life's Fourth Division together. Everything was temporary...

Feet numbing to new found confidence, I moved on with a smile. 'Up The Blades, Stan!

I snared Sam's beam through a sash window and responded in kind. He looked otherwise occupied. Maybe Dave was with him. Making up the side path, I spotted Mick in my dad's chair, facing the gas fire. Nothing new there... or not until my dad loomed to the window with an angry glare, for no reason I imagined. My mum was silhouetted between the kitchen and front room, poised for meeting me at the back door.

This last stage, by my dad's now famous gable-end, felt longer than my trudges through Wigan, Manchester and Sheffield together. This twenty to thirty feet throughout which the afore-mentioned optimism fizzled away like one of my dad's *Andrew's Liver Salts*...

'Where *have* you been?' my mum attacked, opening the door.

'*Joan,*' my dad rushed through, 'let me handle this.' And posed the same question in the same fashion: 'We've been worried bloody sick!' He freaked at the sight of my feet.

'I'd have done better myself,' huffed my mum.

Mick calmed things, making over to the kitchen under his own steam: 'He's here, that's all that matters.'

'Where is everybody?' I could but wonder. The house should be full at a time like this.

My mum glanced upward. 'Sam 'n' Dave are *at* it,' she said, for something else to say.

Mick deemed I was a good lad, but that someone ought to sort out my feet, pronto, while he should get back and 'face the music.'

'Poor Mick.' She'd held on until...

My dad ran hot water like a false hope. 'Bloody United...'

'What's goin' on?'

'Not too loud,' he whispered. 'Sit down, I'll get the turps.'

'Get what?'

'The... *bloo*dy *TCP,* I mean... 'not with it, force of habit.'

My mum wiped her eyes in front of the unlit fire.

I pitched my jacket into the storm cupboard, rolled up the slacks and fell into my dad's chair. I dipped my feet into the bowl – *'Christ* all bleedin' mighty!'

'How's this happened?' he asked.

'Someone threw a...'

'Where, in Wigan?'

'No, Man...'

'Neil's dead,' he cut in once more, like he'd waited for a suitable moment, and that was it.

But it wasn't as far as I was concerned.

For despite how my mum thrust her hands back to her face, I wouldn't submit to another of Macca's, or any of his aliases', or any of the others', eclipsing acts today, I'd outshine them this time: 'Somebody nicked my Polka Dot!' And what about Don Downing's *Lonely Days, Lonely Nights,* I'd forgotten about that one – 'Thievin' bastard!' And as for United, not that anyone cared to give me the actual *score,* 'they're crap!' No, if they hoped to learn anything at all about suffering, they'd have done better to stand beside me outside St Michael's an hour ago, or outside this window ten minutes ago – 'I listened to Hall an' Oats the whole way through...!'

'Phill...'

'I'm barred from The Grouse, Dad...'

He put a hand on my knee...

209

... a wet one: 'Watch it, you'll take the dye out o' my trousers!'

I awoke from what may only have been a second's drift, feet in the no longer so insensitive water, like I'd... died and returned, floated back into my dad's chair, to more anxious glares.

'While your mam's here,' he said, paused, and once more asked: 'Do you take drugs?'

My mum looked frantic for the right answer. 'I'm here... aren't I?' turned out to be the one.

'Jenny's gettin' married,' she said, like we'd been discussing the weather, an indirect demand we drop the other subject forevermore. ''Couple o' weeks.'

'Registry office,' muttered my dad. They've been round this mornin'.'

'We didn't know she was three months pregnant, either, so if anybody on the street asks, tell 'em they're married already.'

I didn't know whether to laugh or cry.

Back from the cupboard with a bandage-roll, scissors and a groan, my dad kneeled again. *"When sorrers come, they come not in single spies but in battalions."*

And so I cried a little more.

I hoped my mum might conjure up the force for an egg sandwich, to get me through, as if she'd say no. I swallowed the last bite to my dad's army-wrapping completion.

My mum suggested shouting Sam and Dave down, but to the faint opening bars of Dutch Robinson's *Can't Get Along Without You*, I reckoned they'd be alright for five minutes more.

I made it clear I'd get up when ready.

'Don't say anythin' to Sam,' one of them begged.

If the boys looked eager, routine's hand would pull me through the questions offensive to the end of said tune: 'Yep, Yep, Little accident, No.' Oh, and, due to my accident, I'd be obliged to stay home a good number of weeks. I congratulated myself on the quick thinking.

'Any requests?' asked Dave, for solace.

Sam recommended 'Mr. J' in such circumstances.

I could but smile... and yet there *was* someone I fancied hearing before hitting hay. I might never have slept without him: 'The Duke.'

210

'Gene Chandler,' Sam enlightened, and warned: 'Watch him, he gets ratty when you read 'em out.'

'I won't anymore, Sam.'

Dave pulled up a handful: *'Nothing Can Stop Me?'*

'That'll do,' I said.

Sam looked incredulous, while proud of Dave's bit-less handiness.

And as they clicked their fingers, I looked beyond the branches of an unfortunate sycamore, grateful the house had its back turned on Wigan…

*… Off, the forever young fop raced… thumbs-up strut down an old school corridor…*

However would they fit all those names on the headstone…?

I contemplated sleeping through Sunday altogether. I'd build up my strength, even if that meant waking on a Monday morning. Tough journey ahead, but then controlled breathing, I'd come to learn, was the key. I could think of worse places to be, a man of my age.

And hadn't my dad done well with these young feet…

5

## 36

*'I am a dreamer. For a dreamer is one who can only find his
way by moonlight, and his punishment is that he sees the dawn
before the rest of the world.'*

There was no stopping Sam with the vinyl now. And I'd got a
full evening of it yet.

My mum and dad had just gone through the door, out, together,
as a couple, for what was, barring a recent wedding and holidays,
only the second time since I'd known them. I'd babysat for them
last Thursday as well; the start of a ritual.

At least it was nice to see the two them stagger home, comical.
My mum couldn't hold her drink, and so, whenever my dad
tippled into one of his customary post-ale-and-plentiful
perspectives, she, under equal influence by proportion, was able
to rescue the rest of us by pulling him back: 'Shut up, silly
bleeder!' Margaret Lockwood went right out of the window last
week. Though the really comical part was that, even when
recognizing the ineffectuality of his ramblings, he wouldn't be
outdone. And to a Gloria Jones backing – *Dansette* down for that
evening also – he got out of his chair and performed a stirring
Mark Almond impression, inspired by the young man's graceful
efforts on some recent episode of *Top of The Pops*.

'Dad,' Sam protested, 'he's nicked it!'

It was good to see the old man take a well-earned break with
his other half, and good that she'd at last agreed to it, that she'd
drawn herself away from the cleanest net curtains in history –
'still time for passers-by to notice, in these last weeks of
summer. It was good *for* him, too, since debate-worthy events of
late appeared to be piling around him all the more, while he
forever believed himself capable of taking them on.

England was on fire.

Or at least its inner cities – barring our own; *'Sheffield Coppers Are Hard,'* reminded the local paper. As my dad illustrated, half of our nation's women were batting their eyelashes like Princess Diana for their getting richer husbands, while the other half, living in slums like us, were getting stuck in with their getting poorer husbands, 'battering police riot shields with Molotov cocktails, all to impress this bleedin' wicked government!' He'd then recall having warned us, only we'd not listened.

The back end of summer '81; September's second half – 17th, 18th... – a country more divided, 'and us in the wrong half, like a lotta decent folk!'

For the slums, I'd not noticed any difference. For the eyelash-batting, I couldn't agree more. My sister must have spent months studying the future princess' every blush on the Nine O' Clock News.

* * * * *

On the happiest day of Jenny's life, business took place in the belfry-free surroundings of a modern Sheffield city-central registry office.

'Has she got somethin' in her eye?' whispered Auntie Pat, in the row behind.

'And she's more than three months gone,' coughed Uncle Jeff.

I was more concerned with the way my soon-to-be brother-in-law chewed making his vows, that on his 'I do, aye', the registrar might cop a *Wrigley's* in *his* eye.

'Get on the dance floor, mix!' ordered the groom at the evening bash, mike at hand. 'None o' that different-families-in-their-own-corners crap!' Having then tumbled from the stage, he saved his embarrassment with a trouser-drop, triggering the nervous titters, girly giggles aplenty. Pegs returned to rightful place, he took the ever blushing bride by what appeared to be growing bigger by the second over a red leather miniskirt and awarded the rest of us a performance for posterity, from one end of Duran Duran's *Planet Earth* to the other.

They'd been practicing.

Pageboy Sam, who'd insisted on braces and *Dr Marten* shoes for the occasion, was overwhelmed for all the wrong reasons. The nearest he got to donating a performance was to Shakin' Stevens' *This Ole House,* and that was only through frustration. Or cousin Avril offering his arm. He fancied her whether he'd missed out on the Hot Pants or not.

Our evening was Northern Soul-free because the bride had threatened the deejay, sure as I was, for fear Sam and me should steel her limelight. The giveaway was my attempt at a request, when said jock forgot himself, or who I was: ''Can't, she... I mean, errr 'not brung, errr...' Frantic, he was.

Duran Duran played one in three: Jenny hadn't wanted anyone to get bored, 'like a lot do at weddings.' We thus suffered only two out of the three wedding classics, of which Terry Wogan led the way.

It at least granted my dad a surface laugh: elder son, I recognised he was, in fact, howling with grief. 'And no,' he said, making back to the bar, 'I think your grom's better off where she is.'

\* \* \* \* \*

Then again, he got his way regarding the long-mulled-over kitchen wall, by knocking it through to the outside toilet, three Saturdays on from the other, just cited disaster.

It was down to the French, what I understood, or 'that bleedin' excuse for a nation', who'd 'all be over here again if anything started.' They'd been building a nuclear plant in Iraq, for the Iraqis, near the capital, until the Israelis decided they were having none of it. With fighter jets, ''it'' was obliterated in one fell swoop, before the Iraqis were able to obliterate *them.* The lump hammer didn't half twitch that Sunday evening.

'Pete, you'll kill yourself tryin' to knock through that' – storm cupboard – 'floor, you need one o' them drill things. Ask 'em to do it when they come to modernize.'

''Be too late.'

If he once more capitulated before mum's common sense, the wall partitioning the kitchen and toilet came down for consolation, cistern and all.

215

The Council agreed to repair the wreckage, while we, duty calling, exploited the porch toilet of any neighbour who happened to be in at the time, barring Bashforth's, should we get locked in and rammed into a half-nelson. They also fined the home wrecker for gross negligence, rough and ready damage cost in instalments, which were added to Shylock's Friday evening bills. ''Could've brought the whole house down,' railed some spotty Council assessor in a black Mac, waving his clipboard toward the bombsite. One glance and finger-jiggle from my dad, and the power that had gone to his head crashed down like the water tank by his feet.

They got the place inhabitable for Royal Wedding Day, last weekend in July, the majority of work being carried out Saturday mornings by 'an' excess o' staff on treble-time', going by the work's supplier. We spent that summery day in celebratory mood, with cans of *Younger's Tartan* and crisps – Sam left the records beneath the bed for an afternoon and surreptitious swig. And when we got tired with the telly, ''Just nippin' to the toilet' was sounded and *off* one of us gaily jaunted. It was nice having it back, outside or not.

It seemed my mum would always be hampered by my dad's hammer swinging whims at walls and telly buttons. But then I'd got my own share with Sam's colourful language fits, aimed at those on his Div hit-list: everyone except his friend Dave; and even he'd been singled out for not demonstrating enough enthusiasm for Mr. J's *Love Lights.* Teachers were included, mainly the one in music who'd had the class spend an evening learning the words to Cat Stevens' *Morning Has Broken,* for some Harvest Festival concert, an evening which, like any other, clashed with his own music-worship time: 'He said it was a classic, the dopey sh...!'

'Sam, I've told you not to...'

'But he's not even heard o' Candi Staton!'

I was grateful his musical taste reflected my own. It was more how he reflected me in every other way at that age, the part of me *I* didn't like anymore.

My fears ran deeper. Jed gone, Sam would remember him for the impertinent peacock he was – the swagger, the wink, a packet of Lincolnshire's finest – and so remain intrigued as to his whereabouts, the truth of which being right up *Joe Hawkins'* street. I stuck with what I thought best, showed a lessening interest in what had gone before, save the discs beneath the bed – I still couldn't have him coming home one afternoon and telling me he'd borrowed Nigel Nuttall's Queen LPs... or whatever his name might be.

* * * * *

For 1st July, I deliberated the matter the whole of my long, lacklustre ride home, as with the thirty minutes' sit *Chez* Geoff, where I also mused on which object my barber had thrown out first: the lacquered-radio or the gregarious Angela.

This would be the evening, I concluded, while the Friday night iron was hot.

''Comin' upstairs?' Sam invited.

I feigned interest in *Look North*, waiting for a report to first get Sam on my side, say, a King Arthur appearance, and his proclamation that people would 'allus need coal'; that one riled my dad every time: *'Steel,* silly...!'

But as nothing was going, I stepped up the pressing movement. And mumbled something like: ''Don't know why I'm takin' so long anyway. Wigan's been closed a few months now.'

Brainy alone looked impartial.

My mum and dad caught on the instant Sam flew upstairs.

I asked my mum if she'd finish the trousers.

'Bullshit!' Sam welcomed, pointing to a blackened wall of *Black Echoes* cuttings, where once had reigned Slade and David Cassidy, and to a freshly, however retrospectively, stuck piece reading *Wigan Friday Oldies All-nighter! 3rd July, 1981.*

I extended the lie for all it was worth: ''Printed before the place burned down.' Though I shouldn't have blamed the Yetis.

'Bastards! Nigel Nesbit's gonna cop it Monday – Queen Fan, 'looks at tit!' Slight pause, he asked: 'What's Jed doin' about it?'

''Got a bird in Ilkeston – Ilkley,' I said, off the top of my head. His world looked like it had collapsed either way. 'It's for the best, Sam. 'Part from that, it's not the be-all-an'-end-all. They'll be plenty more Wigan Casinos.'

217

'Why's Jed got a bird?' He rubbed the cutting with an index. 'He's not gone poof, has he?'

'No.'

During that same weekend, my brother came round to both ideas. And I left it until late Sunday evening to suggest he let poor Nigel Nesbit be, since the would-be victim was already handicapped, with or without the name. Sam's rebellion needed care and attention, and I would never have gotten round to addressing it without May's distressing events.

Keeping that from him had proven challenging enough.

\* \* \* \* \*

On the funeral's vigil, as Sam perfected swallow dives from his bed – you could tell the moves by the way the house vibrated – my dad instructed me to look after Mick, implying he himself wouldn't be making the graveside.

I didn't ask why, just did as told: I stuck by Mick like one of the anguished family, and was treated as such in return. He appeared glad of it, too. More visible, though, than his natural pain, was his aura of controlled rage, like a corona. I'd never know whether the rage was directed inward – maybe he felt responsible for this fearsome day, for having turned his back the moment Macca bought his one way ticket six feet downward – or outward, at the majority of the crowd and its influence – the Sheffield crew had turned up in its entirety, as well as others from further afield, some looking like they were here to book their own plots for the coming weeks. All I knew was that Mick had a problem carrying it, and no matter how hard he strove, the nudges, the shattering smiles, he wasn't going to make it.

Slicing the service in two at some path of righteousness, his voice ricocheted white wall to white wall: 'You!' The index was sword-like, indenting the axis of its target, opposite aisle: Wiffa's back-to-front swastika. It looked like it had popped up and presented itself for the cause.

'Gentlemen, gentlemen,' entreated the pastor, 'in these sad times, troubles burrow deep, where emotions rise high…'

'Out!'

'*Please,* gentlemen!'

'Mick, Mick,' the name ferreted through from all sides, reminding me, of all the nervous moments, of a computer game recently installed in The Grouse's main road end: a *Pac-Man*; the new crowd aimed for that thing before the bar.

I was ready for anything, here or afterward. My dad had ordered me to look after Mick.

'Please, gentlemen,' echoed the appeal. Still, the next line did the trick, amazing the Soul congregation, baffling the family, and putting Mick's wrath in check: 'This is the *last* thing The Duke would have wanted.'

Only an uncontrollable, understandable, titter broke the hush.

Jed elbowed his friend, nodded toward the arched entrance and got up. 'Sorry,' he whispered to all *en route*.

''Sort that bastard out later,' Mick promised, beneath a cough.

Vowing to be by his side, my use of 'brother' was inept. But then it didn't take Mick long to readjust that figurative visor. I could never be so strong.

We vacated the chapel to a backing of *Nothing Can Stop Me*. The pastor sang along.

After which, the Soul contingent congregated at one side of the hole, the family at the other.

Sharing hugs and tears between the two groups, April asked me where I'd gotten to, or had been, this time for something to say. My feet hurt, I told her, laconic as it sounded. She called me 'precious', like it seemed she always would, squeezing tight, wetting my neck; she'd warned me not to walk about in bare feet, she said. And before moving on, she reminded me to keep the faith. Her clenched fist punched me sideways...

It was the same evening my dad invited me to a drink up at our local, an invite sounding not as far out of the blue as he would have liked.

So words had been spoken.

He pointed to the shelter's graffiti like he'd just noticed, said it looked like somebody had got it bad. His head was back to the fore when he alluded to the girl whose name he hadn't pronounced for however long: 'She'll come round again.'

I still believed he possessed magic powers: 'Nathalie?'

'No,' he laughed, dropping his head. 'One like her, mark my words.'

Our silence articulated the rest, everything we'd hoped to say for a while.

Mick and Uncle Pete were waiting for us inside. They held out pints on our approach.

The evening was a reflective one, for obvious reasons. I couldn't remember feeling so close to other people.

\* \* \* \* \*

The Entrance Bar turned into a bit of a routine – *I* now barred myself from the other side, where someone would unendingly feel the need to accompany his/her drink with The Detroit Emeralds...

We didn't limit our summer evenings' conferences to The Grouse alone, either, Mick and me. At weekends, with nowt to lose and a police escort resembling two lines of dominoes from the outskirts, we took in every existing night club the city's centre had to offer, rubbing shoulders with the New Romantics and the staunch-if-exacerbated-by-it-all Jam disciples.

That said, we didn't go looking for girls, because Mick was happily married and oozed such sentiment. And yet they, too, seemingly flowed on tap. Whether our indifference was the key, or Mick held some female-attracting magnet like an old habit in that pocketed left hand of his, I couldn't work out. But the bigger the club, the bigger the party.

I suggested that on future outings we stick to the Crazy Daisy – or 'Crazy Daisies', as the Two Petes called it – one of the smaller, Heaven 17-type joints. Mick may have been used to the lustful adoration but I wasn't – Geoff's last Angela showed *far* more interest in me of late, more than she ever had back in the chair.

The more genuine interest came from another, equally cycloptic, auburn-wedged lady.

'You go in The Grouse,' she called over, breaking off from a futuristic, lopsided groove. 'You stand in the old men's side.'

Well, I told her, if she ever hoped to see me back in the young side, I'd need to see her other eye first. Yes, they looked great together.

*Love Action* calling, she returned to the floor with another chuckle.

Mick deemed she was a model with a sense of humour. But we'd be entering those winter months before I'd pluck up the courage to ask her out.

Summer rolled on, my sole break being one of the two August 'Sheffield Works Weeks' I took in Skegness with my mum, dad and Sam. I'd begun to feel sorry for them without my grom and me – it was worth it just to see my dad's face when I suggested it. In truth, I also missed that murky brown sea. And Sands, which I made for the last time, thanks to *two* young things from good old, reliable Ilkeston.

\* \* \* \* \*

That Monday evening, as my dad and me soaked up the *Courage* in the Jolly Fisherman, the interested ladies caught my eye the moment Smokey R's *Being With You* caught my ear. I showed off the Mick-training with a fair-minded wink. Straight after which, they, looking like they'd had no training whatsoever, made a semi-reddened rush over from the other side of the bar, to enquire whether we'd be escorting them there, to Sands. If competition was inexistent, my dad still looked impressed... and still thought he'd run a mile, to a caravan between Skegness and Vickers Point, post-a furtive 'If you can't be good, you only get *one* pregnant... 'Can't afford both.'

He'd come to overestimate my ability with the opposite sex: *I*'d brushed off a lady with a French h.

He needn't have worried. If I entered Sands with one on either arm, it wasn't the case on exit. It wasn't like I cared that much, either. For when our deejay informed us he'd received a nameless request for Gene Chandler's *Get Down*, like in thumbs up ad infinitum, à la Macca, I did just that. I celebrated who and where I was.

I'd gotten it right.

221

Sooner or later, the entire club got down. Or rather sat down, in unison, silken, sun-kissed legs and arms enfolding me into delirium, as dictated by The Gap Band's *Oops Up Side Your Head*; the faster I rowed the faster I'd reach my sub-pier rapture.

Emancipation, however, came too early, bare back of the girl in front copping the lot, slapped on like an ultraviolet continent.

She sprang to her feet: 'Dirty gett!'

Not that she'd minded being bitten to pieces.

I didn't dare to ask her, or the one behind, for a moonlit stroll after that. I'd had my fun and would live to be sick again.

The stuffed dog in the old bat's window looked more amusing a second time round, too.

But then leaving at the end of the week was as difficult as any other...

\* \* \* \* \*

Dealing with these verging-on-winter evenings was more so.

September's second half, darkness not creeping but pouring in. Obliged, as I now was, I felt, to heed Sam's passionate play-lists throughout. And to be considerate toward his untiring demands I recount stories of old as new – I had no new ones to tell.

Favourites being the likes of when, a year or two back, we'd ended up in The Limit Club, in town again, where Paul Young and his Q Tips had adopted a soulful reputation.

I'd never known such a booze-ridden sticky floor, though it hardly merited the number of times Jed fell down onto it: 'Not bad for some white bloke!' Down he went. Out there and by my side at the same time. ''Like his cravat.'

I hadn't noticed anyone's scarf for looking after him.

But sticky wood it would always be for Sam's sticky ears.

\* \* \* \* \*

Or a winter-weekend coastal adventure, the less said about the vehicle the better.

My best friend and me were off to a Cleethorpes all-dayer with three Wigan bandits, who got up to all sorts of nefarious activity *en route.* Jed's main supplier was waiting in Grimsby – I'd told Sam he was owed money for some far off tiling job. I was to play straight minder, strength in numbers, as if. Our bandidos decided they were only dropping us off after all, and couldn't have escaped more speedily.

It wasn't the twitching curtains for lack of. But the twitching eyes.

Floodlights to the fore, I fastened the trench coat and begged Jed not to mention football. He scanned the street's habitation like he'd come to buy the lot, climbed a pair of steps and knocked against a door twice his size, which had possibly been made to measure, going by the size of the lady who welcomed us through. We were told to wait on as able-bodied a sofa as the vehicle we'd landed in.

She didn't say anything else, for busily scrutinizing yesterday's local televised match and ogling girls in *Vanity Fair* in one go.

The much younger thing was the personality.

Strictly underage, she tugged at my leather sleeve and pleaded in whispers that I follow her up the *Adam's Family*-esque stairs. And when I smiled my best smile, sighed my best sigh – ''Got to get off, I'm afraid' – she tried her luck on Jed. And then back to me, as in doggedly as does it, like I might have jealously changed my mind.

The part at which Sam convulsed was the 'rescue' scene, as the kitchen door flew open to a background grind of a washing machine, and there stood our hostess' partner in a blue and white, Polka Dot one piece, which fell above hairy knees. However short the dress, it still outdid the beard, which dropped only to stick-straight hips. ''You here for your stuff?' s/he asked, *Kojak* cigarette bouncing between teeth. S/he didn't wait for an answer, but pointed to the minimalist number our young nymph was barely wearing above her waist: 'Roxy, get that off!' The top should have been in the washing machine with the rest.

I wanted to run, proposed we do so, to find Jed on his knees.

'Yeah,' he replied, for the stuff, concealing himself behind yours truly. His damp cheeks plunged into my ear once he'd made it back up.

Roxy removed the top and little-finger flung it to our hirsute Greta Garbo, before sitting her flat-chested self on Jed's knee and stroking his hair, guessing he'd shown the first signs of cracking.

'Go an' get 'em,' Greta nodded, to our randy Roxy.

'Come on,' purred the latter, twiddling the old French crop.

'Go an' *get* 'em!' bawled the enormous hostess, an explosion. ''Tryin' to watch a match!'

We regained composure to the thud of feet on the stairs, in slow but evident descent.

'Alright, lads?' the young bald twins greeted in chorus – Greta's antitheses, eyebrow-less – post-a moment's weighing up. They were identical to being... one being, appearing to move and speak at the same time. When one looked as if he was going to pull the gear from a matching combat khaki, thigh-side pocket, it materialised from the adjacent pocket of the other.

''From Sheffield, yeah?' enquired whichever.

'Yeah,' my best friend smiled, ''all got us crosses to bear.'

They laughed simultaneously.

Jed glimpsed inside his parcel and turned out another crumpled fiver.

''Got an all-dayer to get to,' we said, rising simultaneously.

'Who put you on to them?' I asked, panting past the football ground, tears of comic relief flowing like rain.

'Some bloke I know from Leeds.'

''Can't wait to meet him!'

* * * * *

I never told Sam that, just before we'd left the mad house, the twins had offered us a 'quick un' with Roxy at a tenner each, or that only Jed's quick thinking had saved us from any kind of further sexual harassment, his expounding on the idea we'd come straight from Wigan and so 'it' would have been nigh on impossible on a night's worth of gear. What I told him was they'd hoped to sell her because she embarrassed them in front of every man that called by.

'Embarrassed *them*?' he spluttered.

224

And this was my dilemma, with these rituals: my deviations meant his heroes remained his heroes.

It was Mick who'd asked that Sam hear nothing of *his* brother's fall, same day as the burial, and I'd got an even bigger load on him.

One of Sam's favourites was just after Christmas, a Sunday Windmill session, the evening The Duke had almost lost his life but for deflecting the inebriated knife blows onto his arms.

We couldn't work out how he, of all regular states, managed to pull that one off.

\* \* \* \* \*

Again it was all down to Wiffa, for provoking five or so, then harmless, partiers heading on to an estate further afield the week previous. Seven ale-evenings passed, I hoped they'd have forgotten.

For this Sunday, they turned up in bigger numbers.

I thought it done with spitting a tooth from three or four punches thrown as we made our stumbles down the stairs; I felt happy supposing you won and lost some. Observing the twenty odd pile off at the next stop was to realise they'd lured us into a false sense of security.

'Split up an' run!'

If I despised taking an order on Wiffa's part, by then I was already running over moving cars on Tinsley Viaduct.

The constable – another 'belter', as my dad would go on to portray her – knocked on our door at two the following morning, to inform us 'Neil McIntyre was caught and stabbed after a skirmish on the 35 bus. Am I right, Phillip?'

'What?'

'That there *was* a skirmish?'

'Oh, yeah...'

'He'll be okay,' she assured, 'thanks to his reflexes. I think he frightened them off.'

I assumed she'd got the wrong name. But then came another worry: April.

'She's fine. She was caught with' – looking down to her pad – 'Chris. They let him off as well, for staying by her... according to *his* statement at any rate.'

So chivalry's not dead, read my dad's half-smile.

She agreed, peeking from beneath a chessboard headpiece.

Whatever my take on it, Sam would never sleep again.

It made the front page of the local that evening, columned under the heading 'In Brief', title incorporating 'Gang War'. The short article depicted how one valiant young man had battled off a multitude of blades to save his princess, while another had whisked her to safety in the meantime. Or words not too far off that effect.

I scratched my head. 'This paper makes 'em up better than me...'

\* \* \* \* \*

It was in this exhausted frame of mind – it had already been a long evening and my mum and dad wouldn't be back for an hour yet – I decided to take a bum-freezer cigarette-break on the doorstep, along to JJ Barnes' *Baby Please Come Back Home*. I embraced a full-featured full moon, and wondered why it all now seemed so clear. A good half of them, Soul singers, bemoaned the same: having been unable to see until now.

And with every nicotine inhalation, I exhaled a cord of independent halos, each encircling and hugging that golden coin before withering away through its own passion. Was it really *the*...

'... 'Same moon,' nodded my old hero, propping up my mum best he could, for fear she'd use his roses as a bed – he loved those roses. He conceded it would look nicer still over 'that North Bay' of mine, the one I 'kept goin' on about.'

I was ready to ask why they were back so early, but one look at my mum and everything was as clear as the night sky.

'An' where's that young Soul *f'natic*?' she slurred.

'Aye,' my dad sighed, 'she's a beauty', referring to the moon. And, ''Can't take her anywhere', referring to the obvious. He tapped me with a foot to let him pass, just as my mum decided she'd let me off with the three pounds I'd need to pay back tomorrow evening. He reminded her I'd not borrowed them in the first place, as with last week.

'Oh, yeah,' she sang, tapping the sofa's lap, 'well *if* you had, cos... cos...' All Guess-what-I've-gone-and-done-like, she fumbled with her purse and tried a semi-functional hand at creating a fan from a fistful of pound notes: '... der derrrrrrr!' Which spread across the carpet like from an autumn gust of wind, one lying flat across Brainy's bemused face, another wedging itself between the bars of the gas fire.

My dad made the dive: 'Christ, Joan, get a grip!' And smiled: 'Twenty-eight quid, eh!' A few more of those and he deduced he'd be able to give up the grind.

Thinking records and *Fred Perry*s, Sam harvested the rest of the bingo-win, while his mum stabbed at his midriff with her fingertips: 'My likkle Soul *f'na*tic.'

It took no more than a joke on my part to set my dad off, that were my mum to make the win a *twice*-weekly habit, *I*'d give up the grind, too.

'Phillip' – rarely did he call me Phillip, his own bingo-win comment no longer relevant – '*how* many times – We can't live without it!'

I pointed out that enough people were doing so.

'That's different!' They weren't living at all. 'Imagine what's being bred in this country as we speak, the lot for nowt, that's what they want. An' the genuine folk cop it every time.' You had to earn in this life. There was nothing wrong with the system when not abused, but 'by God, it's abused!'

'Phyllis,' my mum endeavoured. 'Phill... Pete!' And nodded off again.

''Knockin' out kids like rabbits for it, they are...'

Abandoned, my mum's intoxicated interruptions neither frequent nor generous, I argued the case for the system abuser.

'You can't think like that, not wantin' to work an' still wantin' the lot!' It only led to disrespect for everyone, 'not workin' an' pullin' together...'

But Toby Legend's *Time Will Pass You By* cut his flow; Sam knew what he was doing.

'We never had it so good, kid,' his dad eventually sighed, no longer speaking for a previewed future but a reviewed past. He turned his head to the fire, and half-whispered: 'I did my best, you know, for Jed.'

Sam's finger braked dead in the *Atlantic* section.

As hard as it was, his dad went on, 'seeing an adopted son go down in the line o' fire', well, he had to protect his closest, the army taught him that. To slice a solemnity he'd not sought to create, he asked whether he'd ever mentioned his having *been* in the army, which didn't work, and he was showing the first signs of lamenting the coal's absence. His 'blood sons' were the ones that counted in the end – 'It's bad enough worryin' about two.' But he was proud of them, even if he didn't say it enough…

My mum then sliced the atmosphere with a wail: 'The *room*'s spinnin'!'

Ignoring her a second longer, he pushed me to give Jed his best, judged we'd been on too many holidays together to not care. And his eyes widened: 'If *you* can sort him out…'

My mum now attempted to raise herself without use of her legs, a stranded whale of sorts: '*Pe*ter!'

And as my dad hauled her to the kitchen sink, I ruffled Sam's hair in a sign it was all downhill from here…

'What did he mean,' my brother asked, watching me tuck him into bed, fall onto my own, and fiddle with the transistor, 'about Jed goin' "down in the line o' fire"?'

''Fired from his job,' I said, in a tone of closure.

'Haah… cool…'

I was tired, felt as if five years of insomnia had regrouped, were staging all-out attacks. But I wouldn't complain, for my nights still formed the best part of my days. Here where I sailed on a bed of imaginings.

'And *what* a Dylan – That's not singin'!' Sam sniped, to Bob's *I Shall Be Released*. Or did I just imagine…?

*'… Did you say something about stroking my violin, Phillip?'* as ever she teased.

*And so I readjusted my posture best I could, given my amorous little reverie didn't want to… let go…*

'… Get up, Phillip…'
'… Let go.'

'… Get up…'

'… Let…'

'It's your dad,' she spelt out, in all its uncomplicated severity, when I'd never so wanted to dream, to put this thing down and move on. Except this thing, via bilious breath, wouldn't let go: 'It's your dad, love.' This crossroads. Pleasure cruise cancelled, sir. Time to be a man.

Again I readjusted my posture: 'What do you mean?'

Afraid she might scream, she clutched, whispered: 'He's very ill, love.' Before tendering me the cruellest of batons, along with a bit of a Dad-ism: 'So get your clothes on, get to that phone, and run like the wind.'

I skipped the stairs for a leap, shoes for time, and accelerated with every barefoot step into a neon fright of dark, chased by the horns-less devil himself. And I ran and wept, and I ran and wept, *"It's your dad, love"* carving me up for violent want of a never-nearing line, a red windowed box… run… run… run… nine… nine… nine…

'Which service do you require?' enquired a young female voice.

'My dad.'

'Okay, so which service do you require?'

'My dad.'

'And what's wrong with him?'

'He's…'

'Yes?'

'… very ill, love.'

'Where is he?'

''Very ill… home.'

'Where's…?'

Where – oh-where, like it might still be if I squeezed hard enough! But it was too late. And so I spat my wasteland thirst: 'Fif two… Wellin'ton Street.'

'Okay, we'll be…'

Getting back proved quicker. To lightened bedrooms, to rotting sashes risen, cheeks between palms, moonlike eyes. And to the gravest cut of all: there, eclipsing Stan's ageing milk float, hovered the surgical advance guard, coruscating blue bullet beams in knowing search for the culprit, for the enemy of wrongs, like a nocturnal Nazi arrest.

They'd come to take him away, my dad, my hero, first ever.

Arms now free to cling one to the other, he halted before the vehicle's shutters and, as in some last request, turned and hurled me the ever engrained gaze. Eyes washed out, lips dead blue and dead. However could it be? That they could they say everything, word-free?

They were taking him away, my dad, my hero, first ever...

'Why didn't you knock me up?' Stan tapped in gentle disapproval, smocked as yet uncapped, eyes collapsing to these bare, bloody stubs, like I looked for any excuse. '*I* don't know,' he told some imaginary friend, 'the first time I need him to, he flies straight past...'

Only on catching a bit of Sam, lost in a daybreak world of neighbourly hugs, would I know how to reply. It was called having the world at my feet, I said. And I thought I'd start making proper use of them.

I contagiously dropped my head.

37

*'Thy friendship oft has made my heart to ache;*
*Do be my enemy... for friendship's sake...'*

I'd been pacing the perimeters of this exclusive unit for some time. Thirty good hours, going by my mum's count, four o'clock on a Saturday afternoon.

'Come and get a bit o' tea!' she tried again.

I wanted to tell my sedated dad how United had done.

An ever supportive Stan had contacted Jeff immediately. But my uncle's generous body would then need propping away from the phone by the generous body of Auntie Pat, before he could get down here.

He proved stronger today, for Sam's sake.

'Come on,' said Stan.

Stan had finished his shifts and sailed down on a milk float, twice, as well as floated off around seven yesterday evening to get Mick here in the quicker vehicle. The young milkman reckoned no-one in their right mind would want to know how United had done.

Mick didn't say anything, just bumped my arm.

Indestructible, he'd looked yesterday, set for another night on the town with his adopted brother. Once here, I'd had all on getting rid of him, as with bringing him round to his Saturday morning shift – he now delivered bread – which he completed by nine and was back donating a *Younger's* bitter breakfast from beneath green grapes bought lord-knows-where.

Uncle Pete, my dad's old partner in laughs, deemed things were depressing enough, without telling him how United had done...Fine mess they'd gotten themselves into this time.

He'd not made yesterday at all. Rather than accept a lift from our herald of woe, he'd "just about collapsed on the spot", quit

231

The Grouse by the back and run on home, ''crying like a baby''. He got here this morning. And here he'd remained.

The final backing derived from someone resembling another unofficial relative, newly cut pinstripe below an old Tony Curtis. My dad's foreman. Inspector Comrade; the all-rectifying tool merchant, as I'd deduced a couple of hours ago on his tendering my mum a wage packet and bouquet of flowers. Straight after which he grasped one of my dad's needle-infested hands and broke down: 'Sorry, sorry...' As if troubled by something greater than this: 'I'm so sorry...' My mum consoled him, patted a shoulder and offered a hanky. And he, appearing more fragile than young Sam for a while, collected himself in time.

If only my dad could have witnessed it all! And I knew what he'd make of our nurse: a young belter was how he'd describe her, no sooner free of this wiry mess.

She told us he'd 'suffered a massive heart attack, and so could remain in Intensive Care for up to two weeks.'

'At forty three?' No, she'd gotten it wrong while ever my brother clung to my side.

'He's not on his own,' she said, rubbing a thumb across Sam's soothe-soiled forehead, digging for something more encouraging. ''Seems to be an epidemic. But we've managed to save him, so he'll be fine.' She dropped her eyes: 'Won't he!'

Sam had heard promises of this kind before.

When my mum beckoned him home, he held his head my way, searching for support I was no longer able to give, looking every bit the young boy he once was.

Uncle Pete reckoned he'd done longer than Ken Dodd. Except Sam didn't twig.

Mick got there with something domestic, asked how he felt having gotten through his first all-nighter, and whether he believed them overrated.

My bushwhacked brother.

For all I'd striven to keep from him, never had I envisaged anything like these last thirty or so hours. And as I wouldn't have left my dad's side like I owned the place – visiting hours were broached a couple of days on – he wouldn't have left mine. He spent most of the time with his head resting on his dad's bed, lifting it only for our angels in peaked caps, who'd wake him

232

with lemonade and hospital food – the 'poor little soul' copped more than your average helping of ice-cream, too, if my tired eyes served correctly. Staying put also meant allowing our mum to go and cry her heart out on pretext of feeding the cat. She'd prop us up again back here.

Good old mum… but the poor young soul.

\* \* \* \* \*

It was for Sam's sake I wished I could have restrained my ire yesterday, and not, no sooner his dad hurtled away, gone about a barefoot-beating of that chair, blaming the – 'Bastard!' – thing for all this, persuaded it had been eating him alive: it already looked bigger. A huge, imitation-leather-clad smirk.

My mum squeezed her youngest for all the world.

I flew upstairs and ripped out the big black box. It was, in effect, a revulsion-teeming-heart of a rip, the – 'Bastard!' – thing opening out to nothing but vinyl… if still unsnap-able. I pulled a second – third, dazzling labels breaking *me* to pieces, backed by the eulogy of *'a bit o' Garnet Garnet…'*

And it was here I captured the genuine leather-clad peacock of old: creases, smell, grin – right where my beef lay. My dad got on fine with the records, it was more they represented slices of 'him' beneath my bed. He who'd turned his back on his real family the moment the going had gotten tough. No, he hadn't gone down in the line of fire, but chosen an easier path.

I placed the vinyl back, for my dad's sake, I told myself.

And so to the books.

I'd hidden them beneath Sam's mattress, work of an ingenious mind, I'd judged. If they were no longer in the precise place or order, the top of the pile remained the same. Front page glorified, was he: *Suedehead,* for we, the too young and impressionable. I poked, bent, prodded and punched, trod on and kicked. And might have torn had I opened the pages.

I pressed them down on Sam's sore snout, pointed to where they were heading; said he was 'lucky' it wasn't the records!

'Whatever you say, Phill,' his red eyes replied.

I dropped the thumbed pages of my chosen school reading-list into the backyard bin like scraps of an evening's fish and chips supper. Or as uncaringly as *Hawkins'* arrogant *Abercrombie* would allow, covering them with the new, less boisterous rubber lid.

'I think we all know how lucky he is,' said my mum, as I fell into the sofa at her other side, opposite Sam…

* * * * *

We'd take the ray of a mid-September sun-up as a signal to get here, via a smoky top-deck, rubbing shoulders with a hoard of payday merry workers. Here, to this exclusive unit, where I yielded to the common sense of these good people, here when it mattered. And swallowed the bitter taste of those who were not.

They, who'd pop round solely to see my dad, whether admitting it or not. They, who'd disappear from the concert room for half an hour... Okay, so Macca had an alibi, as did Jenny, for that matter: she was in Malaga enjoying the first of many foreign holidays to come, until Sunday, recovering from the 'early' birth of the first of many babies to come. Little Loretta was residing with her other grandparents.

But, oh, Jed…

Mick made headway assuring us my dad would still be here when we got back.

Duty prevented me pushing him on it.

We men thus gave my mum a private moment, by floundering into the real light of day, promising to meet up later for a pint. Sam received congratulations abundant for his bravery, reward: a night from the front. To get his head down and restock for the day ahead.

Jeff escorted Uncle Pete. The rest of us huddled into Stan's glossy-green wotsit, to a light backing of *She's Gone,* Tavares' version.

Sam wouldn't be up to educating this time round.

My dad's inspector had gotten here by bus and wouldn't put anyone out accepting a lift. He cut something of a lost figure, faltering away to the iron-gated entrance…

Mick stayed over for one of my mum's real cups o' tea, so he insisted. Sam was already being put to bed.

It was an odd moment, awkward, Mick and me gravitating to the kitchen. He stood by the stove, I burrowed into the trench. And out we peered into what looked like an empty room, barring that chair...

... that chair. From which I heard a voice of hope. A voice assuring me Tony Currie was leaving our United for Leeds only because he wanted to stick around in Yorkshire until it was time to come home again. I heard a pledge through Saturday night-ale breath, as *Emma Peel* walked out on *John Steed*, that I'd be in love with the new girl a Saturday on. It was actually seconds on: *Emma* twiddled an index, said *Steed* liked his tea stirred anticlockwise, *Tara King* smiled, and I stopped crying right there.

He did that, my dad... said the right thing.

Mick thought we'd have to 'start gettin' us *Lucky Bags* from another shop.'

And at this never-so-right a juncture, I spilled the beans. 'I met this girl,' I said. 'Nathalie. With a French 'h'.'

Mick offered no trace of what he was thinking, gazing somewhere in the direction of the gas fire. 'Where are they now?' he asked in time, without shifting his eyes, or elaborating on who ''they'' happened to be.

'Maybe I chose the wrong song,' I said.

He suddenly made for the front door, forgetting the tea for what looked like a need of fresh air.

'Does that chair look bigger to you?' I asked him, passing through.

'No,' he said, categorically, stopping in his tracks. 'And besides, I reckon that Chuck Jackson o' yours was only ever a black Tom Jones anyhow...'

I reciprocated the smile, familiar with his benevolent game.

'You'll never change,' he winked, once outside.

'We don't change, Mick, we evolve.'

'What happened to him, by the way?'

'Who?'

'Tom Jones?'

'No idea.'

'Me neither,' he said. 'With a French 'h', eh!'

And off he went.

I had no idea how long I'd been gaping out at the Shirecliffe skyline, its unflagging antenna amid already gilded-leaves, when I spotted the French crop ferreting about the top of Bashforth's privet, like a long-legged hedgehog.

He'd gotten word and turned up – I knew he would. I closed the door, to rehearse a lean against the outside wall, and then opened it again.

Jed peeped over the hedge-top, at the living-room window, as if nailed to the spot, prior to showing himself for what he'd become: an unsightly muddle barring the hairdo. 'We've got to be there tonight,' he half-whispered, 'it's the last un!'

I must have looked clueless.

From a shuffle up the path, he whipped out a pair of tickets, not quite planting one on my nose, tickets claiming Wigan Casino's immediate closure, as of this last ever all-nighter. And he called me 'bro''.

'Where's Wiffa?'

''Got five years, for nicking' a lollypop-lady's lollypop. If you get my meanin'.'

I didn't get anything.

'But so what,' he shrugged, another peep to the window, 'it's us two, bro', 'got to be!'

I'd never known anger until this instance, I realised. And a very visible anger at that, going by how my old friend reeled back. ''No good lookin' up there,' I said, 'he's on a life-support machine in an Intensive Care Unit... if you get my meanin'.'

Jed clasped a ticket as if to stay standing. The second fell, he none the wiser.

'So you can pick that shit up' – he could keep his fallen ticket. ''Be goin' long after you, that place.' And I gently pulled the trigger: 'Now fuck off before I kill you.'

He lurched away, fell at one point. And I should have felt better for it.

I'd have felt much better had my ex-style-counsellor supposed this great gag had gotten out of hand.

There the ticket lay.

I rummaged my head into hanging coats, hunted a major loss. And for a moment, I seized the scent of a wintry night gone, in a word or two: *'Lucky bastard, you... Do you know?'*

'He will, won't he?' Sam probed, tugging at my shirt without looking up.

'What?'

'"Come back"? My dad.'

''Course he will. Come on, you're supposed to be in bed.'

'But what's Jed done?'

His dad's *Old Spice* at hand, my mum was quick to ask: 'What are you doin', effing an' blinding in the street?'

''Never blinded once.'

''Hardly recognised the poor sod.' And as we tumbled to the sofa, she insisted I get out and make it up with him.

Instead I pulled Sam onto my knees, for the first in too long a time.

My mum thought I'd have done better telling Shylock to, '... you know...' – miming – '... f... off. For a month or two at least.' He'd be round this evening; we were out yesterday.

When a knock *was* sounded at the door, Sam sprang, believing Jed was back for a retry.

'Does this belong to you, young man?' my mum's prediction asked our boy in stripy pyjamas.

The reply was terse: 'Fuck off!'

My mum stayed put.

There was no second knock, though Sam did take his time returning to view. Doing so, he thrust the door open like a boy on a second mission, brandishing a spotless pink and white striped ticket below indignant eyes.

''Thought you said Wigan was closed!'

6

## 38

*'We are all in the gutter, but some of us are looking at the stars.'*

And so back to my recurring dream, the one I was once woken from on my 49 bus, by the rare attraction in the coat. To the same musical backing of Mr. J's *I Only Get This Feeling,* it went like this:

*'That's how to spill coke down your shirt,' Jed laughed.*

*But some things were worth it, I supposed, if very few. 'On my way,' I promised, to the one Soul brother who'd understand me like no other.*

*Witness to another miracle* (you know the one), *he returned my fervour with an incredulous nod – Boy, he oozed chic! Copper-coloured, fully-buttoned Fred Perry shirt, red and white stripes embellishing the collar. The matching red Levi's; 'deserts' to die for. And the black, three gold-buttoned box...*

'... duck. Your box, duck – I say, you've dropped your sandwich b...'

'Oh, so I have...'

''Must've dropped off yourself,' she snorted.

'As always.'

''Young lad like you, on a Friday night?'

November's first. Season's lights up a month already, bus stuffed with end-of-week factory fall-outs and the ''Like to get my Christmas-shoppin' done before the rush starts' contingent. Hence why I'd opted for the Attercliffe bus in the first place – my regular was full. As was this one, like I said, stuffed. I'd used the lady's shoulder because somebody was sitting on one of mine.

But then it wasn't like I was learning anything new.

''Nice box,' she added, as I pressed the sea-blue, see-through number to my nose. 'You want to look after it, 'last you a lifetime, money well spent.'

Failing to locate another world, I became anxious she understood the purchase wasn't my doing but my mum's: '*I* was happy with a bread bag!'

She deemed my mum was right, folding her arms before changing the subject. The lights weren't what they used to be, she said, and chuckled at my telling her I'd not noticed, that I'd already dropped off. I wouldn't go into how I believed them too early, or why I'd slammed my forty pence down on the driver's tinny counter for whistling that *Wish I Could Be Home For...* thing too loudly, as I was sure she'd view me as some prematurely ripened humbug. What I would like to have done was to keep talking more about my mum. I'd have sung her praises till the cows came home.

But the moment seemed to have passed me by.

My mum.

Burdened, she was, with my dad's entrenched depression, which had dug in whilst he was out in Intensive Care; as well as with his refusal to claim benefits – he preferred pride to shame. Propped us up proper, and I'd no idea where we'd have been without her. Cleaning jobs here – paid in hand, needless to say – shopping there, meals in between, dusting upheld on a subsidiary level.

I helped out where I could. Tried harder at work, got in on Saturday mornings – Alcrap didn't know what to make of it. And I gave her more board, never losing hope my efforts be of a provisional measure.

She had all on.

As for my dad, at least he was now able to see Madame *Shake 'n' Vac* for what she really was: 'The bleedin' idiot!' Though I'd have preferred the gormless glance. King Arthur had evolved into The Antichrist, The Ripper into something worse – they'd been in league all along. And this was after the doctor had advised him to refrain from watching the news until he was up to it again – like he'd never been up to it. Had he managed to lift the lump hammer, he'd have cracked the world in two, what with this new free time he had on those ex-rocky-calloused hands, hands that were fast beginning to look like they belonged to young Sam.

Mick was wrong about the chair, by the way. It *had* grown, by a good three stones' worth to my reckoning.

For the twice-weekly visits of Uncle Jeff, Pete, Mick, Stan and Comrade Alan, it was like being back in The Grouse. Until they left. With heart-splintering honesty, 'Has this really happened to me?' my dad would ask, waving them on with a sorry smile through the double sash, before declining into his hanky.

My mum would then step in from the kitchen to pick up our chins.

Jenny's visits were also more frequent. One minute baby Loretta would be butting 'grandy''s nose for lack of head-control, the next, both would be sobbing for England – she'd just be hungry. And the rare wave of family joy would flow away with the undertow.

''Think she'll remember me, Joan?'

'Here we go,' we'd chorus, whisperers all.

As for little Sam, his life had become a strain, too. His dad was unable to veil his fears, petrified he might never see his youngest grow, be there as he'd been for me. And the lad had a couple of hours to swallow before I got home.

To shield him from the downstairs gloom, once more I did my bit: I nursed his withering interest in the 45s. The next step would have meant me packing in work, but I couldn't think like that anymore.

Sam's once wondrous world, the snow-sprinkled, golden-maple pledges – my old wood, talc and Mr. J – had crumbled to pieces. Why had Jed looked 'such a mess that day?' he'd ask. And in line with some classroom rumour, was it true about Macca's fatal accident?

Worse than all of this, he knew he'd never again use 'My dad could fight your dad' in the old school battleground.

Ferocious, was his cynicism, for such a young boy.

The place to channel his anger, his incomprehension, should have been down at his brother-in-law's new martial arts club a couple of evenings a week – which the latter had opened on the new parents' return from poor old Malaga. The glitch being Sam was returning home black and blue, courtesy of the somewhat over-keen demonstrations. But it was our zealous brother-in-law's first club; things would surely calm down in time.

Besides, I was positive Sam would get his own back one day...

And for the old crowd?

Well, Chris and April looked happy enough, as I made out bumping into them for the first time since that black day. If anything, April was looking younger, renewed, like... she'd also calmed down a tad. She was always going to tease me, ask what on earth I'd had better to do with myself the night of Wigan's supposedly last-ever overnight attraction – it could still have been open for all she knew. She then expressed regret at the news of my dad, and, link not so tenuous, went on to depict how Paul had sold the vinyl, in one great bulk, to buy some flashy new car, his dad having put the other half toward.

I'd never have believed Paul, of all people, was capable of selling his Soul.

She eventually offered due relief concerning Jed, who hadn't ended his days in Wigan Wallgate after all, for a woman he'd needed to get home to: some young hairdresser he'd met, as luck would have it. A certain Vicky from Ilkeston. April pinched my cheek, said they'd been going steady for some time. Over two years, according to Chris, who reckoned Vicky was even worse than Jed for drugs.

Ilkley. Ilkeston... easy mistake to make.

My reaction was to bring up something unconnected: I described how, weeks previous, one late evening, with my dad locked away in his private room, I might have ended up in a ward akin. The Grouse behind me, I'd debated whether to get straight home or first indulge in a Coronation Butty, when a stolen, police-pursued vehicle cancelled my dilemma by cancelling out a red light and disrobing me of my *Levi's*. At Casualty, I spent the night consoling some young sweetheart who'd trodden on a broken bottle outside Penny's Night Club.

'*You* and feet!' roared my old Soul sister...

*Jed was alright, then, whatever that meant. A pair together. And for quite a time...*

Then again, he wasn't the only one. I now had my own senorita to think about, of the auburn wedged variety. My Human Leaguer.

We were off out tonight.

I was meeting Angela – who'd never set foot in Geoff's – outside The Old Blue Bell – Crazy Daisy's neighbour. And because today was Friday, Mick and his wife were escorting me there, since he wouldn't play gooseberry and I wouldn't forego his company.

I wouldn't stay out too late, mind you. Not with work tomorrow.

I'd been seeing her off and on over the last month, in The Grouse's re-refurbished concert room, or 'Entertainment Suite'; more emphasis on the acts, a watered down jukebox, and a place looking entirely new – Mick and me were avoiding the old men's side until the comedy resumed; Pete was avoiding the place altogether.

She turned out to be of Irish lineage, Angela, her parents the couple of which the inebriated husband had challenged me to a swearing duel. He didn't remember, of course, as she'd report back, but I'd still try: 'My mate had noticed a couple o' girls, so he poured his vinegar supper down my mohairs.'

'Down your what?'

'My mohairs ... – You an' your Human League!'

'What did he do that for?'

''Cos he was wapped.'

'What'?'

'Christ, it's not like I'm talkin' Godward...!'

'Talkin' 'what'?'

'Never mind.'

'Well, you'd do good beatin' my dad at swearing. He's won prizes for it – He's Irish!'

I had to laugh.

And how effortlessly I found myself at the back end of the brisk evening recalled. Or the front end of a breathtaking night.

243

But yes, it wasn't the first time…

\* \* \* \* \*

And anyhow, all that's history.

''Lookin' a bit white, darlin',' my travel companion nudges from nowhere, or another silhouetted mill. ''Nothin' *I* said, is it?'

'No.'

I observe an elderly man step onto the bus, triumphant. He parks his backside up front, chatters with the driver, as might a best friend, like he's known him all his life. And I recall my grom pointing him out some years back.

He hasn't changed much. Or evolved.

How fortunate for me, then, I've come a long way. Upshot being the old factory aficionado won't have the same effect on me this time round.

Or not as much.

I've learned a bit on bridges crossed between then and now, on buses in particular. Like what's meant by keeping the faith. Or how to control my breathing during moments such as these.

The funny part, though, has to be the ancient soul's sandwich box. Same colour as mine – now there's a fluke if ever there were! That very same…

My travel companion offers me an empty sachet from an off-white shopping bag. But I push her hand back, gesture sufficient to restore order. I can't see what her problem is.

Which leads me to something else I've learned: everything is temporary, this sandwich box being no exception.

My time is still before me.

More important – and I suppose this is the thing – is to know that in future I'll need to examine a song-title prior to trusting in it. To pause before I leap, as it were – in the gutter but learning to fly, my dad once said, or something in that vein. Our main man's *I've Got To Be Strong* sounds a tad too self-evident, for a self-educated young man like me. Whereas *Any Day Now,* yes, that sounds apt, before all the time in the world.

An old song for a new dawn, then. Now, there's a choice.

And if it's good enough for Mr. J…

244

*As they strolled away, I observed how Raquel placed an arm through Jed's, like she'd known him years but not seen him for years. I'd no idea what he said but saw her gaze up to him and laugh, how her head fell onto his shoulder in a state of complicity, as if they knew something we didn't, had planned it all along. What I knew was that they were happy. As was Victoria. However brief this bliss, it would for all time spin its merry way back round, like the letter and number-box on our favourite record machine... and not a second of it would be wasted. Such were our viewpoints and values founded during those wagged school days. It was easy for us: we were invincible... weren't we?*

# Chapter Headings

**Chapters:** 1 – ('*… We are such stuff…*') *The Tempest,* William Shakespeare.

2 – ('*Now is the* winter…') *Richard III,* William Shakespeare.

3 – ('*When beggars die…*') *Julius Caesar,* William Shakespeare.

4 – ('*There's nowt as queer…*') Anon.

5 – ('*Beauty is the wonder of wonders…*') *The Picture of Dorian Gray,* Oscar Wilde.

6 – ('*… his addiction was to courses vain…*') *Henry V,* William Shakespeare.

7 – ('*Vows are but Breath…*') *Love's Labour's lost,* William Shakespeare.

8 – ('*Deal mildly with his youth…*') *Richard II,* William Shakespeare.

9 – ('*Now, soldiers, march away…*') *Henry V,* William Shakespeare.

10 – ('*Man can believe the impossible…*') *The Decay of Lying,* Oscar Wilde.

11 – ('*Time eases all things.*'), Sophocles,) William Shakespeare.

12 – ('*…neither a borrower nor a lender be!*') *Hamlet,* William Shakespeare.

13 – ('*All the world's a stage…*') *As You Like It,* William Shakespeare.

14 – ('*The road of excess…*') *The Marriage of Heaven and Hell,* William Blake.

15 – ('*Silence is…*') *Much Ado about nothing,* William Shakespeare.

16 – ('*Yet every step…*') *To Jessie's Dancing Feet,* William De Lancey Ellwanger.

17 – ('*All that glitters…*') *The Merchant of Venice,* William Shakespeare.

18 – ('*United and unite…*') Anon.

19 – ('*Is this the region, this the soil…*') *Paradise Lost book 1,* John Milton.

20 – (*'Yet from those flames No light...'*)
*Paradise Lost book 1*, John Milton.

21 – (*'Speak, father, speak...'*) *Little Boy Lost
(Songs of innocence)*, William Blake.

22 – (*'When the wind of change blows...'*
Ancient Chinese proverb.

23 – (*'Thou know'st 'tis common...'*) *Hamlet*,
William Shakespeare.

24 – (*'... The fewer men...'*) *Henry V*, William
Shakespeare.

25 – (*'Darkness had set in...'*) *Oliver Twist*,
Charles Dickens.

26 – (*'For once she was...'*) Anon.

27 – (*'It was on...'*) *The Strange Case of Dr.
Jekyll & Mr. Hide*, Robert L. Stevenson.

28 – (*'Men of few words...'*) *Henry V*, William
Shakespeare.

29 – (*'O most lame and impotent conclusion!*)
*Othello*, William Shakespeare.

30 – (*'... and may fleets of angels...'*) *Hamlet*,
William Shakespeare.

31 – (*'Give sorrow words...'*) *Macbeth*, William
Shakespeare.

32 – (*'Out of the day...'*) *A Lament*, Percy
Byshhe Shelly.

33 – (*'We are time's subjects...'*) *Henry IV part
II*, William Shakespeare.

34 – (*Come what come may...'*) *Macbeth*,
William Shakespeare.

35 – (*'Excessive sorrow...'*) *The Marriage of
Heaven and Hell*, William Blake.

36 – (*'I am a dreamer...'*) *The critic as Artist*,
Oscar Wilde.

37 – (*'Thy friendship...'*) *The Poetical Works*,
William Blake.

38 – (*'We are all in the gutter...'*) *The Picture of
Dorian Gray*, Oscar Wilde.

Chris Rose was born in Sheffield, many moons ago, and *Wood, Talc and Mr. J* is his debut novel.

He spent his 'early' formative years on the Northern Soul circuit, pretty much like *Phillip Rowlings,* the Casino Club being his favourite haunt; and a place he believes set him up for life's wondrous journey. Each year is a formative one in his eyes.

He is a Francophile. Indeed, he wrote *Wood, Talc and Mr. J* whilst living in France. He is a linguist; he speaks French and Spanish, and has the basics of Italian and German. And he taught English as a second language for many years, both in England and in France. He also translates, primarily from French, and has a Masters in Literary Translation

He loves the theatre and performs annually in what is believed to be Britain's unique, established French theatre company, at the UEA, in Norwich.

Otherwise, when not lost in a book, his own or someone else's, he loves to just lose himself in one of his steel stringed guitars. His beautiful partner and eight year old daughter are very patient...

Chris is currently working on his second novel, *Nancy Boy.* If you'd like to learn more about, and maybe interact with, the author, here's where to find him:

**Website:** http://woodtalcandmrj.com

**Facebook:** https://www.facebook.com/WoodTalcandMrJ

**Linkedin:** http://www.linkedin.com (Chris Rose-Writer/Translator)

**RebelMouse:** https://www.rebelmouse.com/Chris_Rose/

**Twitter:** https://twitter.com/WritingOnACloud

14077591R00141

Printed in Great Britain
by Amazon.co.uk, Ltd.,
Marston Gate.